we are not in P

Other fiction by SHAUNA SINGH BALDWIN

English Lessons and Other Stories
What the Body Remembers
The Tiger Claw

Shauna Singh Baldwin

we are not in Pakistan

Author photo by David J. Baldwin.
Cover image © Irina Opachevsky, istock.
Cover and interior book design by Julie Scriver.
Printed in Canada.
10 9 8 7 6 5 4 3 2 1

Library and Archives Canada Cataloguing in Publication

Baldwin, Shauna Singh, 1962-
We are not in Pakistan / Shauna Singh Baldwin.

ISBN 978-0-86492-488-9

I. Title.
PS8553.A4493W4 2007 C813'.54 C2007-903124-2

Goose Lane Editions acknowledges the financial support of the Canada Council for the Arts, the Government of Canada through the Book Publishing Industry Development Program (BPIDP), and the New Brunswick Department of Wellness, Culture and Sport for its publishing activities.

Goose Lane Editions
Suite 330, 500 Beaverbrook Court
Fredericton, New Brunswick
CANADA E3B 5X4
www.gooselane.com

for Adesh Bhuaji
who said to keep my stories short
and Manjit Uncle
who said to keep them long

Contents

9 *Only a Button*
61 *Naina*
73 *Rendezvous*
97 *Fletcher*
125 *The View from the Mountain*
141 *We Are Not in Pakistan*
169 *Night of the Leonids*
187 *This Raghead*
199 *Nocturne for a Blue Day*
217 *The Distance Between Us*

273 *Acknowledgments*

Only a Button

October 1985

The front door flings open — Viktor. Breathless, as if he took the stairs two at a time. "Olena, I'm assigned to the Lenin Power Station!" Off come his coat and shoes. His arms are strong around his wife. Her feet leave the ground, the kitchen whirls. Kisses jab her cheeks.

She is laughing, kissing back fiercely, but her inside voice is saying *oh, no, oh no . . . we will have to move. Move from Moscow, close to Kyiv. Close to Matushka.*

Why must Olena call her Matushka? Because that's what Viktor calls his mother.

A lock of dark hair falls across his forehead, words spill from him as never before. Viktor is delighted; Olena should be happy. The station is in Ukraine, near her home.

She brings out the vodka, raises a glass. "Shalom, Viktor!" The secret greeting comes to her lips as though warding off the future. "Omayn!" he says, downing his drink. So excited he doesn't even tell her to hush.

But behind the locked door of the washroom, anger makes her heave and retch. Emptied and exhausted, she sits on the toilet seat, legs straight forward, an auburn veil of hair obscuring her face.

This man she loves is the one person she can't tell how she feels.

At seven, Viktor stood with other school children chosen to hail the man code-named Borodin, "The Beard": Igor Kurchatov, father of the Soviet atomic bomb. Viktor was chosen to study Borodin and more Borodin. While Olena was reading folk tales in school, Viktor read Dollezhal on reactor design. When they met, standing in line for Bulgarian cigarettes, she was a teacher of seven-year-olds, and he was almost through his six years at the Moscow Institute of Physical Engineering.

Olena rises, moves to the sink and splashes water over her face.

Viktor used to call her his Ukrainian samovar — and it's still true that she has a small face, slender arms and a long narrow torso perched on the flare of her hips. And he's still a methodical fireplug of a man with a rare but wide smile. A hard-working man, which makes him different from many husbands. And a member of the Party.

She cups one hand beneath the faucet, releases a trickle of water with the other. She rinses her mouth.

Matushka and Viktor — and Viktor's father when he was alive — always belonged to the Party. Olena's family never did. Dedushka, her grandfather, was "detained" by Stalin. Her grandmother too. Detained in a camp for years, despite his Stalingrad war medal, just for hiding a kulak from the secret police. Olena's mother was born in that camp. Still, Dedushka calls Party members "crownless clown tsars" and "the new feudals" — how lucky Olena is that he is seventy-one and alive.

Her father came from good proletarian roots. The son of a blacksmith. But he came to Moscow and was so seduced by the Lenin Library that he became a perpetual student of Chekov and Dostoyevsky. Olena's mother said he was living in someone else's story rather than his own. They divorced when Olena was only two, and her mother took her back to Ukraine and Dedushka. By the time Olena met Viktor, her parents were gone. And marrying Viktor washed her clean of her family's sins.

For Viktor. But never for Matushka.

Olena squeezes paste onto her toothbrush and begins to brush slowly.

She was so young then, so naive. Newly married. Living in Matushka's Moscow apartment until Viktor graduated and his name came up among the thousands on Moscow's waiting list for housing. Hoping to win a single smile from her five-foot Tartar-faced mother-in-law. All those two years, Olena thought obedience would make Matushka love her. But even after the unthinkable, Matushka's lips stayed permanently pursed, as if she wouldn't deign to spit in Olena's direction.

Foam and water swirl down the drain.

Five years ago, during all the excitement of the Moscow Olympics, soon after Viktor and Olena first moved to this apartment, Olena came home from work to find Viktor and Anatoli sitting at the kitchen table. She thought Viktor had invited the swift-talking, lighthearted Anatoli to help her celebrate her twenty-fourth birthday, but no. The same Viktor who, two years earlier, when he couldn't afford a present, had given her a large box with a small card inside promising a thousand kisses, had forgotten it. And so had Anatoli, his college friend, who had known her now for three years. But as soon as Olena mentioned it, Viktor invited two more guests! Olena had spent her whole lunch break standing in line and all she could buy was a sliver of beef. Baby Galina's bare bottom riding her arm, Viktor and three guests to feed, and Matushka called. From Kyiv, thousands of kilometres away.

Viktor took the phone and relayed the message: Matushka lost a button in the apartment during her visit. She wanted Olena to find it. An embroidered button, it's true, but — a button. Worth ten or twenty kopeks? Olena said to Viktor, "Tell her I will look, and if I find it, I will keep it for her."

But no! Viktor stood with his palm over the phone cup, eyebrows a straight line. "Look for it. She needs it."

"Now?" said Olena. A trickle of urine crept down her hip from Galina.

"That's what she said." He said this in Russian, not Ukrainian. Yes, Olena remembers that.

He expected Olena to search for his mother's button, so she did. She propped Galina on her baby pot, then took her into the bedroom. She laid the baby on the bed and began searching, keeping her eye on Galina all the while. Searched through the bedroom, the kitchen, the washroom. Even pushed aside Viktor's shirts in the tub room and looked in the bathtub. She searched for more than fifteen minutes, picked up Galina, and returned to Viktor and his guests. "Please believe me, Viktor, I cannot find it."

Viktor placed a call to Kyiv. "Olena says she cannot find it."

He should have said, Olena cannot find it. That might have kept Matushka quiet. He could have said, We have been trying to find your button ever since you called, and we have looked everywhere, but we cannot find it. He could have said, as one says to a child, Don't worry, it's only a button. We'll find another just like it. Not Viktor.

So, of course, Matushka said, "Tell her to try harder."

Meanwhile Viktor's friends persuaded him to bring out his balalaika, and between songs, they grumbled at the wait for dinner and passed the vodka. Every hour, between chopping, peeling and stirring, Olena searched. She shushed Galina whenever the singing woke her, and she searched. And every hour, Olena told Viktor she still couldn't find the button, and he called Matushka in Kyiv.

Then it became late and he was hungry and shamed before his friends, so Olena got one, then two slaps across her cheeks. Olena didn't blame him. She might have hit someone too if she could — someone so dear he would have to forgive her. She thought this as she muttered under her breath that even her mother had never hit her — never. No matter how frustrated she was from never having enough money.

It was midnight by the time Viktor let Olena give up searching for the button and three in the morning by the time she finished cleaning up. And then to work the next day.

Olena holds a towel to her eyes, dries the rest of her face. Lipstick would make her look more festive, but she has none.

She would rather move to the other side of the world than to Kyiv. But she is like a cloud that must go where the wind blows. Viktor has worked so hard for this. Olena must have faith in love the way Dedushka has faith in his God.

Viktor said they'll be living in Pripyat. Pripyat is two and a half hours — about seventy kilometres — from Kyiv. They will be very close to her old home, Dedushka's farmhouse. Her little mushroom, her sunshine, her Galina is almost seven now, old enough that she'll come to know her great-grandfather.

They will not be living *with* Matushka.

And her Viktor will be happy.

Olena returns the towel to the rack and leaves the washroom.

November 1985

Viktor's ninth-floor apartment in Pripyat, immediately allotted in this city of only half a million, is larger and airier than the Moscow apartment. And the building is so new! It is as if someone had Viktor and Olena in mind: here is a maroon-upholstered sofa set, sheer curtains, their own TV, and a bookcase where she can display her father's collection of novels and Viktor can stack his military magazines and English scientific journals. Viktor's balalaika fits perfectly under their bed. And there's a balcony where Olena can see far across the city as she hangs her wash to dry.

Olena finds four different kinds of cheese available in Pripyat stores, and such short lines. Galina is assigned to a beautiful new school. Olena can take her to the amusement park, where there's even a Ferris wheel. And it's only a bus ride to Dedushka's home. She does have to take a train or a hydrofoil across the reservoir with Viktor and Galina to visit Matushka in Kyiv. But only on Sundays.

Viktor, Anatoli and Anatoli's twenty-year-old wife Laima take Olena and Galina to admire the huge white blocks of the power station. In the shuttle bus, Anatoli and blond, plump Laima steal a long kiss in the seat behind Olena as Viktor points out the turbine halls, the administrative block where he works, the three chimneys of the old reactors and the red and white chimney of the new one, Unit 4. Olena half turns, catches Laima's eye, hides a smile. But Viktor is pointing out a line of pylons marching like giants across sunflower and wheat fields and telling Galina they supply electricity to Kyiv. If he has noticed, he will say Laima should be more dignified.

Anatoli shows them the flagstone commemorating the opening of the power station in March, 1984. He and Laima attended the ceremony, along with ministers, Party leaders from Kyiv, and the President of the Academy of Sciences. Olena wishes they had been here for the speeches, the fireworks, the lights, the Zils pulling up before the entrance to the House of Culture, and so many Volgas in a cavalcade down Lenin Street.

The bus passes a slogan painted on the wall of the plant: Communism Will Triumph! When Anatoli rises, stands in the aisle, and salutes, Olena wonders if he is joking. Laima and Viktor don't laugh, and others in the bus don't laugh, so Olena doesn't either.

"We employ seventy people per shift," Viktor tells Olena on

the way home. "In capitalist power stations, they can only employ ten or eleven."

Olena is proud for Viktor, so proud she could cry.

But a few days later, as Viktor slices into the molten core of Olena's Chicken Kyiv, he says, "It's nothing like Moscow. My title is Assistant Safety Engineer, but maybe it should be Official Signer of Certificates of Exemption. And now I know which workers work and which play cards and read books. Most are happy with grades of four and three."

Olena remains silent. *I too sometimes miss my friends in Moscow, and my little students, but not for long. Viktor will get used to it soon. He must — what else can he do?*

Viktor dips half the chicken in the butter oozing from the other half and stuffs it in his mouth. "But for everyone to get a five and be rated a pyatorka would take more organization and training. Effort that can't be shown off to Party leaders visiting from Moscow."

With that, he licks his fingers and laughs as she never heard him laugh in Moscow.

It's better that I'm at home now. Viktor will never have to wait for dinner. He'll never get frustrated enough to slap me. Many other women are not so lucky.

As she undresses for bed, Olena can smell warm garlic from her special borscht all the way to the bedroom. She made it for Viktor and Galina as a celebration: only a month since their arrival at Pripyat, and already someone is transferred and Viktor has been promoted to Deputy Safety Engineer in Unit 4. He has received permission to own a motorcycle. And a paper Viktor wrote, published under his director's name, as all his papers are, actually came to the attention of Plant Director Brukhanov.

Olena has put Galina to bed and persuaded her to stay there. She slips into her nightgown, then between the sheets with Victor. His body presses hers to sizzling elation.

With the weight of his arm and leg across her, Viktor whispers, "One more promotion, and we'll celebrate without a condom."

Olena's inside voice is saying, *Tell him. Say it, tell him.* But her unthinkable is unsayable.

"I want a boy," she says instead. "To know what you were like when you were a little boy. And maybe another girl. Galina should never feel alone when we are no longer with her. She must not be an only child, as we are."

Viktor rolls away, clasps his hands behind his head and looks beyond her. "When I was a boy, the plans for the RBMK reactors were just approved, and look, here I am, husbanding them."

Husbanding is not the right word. Maybe Comrade Borodin created a new temple and Viktor is part of its priesthood — but Olena doesn't want to say that.

She is drifting but Viktor is now awake. "We move so much faster these days. Can you believe it's taken nine years for a recommendation from the head of safety in Moscow to arrive on my desk?"

"Was it not important?" says Olena.

"Oh, it was just telling us that extra boron rods should be installed here in the Lenin station, because they found they needed more for the Kursk reactor. But nine years!"

"What will you do?" Olena yawns, head on his chest, his heartbeat steady in her ear.

"Do? Nothing. We have heat sensors, water to absorb neutrons, automatic pumps, the Skala computer, and two hundred and eleven control rods installed already. If our reactors were designed by capitalists only interested in profit, maybe I would worry. But they're designed by Soviet engineers for the people.

We have procedures, safeguards, rules, rules — almost too many to remember."

"But what if . . ."

"An accident is unthinkable. And besides, the rods cost billions of rubles! By the time we ask Moscow to buy them, it could be another nine years until we get them."

Olena drifts beneath a leaden shield. Boron rods dip and plunge in her dreams, cooling the core.

March – April 1986

Olena takes Galina to a performance of the Babi Yar Symphony and meets Rivka in the line before the House of Culture. A Belorussian, like many here. Rivka too lived in Moscow before she came to Pripyat.

She has no husband or children. But somehow Rivka doesn't look sorrowful. With her cloud of brown hair, her sharply pointed chin and large eyes, she looks like Princess Diana.

Olena isn't sure Rivka likes her. Olena likes Rivka but she doesn't say that to Viktor. He might say, in his Party voice, She's too chatty, when he really means, Don't see her again.

Two weeks later, in Pripyat's central square, Olena stops to buy radishes from a babushka — she still has the Moscow habit of always carrying her string shopping bag. A big sign above the weather-beaten old woman reads *Tribuna Energetica*. Pripyat's newspaper, where Rivka works.

Olena decides she will apply for an office job, just a few days a week and while Galina is at school. Two salaries will be better than one. She climbs the stairs into the grey concrete building beneath the sign and asks a stern-faced woman for Rivka. When Rivka enters the reception area, the room feels brighter.

How kindly she greets Olena! She even shows Olena her office.

Such a big newspaper with such a big sign is published from only a few rooms. But it's a new city, a new newspaper.

Rivka shows Olena into her director's office and introduces her. The director says to Olena, "Your husband is working at the power station? Tell him a fourth unit is unnecessary, and so are the fifth and sixth. Just hook all the pylons to Rivka and her energy will fuel the country."

Rivka laughs, and a spark flies between her and the director like a little of the current that flows between Viktor and Olena at night. In her own office, Rivka shows Olena a poem she wrote to commemorate International Women's Day. Olena has never met anyone who writes poetry. Rivka asks what Olena thinks of her poem.

"It is beautiful," says Olena immediately. "Believe me, beautiful!"

Without checking with her director, Rivka tells Olena she can start working with her the day after May Day.

Olena feels she has been given a great gift. But then she is not sure . . . how will she tell Viktor?

Back in the square, Olena adds carrots from the babushka to her shopping bag. Then the joke strikes her and she laughs. Rivka asked what Olena thought of her poem — as if what Olena thinks mattered!

Viktor is picking at his food, though Olena has served one of his favourites, fish kotlety. She wants to tell him about Rivka, about Rivka's poem, about her new job. She will tell him that Laima is working too, and Anatoli doesn't object. She is waiting for the right moment.

"Our power station has been ordered to produce consumer goods," says Viktor, washing his breaded fish down with vodka. "Because of Gorbachev and his glasnost." His eyebrows knot and rise. "What can a reactor make but electricity? Personal nuclear bombs and batteries, maybe?"

This is not the right moment.

Viktor tosses and turns all night, worrying, worrying, till Olena rises, fetches oil and massages him. "You'll think of something," she assures him as he falls asleep.

And the next day, over breakfast, he does think of a good suggestion: meat-mincing machines. He leaves for a meeting with his director and Plant Director Burkhanov. But that evening, he tells her they rejected his suggestion. They decided to propose hay storage facilities to Party leaders in Moscow.

"Imagine how that will look: horse-drawn carts delivering hay to the Lenin reactor," he says with a hurt laugh.

Olena will tell Viktor about her job when he is more calm. Maybe on the weekend before May Day, when they are going to Sochi on the Black Sea.

Olena packs a picnic basket with three matzoh in a napkin, a bottle of Georgian wine, and horseradish. She adds a few sweet prune-stuffed pampushky and a lokshyna noodle ring filled with creamed vegetables. No salo, no sausage.

With Galina, she rides an accordion bus that stops at a village with no name. Her grandfather is lean and bright-eyed, and these days he's more hopeful, he says because of the new man Gorbachev and his glasnost, but Olena knows it's because she is closer. Who else will remember to bring him Passover foods he cannot find in old Chernobyl, the nearest town?

Outside Dedushka's wooden farmhouse, the scent of black

earth surrounds Olena as if she were a child again. Dedushka has a Passover present for Galina — a mink purse that belonged to her great-grandmother. He brings out photo albums and gives her a black and white snapshot of Olena's mother. The little girl balances her plate on her knees and chews solemnly as she listens to a story about the night Olena was born. Later, Dedushka goes inside and returns triumphant, the tarnished rattle that once cheered baby Olena clutched in his hand. "I remember things your mother cannot," he says, laughing as he gives it to Galina.

Friends stop to greet him, linger to exclaim over Olena and Galina and ask his advice. A farmer gives Galina a ride in his cart; Olena will bathe the manure smell away when she gets home.

Olena tells Dedushka they will leave on Saturday morning, tomorrow, after Viktor finishes the safety test at the station. She cannot hide the pride in her voice: they will be guests of Viktor's director at his dacha. And now, since Viktor's director is travelling with Director Burkhanov to Moscow to report their progress on hay storage, it will be just Viktor, Galina and Olena.

Six days — just the three of them in Sochi! Olena has made pampushky and berry-filled nalysnyky. Viktor has stocked up on vodka because Anatoli told him Gorbachev will ban it after May 1. Olena has packed cans of dried milk in a suitcase.

They'll be home on Thursday to watch the May Day parades. Galina is excited about May Day, and so are all her friends. Olena too loves the parade, the streamers, the flags, the placards with the familiar slogans.

"Enjoy this week, Olena," says Dedushka, as she kisses his forehead and brings Galina forward to say goodbye. "There'll never be another like it."

As soon as Olena gets home, the phone rings. Matushka, from Kyiv. A message for Viktor: "Ask what have I done that he is not coming to visit his Matushka on Passover weekend."

The column of Olena's neck feels as hollow as if she had scoured it, removed her larynx and other organs. Her anger sours the sauerkraut soup she makes for dinner.

And she doesn't tell Viktor before he takes the bus to work at ten that evening.

She will tell him when he gets back.

There was an accident. At the plant. Viktor's voice is telling Olena this. He says it again. It's five o'clock on Saturday morning, and he is saying to keep Galina home and stay inside. "Not serious," he says. "Don't worry. Not serious at all."

"Are you telling the truth?"

"I'm so tired," says his Party voice. "Stop your chatter. Close all the windows."

Outside the balcony window, past the laundry, Olena sees it — a red column rising over the power station into the dark sky. She closes her eyes and the afterglow pulses against her eyelids. Viktor said she shouldn't worry. Fire engines will be there already. But her inside voice is saying *oh no, oh no.*

Seven o'clock comes and Olena is still waiting. Instead of dawn, a lesser darkness is spreading behind a column of smoke. Red flames glow and grow. What is Viktor doing? Where is he? What is his exposure? Thirty-five rems an hour is the limit. Then evacuation. But a safety engineer must continue working as long as he can. What does she know but the basics? Radiation sickness — nausea, diarrhea, changes in the blood.

But only if a person is exposed to more than one hundred rems in an hour.

Olena opens the balcony door a crack and sniffs.

Trees. The last fragrance of April. A faint scent like rain falling on a dusty road.

Olena can't see the radiation, she can't sense it in her body. But it's there. Is it going into and through her Viktor right now?

Her knees turn liquid. She has a sudden need to pray. She, an atheist. Dedushka would laugh at her. And she doesn't know a single prayer. A Schevchenko poem is all that comes to mind: "No, let us not depart, nor go. It is early still . . ."

She will wait till eight, and if Viktor isn't home by then, she will even pray to Lenin.

Seven-thirty. Another call. Viktor has been taken to Pripyat hospital. "It's only gas," says the nurse on the phone.

Olena leaves Galina with a neighbour. She runs to the bus stop.

Is it the air or fear burning her eyes, her throat?

Ten minutes. She has wasted ten minutes.

She walks and runs all the way to the hospital. Military vehicles pass, soldiers block some roads — she takes detours. Other women, young and old, are running like her. They join her in the crowd outside the hospital. Olena begins to jostle and yell at the soldiers.

Just past them, at the entrance, stands a woman with a cloud of brown hair, a notebook in her hand. Olena screams Rivka's name.

Rivka says something to someone. Olena is allowed in.

So many patients, so many beds in plastic cubicles. A nurse points to Viktor's. Olena rushes.

Then stops.

Viktor is attached to a drip. She approaches slowly.

"I felt faint," he says, taking Olena's hand. "Then I started vomiting. The nurse made me wash and lie down."

The nurse's face is blank. If only she would tell Olena not to worry or say, Your husband will be home soon. But she just takes Viktor's blood sample and leaves without saying anything.

"Do you have diarrhea?"

"Not yet." He closes swollen eyes.

Her inside voice repeats *one hundred rems, one hundred rems.* She doesn't know what to say.

His grip on her hand tightens. "Bring milk and vodka," he whispers. "And BTs."

"Couldn't . . . couldn't that be dangerous?"

"Just bring those cigarettes!"

"Da, da!"

"Give Galina iodine tablets immediately. Buy all the iodine tablets you can. There are a few extra packets in the saddlebag of the motorcycle."

After a moment he says, "We detached from the power grid, lowered enough control rods into the core to reduce power to seven hundred megawatts. But the reactor became unstable. So the shift foreman pushed the emergency A-Z button to lower all the rods and shut down."

"Where were you?"

"I wasn't in the control room. When I felt the thud, such a thud, I thought it was an earthquake. But it could be — we don't know, but it must be — that actor in the White House pressed some button at the same time. Star Wars."

"Like Hiroshima?" says Olena. "Why not all of Pripyat, then?"

"I don't know. All I know is that the reactor did not explode." But his Party voice is speaking, so Olena knows: the reactor did explode. But now what is to be done? Can it be repaired?

"It will be all right," says Viktor. "I saw the smoke moving north, away from Pripyat."

"Get well, Viktor, and we'll go to the dacha some other time soon." Olena kisses his forehead.

. . .

Three days after the accident that was not an explosion, the Moscow Symphony is playing Tchaikovsky on the record player and Olena is ironing with the iron Viktor bought as her first anniversary present. She's waiting for *Vremya* on TV.

The announcer will say that those firemen who so bravely fought the blaze have been evacuated to Hospital 6 in Moscow. They probably won't mention that their wives didn't have a chance to say goodbye. Olena is so lucky Viktor is not a fireman.

The nurse took a blood sample from Viktor — what was the result?

It must be all right because Viktor was discharged from the hospital.

He was called back to work, and Olena is very glad he is not at Unit 4 right now. Instead he's escorting a KGB general and Party leaders from Moscow who have come to assess the damage. His director told him that, as he flies with the leaders in helicopters and rides with them in Zils, he must remind them that Soviet reactors do not need contingency plans and that there are not enough gas masks for the entire population. And he must reassure them that the reactor will be functional again very soon.

Was it right to send Galina to school? She took her iodine pills with breakfast, but . . .

It must be all right because the May Day parade has not been cancelled.

Olena stands her iron up and goes out on the balcony. She pushes the wash aside and peers across the city.

The red glow at the base of the spray of fire seems diminished. Smoke still billows up and descends. But now it's leaning toward her, toward Pripyat.

Oh no, oh no. The wind is changing.

Was the sun so bright at this time last year? Did the cherry blossoms shine as pink? Was the scent of pine trees as strong?

She hasn't been in Pripyat long enough to know.

Oh, let it not rain. Viktor said if it rains, radioactivity can enter the reservoir of the Pripyat and Dnieper rivers and poison Pripyat's water supply.

The neighbour who looked after Galina the morning of the accident said boiling water will purify it.

Olena returns inside and shuts the door tightly.

Almost at the end of the news, the announcer reads, "One of the atomic reactors has been damaged. Measures are being undertaken to eliminate the consequences of the accident."

It went by so fast. He said it so fast — was she mistaken?

Olena keeps her gaze on the TV while she answers the phone. It's Rivka. She wants Olena to ask Viktor, now he is better, what really happened.

But of course Viktor won't tell Olena, and if he did how could she tell Rivka? Because what if Rivka is working for a foreign government? The most charming people usually do.

Rivka says she heard on Voice of America that there was a massive steam explosion followed by a rapid reaction. Then the thousand-ton roof flew off as a second explosion blew the core. Glasnost or no glasnost, Olena knows better than to listen to Voice of America. And if Rivka did listen, she shouldn't admit it — a counter-revolutionary act like that could cost Rivka her Writer's Union card. But Rivka seems to have thrown caution to the wind, the changing wind.

Rivka's angry — she's good at being angry. She doesn't mention that trucks, trains and buses have been commandeered by the army, or that reservists who expected to be summoned to duty in Afghanistan are being trucked into Pripyat. Or that a commission of inquiry was appointed by eleven o'clock on the morning of the accident. Rivka is angry that Director Burkhanov has wasted thirty-six hours before coming to the decision he should have made immediately: *Evacuate*!

Olena tries to explain that Director Burkhanov could not have made that decision. A decision affecting half a million people and possible panic must come all the way from the Politburo, from leaders in Moscow. And as for the delay, *Shcho zrobysh!* What can you do? Rivka must understand that people like Viktor and Olena are their comrades, not their wives, brothers and sisters, sons and daughters. Just comrades.

May 1986

Four days later, the balls of Olena's feet treadle a Podolsk sewing machine in Matushka's tiny spare room. She and Galena — and Viktor on weekends — will share the bed and a floor mattress. Only for a while, until they can return or retrieve their belongings from Pripyat. Refugees are pouring into Kyiv and housing has become impossible, but Viktor has been assured he will be allotted one of the first available apartments.

Seams of a night-blue fabric with a sun and moon print join as they pass smoothly beneath the presser foot. Of Matushka's whole cupboard full of sewing machines with the new Energia motors, this pre-Soviet monster is the only one that works. When Matushka saw Olena using it, she pressed her lips as if sewing with an imported machine confirmed her low opinion of Olena.

Olena can hardly believe she is in Kyiv. Instead of watching May Day parades, she found herself snatching up the suitcase and repacking in minutes as two blank-faced soldiers stood waiting at the door. Because they could live in Matushka's apartment, west of the muscular vein of the Dnieper, Viktor could arrange for her and Galina to be in the first wave of evacuees. Laima, who could only find a bed in an army barrack with other refugees, says looters will probably take anything left behind.

The suitcase Olena had packed for the weekend at the dacha

lies open on the bed, half unpacked. No clothes, because Viktor said their clothes could be contaminated. But it's good for Galina that Olena had packed dried milk — real milk now comes from irradiated cows. And Viktor said she could bring the cranberry liqueur and vodka; it cleanses the body, he says.

But what can she give Galina once the dried milk is finished?

Dark clothing, Anatoli said, might be impenetrable to radiation. The infinite space of night sky, the pattern of suns and reflector moons on Galina's summer dress should fill Olena's mind, separate her from earth and its troubles. But thoughts filter through.

She can't stop seeing Matushka counting out just enough rubles for this fabric for Galina's dress and for the bolt of white cotton beside her, then writing the amounts for each purchase in her black ledger book. Again she hears that wordless sniff: the money was a loan to Olena — not Viktor, not Galina.

Olena needs some bright yellow floss to embroider the collar and yoke for Galina. She will not embroider a single button.

If there is enough fabric left, Olena may even make a dress for herself. But first — she glances at the bolt of white cotton — she will make a new shirt for Viktor, maybe even one for Dedushka.

Dedushka refused to leave his house. The soldiers burned his neighbour's house and buried it, but he could not be persuaded — he said he doesn't have much time to live anyway.

We'll see him again soon. Yes, we will.

But he is alone.

She stops treadling for a moment, dashes her fingertips over her cheeks.

Matushka has taken Galina to the park. She will let the little girl play there for hours, letting everyone think she's Galina's mother rather than her grandmother. She will give her chocolate smuggled from Switzerland. Yes, Matushka, whom Olena thought a dried husk of a woman, incapable of love. At this moment she's probably filling the little girl's head with stories about Olena's stupidity. Or with Khrushchev-era slogans which everyone must now forget.

It's very difficult not to remember the many things you need to forget. On the outskirts of Kyiv is the ravine called Babi Yar — Olena tries not to walk in its direction, but that only makes her think of it more. She is an atheist, but she is also a zhid. Viktor too.

Trust no one.

But it's also very difficult to remember what you're supposed to remember. There's a legend that in the 1940s, Russian deportees in a camp here in Kyiv were challenged to a game of football and won against the Nazis 3-0. Dedushka would have told her that story many times if it were true.

Matushka believes it; it's a Party lie.

The sewing machine whirrs faster.

More and more refugees are coming in trucks from Pripyat. But on the telephone last night, Viktor was not worried. It's a precaution, he said. He said this happened before. With the first reactor at Mayak in '57. Ten thousand were evacuated then and many thousands of acres of farms laid waste.

"How do you know?" said Olena.

"A safety engineer is sometimes told what cannot be written down."

Olena could have asked what else he was told that no one else was told. But she didn't want to know. Did she know or dream of boron rods?

It feels so long ago.

Top academicians and other experts are arriving from all over the Soviet Union, Viktor said. He is not in danger, he said. He and Anatoli are working together, phoning Moscow to arrange shipments of nitrogen, boron and lead. But, he said, his life — everyone's life — has been divided into before and after the accident.

Olena understands. Her life was once divided too. The unthinkable was her Chernobyl.

As fabric moves beneath her fingertips, gratitude toward some big spirit begins to sing within Olena. Just think what could have happened to Viktor, but didn't. She has the urge to praise some force that kept him from harm that night and has allowed him to recover so quickly from his stay in the hospital. His hair is falling out, but he is alive. Three of his colleagues were not so lucky, and maybe more have died; glasnost will not go so far as to make the Party tell.

Olena doesn't want to know what might happen. She just wants to know what she should do to keep Galina safe.

"Most possibilities," said Viktor, "become what does not happen."

Possibility means not yet.

Not yet, creaks Olena's treadle, *not yet.*

Fifteen days after the accident that was not an explosion, Olena and Galina are sitting at the kitchen table. Galina is pretending to feed the Misha-bear Matushka bought her.

Matushka has gone shopping for Swiss mineral water for Galina, which she says is better than boiled water, even if it isn't Soviet-made. Radionuclides have been found in the Pripyat River and in wells. Olena has been boiling water for Matushka, Viktor and herself.

"Come, Galina," says Olena. She shows the little girl a paper with hash marks made by Viktor. Each is for a helicopter. Brave pilots flew over the crater of the reactor, Viktor said. Soldiers opened the doors and heaved out gunny sacks filled with sand, boron and lead to neutralize the radiation and plug the hole in the reactor as fast as they could. "But," he said — and Olena heard a click as he bit a nail — "one hundred ninety-five tons of nuclear fuel are still burning."

"Count these for me," says Olena.

Galina drops her bear on the floor.

"How many flights the first day?"

Galina's black curls obscure the paper. She looks up. "Ninety-three!" she squeals.

"And how many the second?"

A small pink triangle emerges from a corner of Galina's mouth as she counts the hash marks on the second paper.

"A hundred and eighty!"

Of all the seven-year-olds she used to teach, Olena can't remember one who is better than Galina at counting. Or one more beautiful, or dear . . . who is more dear — Galina or Viktor?

A centrifuge churns in Olena's stomach each night till Viktor returns from work and calls her from their old apartment. When he comes to Kyiv on weekends, he doesn't want her or Galina to sleep beside him, but they have been together so many years, Olena can't let him sleep alone. And it would disturb Matushka if Galina slept in her room.

The latency period has passed. Viktor's chest and pubic hair comes away in Olena's hand. His testicles have darkened.

Last night he said an expert has proposed that the army build a concrete sarcophagus. "To seal away dust, fuel, two hundred tons of uranium and a ton of radioactive plutonium for at least thirty years," Viktor said, "and the blue glow I saw from the helicopter."

The sarcophagus, he said, will have to be constructed elsewhere and "assembled like a puzzle by liquidators."

"What are liquidators?"

"Army reservists."

"Won't they be in danger?"

"We," said Viktor's Party voice, "will give them lead-shielded vehicles."

He fears more rems, and blame. Blame. Someone has to be blamed, everyone knows that. Olena doesn't want anyone to blame her Viktor.

Olena picks the Misha-bear off the floor and dusts him off.

Dust is dangerous. Olena has become afraid of the stirrings of leaves. Today the pen-like dosimeter Viktor gave her peeped at every vegetable in the market, even here in Kyiv. A babushka from whom she bought sunflower seeds said she caught a huge fish — a fish with long hair instead of gills. Such stories are not only market talk from comrade peasants; the woman in the flat below said she heard a sow gave birth to a litter of piglets without eyes.

Matushka must have heard such things too, because today, even after listening to speeches at her Party meeting, she came home and said to Olena, "You can't have another baby."

In a practical voice. As if she had decided this for Olena. Decided again for Olena.

Galina is leaning over Matushka's proudest possession: Victor's old chess set. She advances a white pawn two paces, then a black one. Then another white one. She pulls up a low stool and sits down. Her brow furrows.

Olena takes the Misha-bear to the spare room. She pulls her suitcase from the cupboard, thrusts it in, and locks it away.

Ten days later, there's a knock at Matushka's apartment door. Olena wipes her hands and takes off her apron. Not Galina — she's at her new school this afternoon. Not Viktor, not on a weekday. He must be at the station right now, answering more questions. It's probably the woman in the flat below, asking to use Matushka's telephone.

But no, Matushka is showing Rivka into her small living room — as if Rivka were *her* friend, rather than Olena's. She orders

Olena to serve poppy-seed cake and tea as if Olena wouldn't have done so otherwise. She offers Rivka a seat on the sofa beside her, then a cigarette. She lights one for herself and slides her brass ashtray within Rivka's reach.

"Tell me," Matushka says to Rivka. "Have they found where the sabotage occurred?"

"It does not appear to be sabotage, comrade," says Rivka.

"But surely it was a spy, a foreign hand," says Matushka.

Rivka glances at Olena and takes a slice of the poppy-seed cake.

Olena pours tea for Matushka and Rivka as Rivka asks about Galina. Matushka regales her with Galina's seven-year-old wisdom. Rivka listens and smiles as if she's really interested.

In the voice of a concerned friend, Rivka asks about Viktor's exposure, his symptoms. What did he see from the helicopter? What recommendations are being made to the KGB and the Politburo? Can Units 1, 2 and 3 really be blocked off from Unit 4? The wind, she says, will carry radionuclides over a million square miles. Miners and metro workers are being trucked in from all over the country — is it just to dig new wells? Is it true what she's heard, that water from the fire hoses has pooled beneath the reactor, and they have to tunnel under it, drain it out and make a refrigeration chamber, or else there will be a second explosion? Does Viktor believe families can ever go back to Pripyat to live? Is there danger to the rest of the Soviet Union? Could Europe become uninhabitable?

Suddenly Olena does not want to tell Rivka anything. For once, she is grateful to Matushka for her expert and polite evasion of Rivka's every question.

"Where are you living?" says Olena to change the subject.

Rivka says the babushka who sold radishes in the central square in Pripyat happened to be one of the peasants choosing townspeople to take home. She chose Rivka and a few others to live with her. But now Rivka has been allotted an apartment in Kyiv, so she can interview visiting dignitaries and reassure the foreign press. She came here because she remembered Olena, remembered promising her a job after May Day — can Olena work with her?

"I didn't know you had been offered a job after May Day," says Matushka. She leans toward Rivka and taps her cigarette into the ashtray. "She forgets things," she says in a conspiratorial tone. "I called Viktor the night before the accident, and Olena forgot to give him my message."

Olena knows what Matushka wants her to say. She hears herself using many words and a deeply apologetic tone to say what could be said in a single word: nyet.

Disappointment passes over Rivka's face, but there's nothing to be done.

She rises. Olena doesn't want her to leave. Not without a smile.

"I'm trying to imagine you," she says, "such a Moscow sophisticate, living in a hut, eating white borsht and potato puddings." It's a joke — a feeble joke.

"Studying life everywhere is my job," says Rivka.

Olena says, "I want to live my own life, not study other people's."

"Then you must want that so much that nothing else and no one else is important to you." Matushka closes the door behind Rivka and says, "You have such individualist friends."

She picks up her handbag, jerks her chin at the crumbed dishes and says, "I have a meeting. I'll return by the time Galina comes home from school."

Olena takes the dishes to the kitchen.

How can any woman ever want anything so much that nothing else and no one else would be important to her?

Viktor is important to me, Galina is important to me, Dedushka is important to me. Matushka too, because Viktor loves her. In the face of their needs, my wants can't possibly matter.

Olena rinses the dishes with cold boiled water. She boils some more, sets it aside for drinking. She pours a tumbler full for herself and watches as the tea leaves fall below the surface. Suddenly, the unthinkable must be thought, the inconceivable must be conceived. Her older daughter. A year before Galina, she lived. At least, maybe she was a daughter. Condoms were expensive — they still are, the Party wants women to produce many babies. Matushka said maybe Olena wanted a baby, but she didn't need one. Viktor's career was more important, she said. And he couldn't afford a child before he graduated, before he had an apartment. How would they raise one without borrowing from her? If Olena didn't agree, Matushka would tell Viktor to refuse to sign the papers so the baby could get a propiska. And without that resident registration stamp, preferably from Moscow, the baby would have no care from any doctor, no education and no right to inherit from either Viktor or Olena. So Matushka sent Olena to her doctor friend, boasting that he made seventeen abortions for her through the years Viktor's father was alive.

When Olena left the doctor she went to the cinema. A black and white movie — she couldn't understand the language. Something Party leaders imported from India to show friendship with a Socialist Democracy. She sat with other living, breathing men and women and let the cramps come. Unseen, a bloodstain crept over her green dress. On screen, a woman with eyes so large they took up half her face shed tears for her, and an actor — she even remembers his name, Raj Kapoor — danced his way through mansions and fields with a smile just like Viktor's, a smile that said, You know you love me.

Would Viktor really have refused to sign his own baby's propiska? Viktor always does what Matushka wants. If he knew what

Matushka had made Olena do, would it not break his heart too? It was too late to ask him, too late to tell him.

As Olena bled away a life that could have been, she cursed Matushka with each spasm. She might have to live with Matushka, but no one could command her to love her mother-in-law. Not Viktor, not anyone.

Olena remained seated as people filed past in the dark, stayed even when the lights came on. Surely there would be another show. Darkness came again and the names of actors began flashing past to tinny music.

She doubled over, sobbing, till she felt a hand squeeze her shoulder. A grandmotherly woman in uniform offered her a glass of water, her handkerchief and silence.

Olena sobs as on that day, tears mingling with her cooling tea. Does she cry for the young woman she left in the theatre or her older daughter?

Matushka has not changed. She is like a cesium isotope, contaminating Viktor with her expectations. Unmeetable expectations. Not one word of concern for Olena since she arrived in Kyiv, and no chance of rest. When Viktor comes on weekends, he might as well still be dressed in that green mask he wears on duty, and she might as well be his butler, personal assistant and cleaning woman. She is expected to do the cooking for Matushka, Viktor and Galina and be quiet. So she does, and she is.

She misses what she never knew, the clean papery smell of the *Tribune Energetica*, a desk, a chair. Rivka, who listens as if what Olena says matters.

. . .

June 1986

Sleeping, Olena senses that Viktor's weight is not on the bed beside her. She wakes. Galina is sleeping on her back, an arm thrown across her forehead, on the mattress at the foot of their bed. But where is Viktor? She listens for clacking and pinging. Since Victory Day, when Viktor heard that Director Burkhanov would be dismissed and sent to a KGB prison somewhere to await trial, he has been using a borrowed typewriter each weekend night. He has applied for transfers to nuclear stations at Kursk, Smolensk, Khmelnitzky and Rovno. He has applied to Austria, where a brand new nuclear power station is being built. He has applied to Italy. He moans that he and Anatoli are the only Ukrainians in the world who do not have relatives in Canada.

But tiptoeing from the spare room tonight, Olena finds only silence and a soft glow from Matushka's kitchen. Viktor is sitting at the table, writing in longhand — a heartfelt plea to the Jewish Social Services of America.

"If they will not listen," he says, "I'll volunteer to fight in Afghanistan."

"But I thought you said . . . the actor in the White House?"

"I said what I was expected to say. But he didn't do it, Olena."

The next morning, Olena takes the metro across the river to the east side of Kyiv to confuse any KGB who may be watching and posts the letters for him.

November – December 1989

The Kalendar Prince movement of *Scheherazade* spins from Olena's new turntable. She sets a small ceramic bowl of sour cream beside a plate of piping hot sirniki on the table and calls, "Galina!"

Galina, who has grown thin and sickly in the three years

since they fled Pripyat, had another headache and sore throat this morning before school. She has returned now but is taking so very long in the bathroom. Maybe she still feels unwell. It's November and changing to winter. Around this time last year, she got pneumonia.

Olena doesn't want to be a radiophobe, but how can continuous low doses of ionizing radiation be, as the Ministry of Health says, an improvement to the body? Especially a child's body?

Olena places a fork and knife beside Galina's plate. She fetches a glass of water from the kitchen.

This apartment is not as large as the one Olena left in Pripyat and its hallways smell of old cabbage, but it's adequate. Soldiers returning from Afghanistan and liquidators of the cleanup don't have apartments this large, or telephone connections. For Olena, though not for Galina, its beauty lies in its location, three trolleybus rides from Matushka's.

Galina will get used to it.

You can get used to anything — Dedushka says so, now all his neighbours have left. All he has is his photo albums.

Olena has torn up worn-out linoleum and repainted Galina's room lemon. She was lucky to find an old sofa and striped purple material for slipcovers. She covered up the mottled wall in the living room by hanging a carpet over it.

If only she had the black and white snapshot of her mother to frame and hang on the wall and the mink purse Dedushka gave Galina. These, the motorcycle, Viktor's balalaika and her father's novels were abandoned in Pripyat.

The carpet on the floor still looks dark and worn, though Olena gave it a good scrubbing in the tub.

"Galina!"

That carpet was still a little wet last week, when Galina's friends sat on it in a circle and ate wedges of her tenth birthday cake. All from Pripyat. Galina said she doesn't have new friends in

Kyiv. More than three and a half years after the accident, so many parents still keep their children from visiting Galina. Maybe they will change, now Viktor has been allotted this new apartment. Maybe they will see that Galina will not be going back to Pripyat but growing up here.

Maybe it is not Chernobyl at all, maybe it's because they know Galina is a zhid.

Olena has told Galina she should be more friendly in school and not hold grudges over small things. She must remind Galina again.

"Galina, the sirniki are getting cold!" Olena opens the door of the tub room. A pale oval framed in wet black curls turns to her from the tub.

"Mamushka," says Galina. Her eyes — so wide.

Olena draws closer. She leans forward to wipe that miserable expression from her daughter's face.

"What? What happened, Galina?"

Water pooling between her daughter's legs flows pinky red.

Olena laughs, she explains, she tells Galina she has become a woman. She holds Galina's wet body close, pulls the tub stopper and washes away her little girl's fears. But she cannot laugh away her own.

Is not ten years too early for Galina's first period? Olena's came at fifteen. And so much blood — was Olena's flow as heavy? Galina's nosebleeds and dizzy spells have kept her home from school more days than other children.

Olena's just-fried sirniki cool. The fourth movement, Festival in Baghdad, plays itself out in the distance. She finds a sanitary napkin, helps Galina dress, brushes her hair. The hairbrush needs cleaning again. Is the amount of hair in it more or less than usual?

That evening, she refrains from telling Viktor about Galina until he has finished dinner. When she finishes, he sits grim faced, a muscle twitching in his cheek. Olena's inside voice begins to say, *oh no, oh no,* as if she could have prevented Galina's period from arriving.

"I had a letter from Vienna today," Viktor says. "The nuclear station has been cancelled."

Another disappointment. Added to the disappointment that all the Soviet power stations to which Viktor applied have halted their expansions.

"And a letter from Italy," he says. "They are cancelling all their nuclear power plans. Anatoli says not to bother trying Sweden — the government there is not hiring. They're phasing out all nuclear power by 2010."

"Protesters?"

"Protesters know nothing!" shouts Viktor and bangs his fist on the table. "They're going to return all of us to coal and steam. They're going to force us into wars for oil. Reactors are safe — if you run them safely!"

Olena thinks of exemption certificates but erases the thought. In the market yesterday she met Laima wearing a scarf that couldn't hide the red, swollen side of her face. And Viktor is as quick-tempered as Anatoli.

"Maybe nuclear power is not good," she says. "Couldn't we harness the wind?"

"Windmills? Yes, and maybe we can design them with hay storage right from the beginning."

"What about the sun?"

"Olena, I'm not trained for the sun, the moon, the wind or the stars. The atom is all I know. After the accident, the Lenin station was supplying power again within five months — can protesters do that? After their protests, they go home to dinners made on stoves, to lights that run on electricity, to refrigerators that draw power from a grid."

"Don't worry, Viktor," says Olena in her most soothing voice.

"Jobs in capitalist countries are not for life — they can hire you but also fire you. So why leave our country? If you don't like this apartment, they are building new ones in Slavutich for all the workers."

"Slavutich is too close to Pripyat."

Viktor cannot trust official assurances that the food is safe, that the water is pure. And he cannot trust what is revealed now because revelation means it was concealed before, and where there was concealment, there may be more to reveal — how can he know?

Lies breed more lies: doctors who sign death documents that do not mention radiation exposure, scientists who sign fraudulent dosimeter readings, directors who tear pages of radiation level readings out of the records. International energy conferences where plant operators are blamed for pushing the emergency A-Z button.

Maybe it would be better if Viktor were like Anatoli, able to read only Russian and Ukrainian, because the scientific journals he reads in English confuse and upset him. International agencies are now saying exposures lower than thirty-five rems can be dangerous. One article said boiling the water does not eliminate radiation, another that the Soviet Union's remaining fourteen RBMK reactors are flawed.

He'd be really upset if she told him their new neighbours say vodka and cranberry juice are useless and may even be harmful. And Viktor is too angry for Olena to tell him, but two days ago Rivka called to say goodbye — she is taking a leave of absence to travel to some villages far outside the Forbidden Zone. Soldiers are taking more radiation readings and moving cows from collective farms and she wants to find out why.

"No one tells our comrades any results," she said. "I wrote an article asking who gave orders for a nursery school to be built beside a radioactive meadow, but my director will not publish it. In another article, I asked why contaminated meat is being shipped to other parts of the nation, and why clean milk and meat is not being brought into the Forbidden Zone. He will not publish it."

Olena wakes at three o'clock and finds Viktor writing to the Jewish Social Services: yes, we'll go.

Plans are secret, Viktor says. Besides Matushka, Anatoli and Laima are the only ones he trusts with the news. So Olena couldn't bid Rivka do svidanya, even if Rivka were back in Kyiv. Goodbye to Matushka will only be temporary, Viktor promises.

If Dedushka could be allotted an apartment in Kyiv, Olena would want to stay. But since he is now forbidden to leave the Zone of Exclusion, it doesn't matter if she is in Kyiv or America. Maybe once she and Viktor are settled, they will let all the people like Dedushka go where they want. Maybe then Dedushka can come to America too.

Anyway, no one has asked Olena. Where Viktor goes, she and Galina go, as if blown by the wind.

Goodbyes to Dedushka are possible only by telephone and through Anatoli, who has an official pass to visit the zone. When he returns, Anatoli says Dedushka looks well, has only a touch of radiophobia. He spends all day writing to the regional authorities — "Send clean products, send Geiger counters, send clean milk, send sugar, send fish. Our wood is contaminated — please install gas."

In the spring he will be forced to evacuate to an apartment in Minsk and given fifteen rubles a month to buy uncontaminated meat and vegetables. Anatoli called Dedushka ungrateful because Dedushka called it coffin money.

The only message Dedushka sent for Olena was, "Go soon. For Galina's sake, go."

It's December, and almost a new decade. A future has arrived when Olena thought there was no future.

She is not ready.

March 1990

Going to America means going to Italy. Soon after they arrive in the apartment building run by the Jewish Social Services, Viktor says he feels better. His burns have faded, he looks stronger. Galina's hair has recovered its curly sheen, and she hasn't had a dizzy spell in weeks. At first her little mushroom wept for Matushka, but now she runs errands and gives the other refugees in the building haircuts. When they pay her in chocolates, she brings it all "home" to Olena in her satchel, her eyes shining.

"No chocolates, you don't need chocolates," Olena says. "You tell them they must tutor you in English and mathematics. Tell them you will pay by haircuts. Or I will pay by haircuts."

Galina is learning Italian and English so fast she even translates for Olena. But Olena worries about Galina going on buses with Italian men — they admire her black curls. They look and look at her, as if she is a prostitute. And Galina just laughs at them. Italian men don't like it when a little girl laughs at them . . . one followed her home and stood below her window all night, waiting. Then Galina didn't laugh.

Olena tells Viktor they should go to Austria, Germany, anywhere. "We must leave now — I don't like this!"

"Germany!" he says. "They have enough refugees and now no wall to keep them out. And I don't speak German. That man will go away."

But then a week passes and the man is still there every night, looking up at Galina's window.

Viktor becomes sure that man is KGB — who else would watch an apartment night after night, maybe in the daytime as well?

"He is dark and short," says Olena. "To me, he looks Italian."

"No," says Viktor, "he's KGB."

"But why would he follow us? Gorbachev and the KGB have enough to worry about — Azerbaijan, Czechoslovakia, now Lithuania."

"Because I resigned from the Party before leaving. Otherwise, how can I enter America?"

"You could have just *said* you had resigned."

"I don't want to begin my life there with a lie."

So again they leave for America, this time by way of Austria, again thanks to Jewish Social Services. On a cool, breezy night, in a rented Fiat.

This is a good feeling, that we are together, just the three of us. And that everything we own can move with us in this car, away from Unit 4.

October 1991

Olena is sitting at the kitchen table of a two-bedroom apartment above the Teri-Oat convenience store in Shorewood, a town on the lakeshore north of Chicago. She is trying to write her November rent check.

She would like to plug her ears against Bette Midler's voice wafting from Galina's room. And Galina's ears too. Her daughter has begun to believe what the song says, "God is watching us," as if the mythical spirit is KGB. And if God is watching, why must he do it "from a distance"? Galina is not the only one who plays the song till it is inescapable; all this year it was the favourite of American soldiers sitting in dusty tents in Kuwait fighting what Viktor called the First Oil War.

A hundred and twenty dollars. How much is that in rubles?

Do not calculate it — just write.

Such a rich country, with no propiska — anyone can just live where they want. But they make their comrades pay so much for housing. And education! Only school is free — how can the state be so irresponsible that it will not pay for college? And so many schools, none of them teaching the same thing to children the same age, no one in Washington telling them what to teach so they can compete with children in other countries. Some people in Olena's ESL class graduated from those schools, born right here in America and can't read their own language. The volunteers who teach her English can't speak Russian or Ukrainian. They teach English as a Second Language, as if Olena grew up like them, speaking only one language.

A hundred and twenty dollars is also the amount she has paid thirteen times now, every month, to Jewish Social Services for the air fares, for their three months in Italy, for the three months in Austria. And she will pay it twenty-three times more.

And Jewish Social Services volunteers are teaching her that Passover, Yom Kippur, Purim and Hanukkah are not just days for cooking special foods. They say real Jews don't eat sausage, or any pork for that matter. They say God is everywhere. Like radiation.

Already Olena has a job; after three months of training last year she works at the Windy City Day Spa giving massages. She doesn't have to speak English for that. She gives "great" massages, say her clients. Olena thought the word "great" should only be used for Party officials or tsars and tsarinas, but here everything and everyone is "great." Her old country, the Soviet Union, is like Great Britain — no longer great. The newspapers and TV all rejoice that Lithuania, Latvia and Estonia have declared their independence.

Would the women she massages think Olena was no longer "great" if she told them she comes from Chernobyl? Maybe they wouldn't want her hands on their skin. She'd become like her poor Dedushka. His letter says no one talks to him in his new apartment in Minsk, no one visits, so afraid are they.

Olena writes the check, puts it in an envelope and seals it. She licks a stamp before she realizes it is self-sticking, unlike Soviet stamps. She presses it to the envelope anyway, not wanting to waste it.

Viktor's English was always much better than Olena's, but he has to learn American English in place of the British kind. He works in a microbiology laboratory, testing and labelling. He tells Olena what food to buy: only brands he has tested in the lab himself. This year she gathers rituals as well as religion: replace foods used, no changes in brand or size. Write checks carefully, add them up each month.

Olena writes the address. Her handwriting looks unfamiliar in English.

She puts the check on the table in the hall and returns to her seat.

Her memory — it's no good any more. Places and faces at home erase themselves slowly, decaying from the core outwards till they are swallowed into black.

She draws a canary yellow notepad toward her and writes to herself in Ukrainian:

Take clothes to laundromat
Write letter to Dedushka
Make lokshyna for Galina
Make potato varenyky for Viktor

. . .

April 1992

Again Olena is sitting at her kitchen table, writing checks. But now Matushka is also here, sitting before the TV in the living room, a notebook and an English-Russian dictionary beside her. Her arrival was a Passover surprise from Jewish Social Services.

Four Los Angeles policemen have been acquitted of beating a black man, Rodney King, and Matushka is trying to understand why people are shocked and enraged by the verdict. If there were a God, Olena would thank it for American TV, which fascinates and persecutes Matushka by withholding what she is expected to believe.

American TV and newspapers all told Olena that the Soviet Union had dissolved, that the Soviet parliament had gone out of existence, but did Olena believe them? She could not believe two republics simply declared their independence and the Kremlin didn't send in troops to teach everyone a lesson. They told her Yeltsin was installed and the Communist Party was powerless, but did she believe them? Not until Matushka resigned from the Party.

Maybe she didn't believe the news on TV because Viktor said Americans give credit to the actor who was in the White House six years ago instead of to Unit 4 at Chernobyl.

On May 1, 1992, one hundred and twenty dollars will come out of her account for the landlord. And another one hundred and twenty for Jewish Social Services. Now Olena has to write another. Fifty dollars, for Matushka. Fifty dollars Olena cannot save for Galina — how much is that in rubles?

If Olena doesn't write this check, will they send Matushka back?

Oh, she will pay, she will pay. Of course.

Olena doesn't talk to Matushka unless she has to. Let her live in her room, Olena in hers. Olena cooks and clean for her, that's enough.

Olena puts the check on the hall table and returns to her seat in the kitchen. She draws her notepad toward her.

Take clothes to laundromat
Write letter to Dedushka
Make lokshyna for Galina
Get vodka for Viktor
Make potato varenyky for Matushka.

October 1992

Viktor is spending hours at the Constant Reader, a used bookstore several blocks away. Every weekend. Perhaps he has found a pretty bookseller there. Olena will surprise him.

The wind is beginning to whip leaves from flaming maples. As she walks, Olena admires the carved pumpkins with which people decorate their doorsteps. A volunteer said none of those pumpkins will be eaten, they will all go to waste. Competing election signs ask her to vote for Clinton, Perot or Bush, but she is not a citizen here. Is she now a citizen of Ukraine or the Soviet Union? American immigration authorities will decide.

Olena tells the bookseller she is looking for language tapes because she can't find the words to say anything else.

She wanders up and down the stacks until she finds Viktor. He's sitting on a stepstool, old copies of Moscow News spread on the floor beside him. He shows her a 1989 article, "The Big Lie." It says Soviet leaders covered up Chernobyl. It is news for the world, he says, and he's glad it was printed. And he shows her another in English about a place called Three Mile Island.

"For the health of so few, the company paid five million dollars in compensation," he says. "And in the Soviet Union, the Chernobyl allowance is negligible. Oh, it's not only the money — we could have learned much from the mistakes of others."

Olena rests her hand on the slope of his shoulders. How thin he is! Perhaps they should take the bus home.

She leads him from the bookstore. At the bus stop, she stifles her habit of staring at dark-skinned people.

Riding home, Viktor says, "So many big lies. Even in America. Nothing is free here — not health, not good education, not housing. Only they say you are free. I think they mean you can buy blue jeans, black jeans, white jeans, so long as they're jeans — this is what they call freedom. You can rent an apartment and it looks same as your neighbour's — just like in Kyiv. You can buy a desk, a chair, a sofa, and there are ten thousand others like it in the homes of other people. And thousands sit before a TV that looks like ours. This is individualism?"

He is decaying as if a half-life had expired. A doctor told him his white cell count is low. But Olena thinks grief for so many lost comrades, sorrow and self-disgust kill slowly.

Viktor shows her a book he bought. "For you," he says. "Taras Schevchenko, in English."

A showcase in Olena's mind displays every gift from Viktor, from the large box with the thousand kisses inside to her iron, a Swiss knife, a blanket from their early days in Moscow. All left far away in Pripyat. Never before has he given her poetry.

Olena looks out of the bus window and back; everything has blurred.

The book falls open and she reads slowly, "In foreign lands live foreign folks; their ways are not your way. There will be none to share your woes or pass the time of day."

She shows Viktor.

He has bought himself a book in English, too. *The Gulag Archipelago*. It looks very difficult.

A few blocks later she says, "You know that Zone of Exclusion they made at Pripyat? I'm living in one here. I can't speak to anyone, they don't understand me."

Viktor takes out his wallet, opens it and holds out a small square of paper. A photo of Galina. Olena gazes at it with him.

"Did you know, she wants to study public health?" he says. Pride, surprise and admiration are mixed in his voice.

Olena envies Galina.

December 1993

After giving three massages, Olena leaves the spa at two o'clock. Sunshine reflects off store windows and snow-furred lintels. It's ten below zero with the wind chill factor. It's good she found a sheepskin jacket and a hat, scarf and boots at the thrift shop. Good that she doesn't have to wait long at the bus stop.

She walks home on plowed and salted sidewalks. Snow trenches come almost to her waist. The wind would freeze her cheeks the same way in Moscow or Ukraine right now.

What's happening there? She has to read Russian newspapers to know — American TV showed only a few seconds of the panic after the ruble recall. Even when Yeltsin stopped the old Communists with a day-long battle that left Moscow's parliament building blackened and smoking, it was news for just a few minutes. But American intentions, they are good. They have even opened a Holocaust museum in Washington.

What is Rivka doing now? And Laima? And the teachers she worked with in Moscow? They are not so lucky. If there's a story about Russian women on TV, it's about trafficking and prostitution.

Olena doesn't look for Rivka among those faces but listens carefully to the names of the reporters. One day she will hear Rivka's.

Does the old country stay the same, frozen, immobile as we wander and wonder? Do we fade as people forget us? Why do so many memories come now, when we are safe? Here, where few seem to have heard of Chernobyl and few seem to care that it happened? Are my memories real or contaminated?

In the mailbox is a letter unevenly plastered with new Ukrainian stamps. Smiling inside, Olena climbs the back stairway to the apartment, puts her handbag on the hall table.

Viktor and Matushka are sitting on the futon in the living room, watching the CBS news. Paula Zahn says many Russian women want rich men to marry them and take them to America. "Prostitutes!" says Matushka.

She comes into the kitchen and says reproachfully to Olena, "Viktor is hungry," when she means, "I'm hungry."

"Da, da!" Olena says, to send Matushka back to the living room.

She opens the freezer above the refrigerator as if about to take out something. She holds the letter from Dedushka to the light to read it.

Her face chills.

A doctor writes to tell Olena Dedushka is no more. Something about a gas connection that Dedushka never got because a politician wanted the connection for his chauffeur. Poor Dedushka must have died of the cold last month — and Olena was not with him.

Olena pulls the freezer door toward her like a shield, holds the handle to keep from falling. Again she reads the letter. And again.

Oh, Dedushka, you who were more father than my father! I am truly an orphan now. You — keeper of memories, witness of my childhood — are lost to me. Forgive me for leaving you.

Now no one of her blood is left anywhere in the former Soviet Union.

. . .

August 1994

Matushka is trying her glass of Stoli with a drop of Tabasco because she cannot find Stoli Pertsovka in the local stores. What a waste of good vodka! But it keeps her sitting before the TV, waiting for Viktor to return from the lab and Olena to serve her holupki. Olena takes her time stuffing beef, rice and tomato filling into boiled cabbage leaves so she doesn't have to sit beside Matushka on the sofa or on Galina's floor cushion.

These days, thanks to Jewish Social Services, Matushka's been retiring to her room at night smiling. "S bogom!" she says, and, coming out in the morning, "Shalom."

"You know the accident," Olena overheard her tell Galina. "It happened because of the communist atheism. They fell away from Yahweh."

What a thing to tell a child. And Galina is still a child, even if she is almost fifteen.

And Matushka has begun opening the door to strangers who offer to replace her television-induced confusion with their certainty — Jehovah's Witnesses, Evangelical Christians. This morning, she accosted Olena as she was leaving for work and made her listen to a passage from the book of Revelation. "The Third Angel blew his trumpet and a huge star fell on a third of all rivers and springs; this was the star called wormwood, and a third of all water turned to bitter wormwood so that many people died from drinking it."

And Chernobyl means wormwood, she told Olena, as if Olena didn't know.

Olena said, "I didn't know Jews believe in the book of Revelation."

And left for work.

Always, Matushka's logic leads back to Olena; Viktor is pre-absolved by love. But what if it is Olena's fault — Chernobyl is her fault? Yet many who believed in God and prayed surreptitiously died there and Olena survives. Which monster God allowed that?

She is still thinking about this when Viktor comes home. Dinner takes a long time now his thyroid is so enlarged. He chews and chews. Suddenly, he says to no one in particular, "What percentage of Russians do you think trust their leaders?"

For the first time in Olena's life, the anger dwelling blue-hot in the crater within her shouts, "What per *cent*? How should I know? Is there no book or magazine in English that can answer your question? Did I just come back from Russia after interviewing every single Russian? Believe me, I don't know! And I don't know how many Ukrainians trust their leaders either, or Belorussians, or Lithuanians, or Americans. And I don't know how many cockroaches fried at Chernobyl, either."

Matushka looks shocked, Viktor merely surprised. He chews more. Swallows.

"Americans," he says in a low voice, as if she hadn't spoken, "think leaders and country and people are all the same — heh!"

Matushka's eyelids flex like tiny bows releasing poison arrows at Olena. Then she turns back to Viktor. Her tone softens and changes to coaxing. Olena too would like to feed Viktor more, but Matushka's solicitousness now stands in her way.

It's good that she pushes him to eat. Everything tastes of lead to him. He's always not hungry, just tired. So very tired.

Finally, Matushka waves to Olena to clear away his half-eaten meal.

"They trust too much," says Viktor. "Just as we did."

Were people too trusting, too accepting? Chernobyl may not be Olena's fault, but, like Viktor, she too failed to speak. Should she have told someone about the many certificates of exemption, the boron control rods, recommended but never ordered, never installed? Rivka, perhaps?

Why would anyone have listened to her, what would she know about too-few control rods? She didn't want Galina to lose her father, perhaps grow up in a camp as her grandmother did.

Oh, that's only partly true.

Admit it now: Olena had not wanted to lose her nice airy apartment, Viktor's motorcycle, the possibility of trips to the Black Sea. After Viktor had worked for ten years, she could have shopped at the kashtan for clothes for Galina, French perfumes and Kashmiri carpets. And should she have been willing to lose all these present and future advantages just to be *right*? She had the habit of obedience, unlike her mother, and by speaking she could have lost her Viktor.

Maybe Olena is losing Viktor, but if ever she could persuade herself to believe in a miracle it might be now — Viktor has survived so long, when so many of his former comrades and thousands of the liquidators have not.

Olena begins washing the dishes.

"Letter from Anatoli," says Viktor. He gives it to Matushka to read aloud. Olena tries not to clink the plates so she can hear.

Anatoli writes to say that without defence contracts, many people have jobs but no pay. Even engineers. First he considered joining the army but heard even they are reducing pay. So now he and Laima have voluntarily given up the apartment allotted to them in Kyiv and moved to Slavutich. They must have stopped counting their rem exposure.

"The sarcophagus around Unit 4 must be tended forever," he says, "or there could be another explosion."

And he hopes that his pay will continue.

"No one is safe here, but is anyone or any place in the world safe now?" Still, he says, there is absolutely no truth to the Greenpeace report that there have been sixty thousand additional deaths in Russia from the accident. And it is not true that there will be ninety-three thousand cancers — Viktor's cancer is caused by food carcinogens in the USA. And how can alarmists say there will be another hundred and forty thousand deaths in Ukraine and Belarus from Chernobyl, when Anatoli and Laima are still alive? And it is all Western propaganda that four to six million people were affected — Viktor should explain this to Americans.

A clipping included in his letter quotes an official study. "Only fifty-six people have died," it says. "There is no evidence of hereditary defects."

If it hadn't been for Matushka, perhaps I could have had two, maybe even three children.

But later that night, when Olena is putting Anatoli's clipping in a special folder for Galina, so she will not worry a few years from now, her hand trembles.

Anatoli and Laima have been married ten years now, but Laima has not had even one child. No child he has mentioned. Can he be sterile from radioactivity or . . .

No evidence, he said. No evidence of hereditary defects.

July 1995

At Viktor's funeral, Olena sits behind Matushka and Galina as the rabbi intones the Kaddish. She tries to believe the words are not only for Viktor but also for Dedushka.

Olena looks at her clasped hands and does not speak as people around her say, "May His great name be blessed forever and to all eternity." It's good of them to come — they didn't know Viktor very long.

Matushka accepts condolences from the rabbi and her friends from the synagogue as if only she were bereaved. It's a short walk to the cemetery afterwards, and Matushka takes Galina's arm, sniffing into her handkerchief as she recounts a story Olena has never heard — something about Viktor winning a chess match when he was six years old. When Olena draws closer, trying to hear, Matushka and Galina seem to walk faster.

Members of the synagogue and the funeral director are kinder — a sad-eyed gentleman with a carnation in his buttonhole has handed Olena two roses. One to toss on Viktor's wooden casket as they lower him into the soil, one to press between Taras Schevchenko poems.

That night, Viktor is not with Olena when she dreams Galina is in labour and she must take her daughter to the same doctor in Moscow. Viktor is not with Olena when she dreams she cannot reach that doctor, so Galina gives birth to a fish with human fingers and toes.

The wind from the Lenin reactor at Chernobyl has taken Viktor from Olena though they fled to the other side of the planet.

June – July 2000

Rose porcelina, pink tulip, hot pink mini carnations, white alstromeria, lavender lisianthus, pompons, galaxleaf, asters, geranium, ivy and limonium — the flowers clasped in Galina's hands dazzle Olena, stab at the root of memory. She forgets she is moving down aisles in a humid cavelike store, selecting this cascade of fragrance, and returns to the day she carried her own bouquet.

How Viktor would have loved this sunny, balmy June! How many moments he has missed, moments he could have shared with Olena and Galina — and yes, Matushka. Proud moments when Kasparov triumphed over Deep Blue "for mankind," or when Ukrainian teams competed in Atlanta. He missed the amazing moment when an American astronaut wore a Russian spacesuit to spacewalk from the space station Mir.

And this.

Could Viktor — could Olena — ever imagine that in the year 2000 her little mushroom, her little girl from Ukraine who just a few years ago watched MTV and sang Spice Girl songs would marry a man from America, in America? A man whose family is Italian and German? When Olena met Galina's fiancé, she told him his great-grandfather and Dedushka must have fought each other in Europe, and they laughed.

Yes, everyone laughed!

Matushka helped Galina decide on a wedding hall and select the dinner menu — as if she has cooked even one dish for herself in America.

Olena has helped Galina choose, order and send invitations. And now these flowers.

Galina insists on paying with her own money, hard-earned from the accounting firm. She did the same for her bridal gown, when Olena could have sewn her one.

"Aw, Mom," she says, "don't worry. I put it on my credit card. More money will come."

Olena says, "Only Americans think like that."

"We're American now."

The door of the flower shop closes with a sigh. Olena blinks in the sunshine.

"I'll make my own dress, then," she says.

"Can you still sew?" Galina asks, as if sewing is something Olena's hands should by now have decently forgotten. She would rather Olena forget all about Ukraine and Chernobyl and that Galina once traded haircuts for English and mathematics lessons. And that she once said she would study public health.

"Yes, of course." Olena squares her shoulders and looks both ways before crossing the street to the bus stop.

She will buy the fabric today. She will sew a drop-waist dress of azure satin with a layer of lemon net. The old and new colours of Ukraine, from before and after the unthinkable. Two colours that must represent the thousand blues and thousand yellows of her old country. She will add a little embroidery — on the yoke, not on the buttons.

Olena and Galina are sitting on the bed in Olena's bedroom. From the living room, Olena can hear the antics of guests on the Jerry Springer show — Matushka now finds them more understandable than Jehovah's Witnesses or Evangelicals.

"Can't you try to be friends with Grandma for one day? My wedding day? Make it a present to me?" says Galina.

Olena tells Galina she would give her many presents, but not this one. That she would give Galina her life if she needed it, but not this.

Galina strokes Olena's hair, takes her hand and speaks to her in Ukrainian. "Why, why do you hate Grandma so much? She can be difficult but" — she looks into Olena's eyes — "what did she *do* to you?"

Words stop in Olena's throat, her tongue twists as if she is speaking English. If Olena and Matushka die like Viktor, who will Galina have? No one. Because of what Matushka did. How, how to explain?

"Please believe me . . ." she begins. And she tells Galina the story of the button. She thinks Galina is old enough to understand. She adds explanations — that in Moscow in 1980 she could not tell a husband he should even hold a baby much less put it on the pot. That she could not say, as Galina says to her fiancé with a sparkle in her voice, "I'll let you make dinner tonight" or "Why don't we make a reservation?"

"That's it?" Galina's hand slips from Olena's. "All this is about a button?"

Olena's heart shrinks to the size of a teaspoon. She doesn't believe it will start up again. Blood has flooded backward, something will explode.

A breath has to be taken, then another.

The lifeline of this moment runs all the way back through Chernobyl and before, when events might have turned out differently. If Galina cannot understand about the button, how will she understand about the doctor, Olena's soiled green dress, the movie actor Raj Kapoor, who smiled like Viktor?

"How many years ago did this happen?"

"You were about a year old," says Olena.

"And that's all?" says Galina. In English.

Does she mean is that all that happened?

"Many such things happened," says Olena. "You were here, every day. You saw."

"Small things," says Galina. "Didn't you always tell me I shouldn't hold grudges over small things?"

Should Olena tell Galina more? Her inside voice is saying *Oh no, oh no. Speak no further or you'll lose Galina.*

One second of decision — yes, no?

The second shivers, then flees into never. Olena is keeper of the memory of her older daughter. She will carry that bitter memory always, like wormwood at her core.

But no one, not even her Galina, can command her love.

After her wedding Galina will go with her man from America. And then? Olena and Matushka will live together? Maybe Olena will find a second job, mopping floors in a newspaper office. Maybe Olena will move to another city or Israel and leave Matushka in a home.

Who will stop her? God? She is not afraid of God.

But Viktor's face comes before her — Viktor wearing his you-know-you-love-me look. Love is a trap, a noose. A tether running from Olena's ankle to his grave.

She can't leave old Matushka all alone.

"You're right," she says, and laughs. "It was only a button. You deserve the most beautiful wedding, where everyone who comes is happy for you and cares about nothing but your joy. And believe me, little mushroom, Matushka and I will be friends."

For that day.

Naina

Naina has carried her baby inside her so long she cannot remember the day her fullness began. Dr. Johnson was just out of medical school then, apple-cheeked, without her streak of grey — Naina remembers her, cold disc of the stethoscope pressed to Naina's mounding stomach, listening, shaking a very solemn head. "Any day now."

And there was the due date, Naina's heels wide apart in stirrups. She remembers every moment of excruciating pain from pushing, pushing, and nothing coming out, not even blood. That she remembers. Then the unwilled dilation, more pushing, more pushing. The brown balloon of her stomach trembling as her baby retreated from light.

She refused the knife that would have sliced from navel to her mound of spiky black hair. Refused so loudly, signing papers, more papers, and no one from the family with her. She remembers her own voice, fourteen years younger, still imitating Asha Bhonsle's soprano because that's all Daddyji ever played on the tape recorder, screaming, "Leave her. When she's ready, she'll come," the pitying whispers of nurses, all the young doctors crowding about her bed, discussing her case.

"I am not a case," she screamed. "Please, please go away."

Naina knew it was a girl from the very beginning. Dr. Johnson didn't have to show her the pictures — pieces of sky collaged to black plastic. Only a girl would be so comfortable in her mother's womb that coming out and needing to grow would spoil her world. By then Naina had talked to the baby for so many months — now so many years — that if the baby hadn't been a girl before she took residence in Naina's womb, she surely became one.

Dr. Johnson confirmed it every month, and by now she uses the same words she used last month, last year. "Yes, I can hear her; her heartbeat is regular. Here" — she clips an ultrasound to the light box on the wall — "see where her toes curl, and look at her hands! Still so tiny after fourteen years."

Also, every month for the past two years, Dr. Johnson says, "That Chinese woman called again to ask if you want her help." This woman swears she's not connected to *Guinness* or the *Globe* or *Star* or *National Enquirer*, but that's where she read about Naina. She calls herself Dr. Chi and says she was a sinseh doctor, but she's repeating her whole medical degree and training so she can practise in Canada. "Shall I tell her you'll think about it?"

By now all the tabloids have written their pieces, had their say. The journals of medical research have taken note, moved on to the next freak show. They still follow up, once in a while, despite Naina's unlisted phone number.

Naina turns wide eyes upon Dr. Johnson, and the bindi above them is a third eye that has become wary of the word "help." "My baby will come when she is ready," she says, as she has said every month.

Dr. Johnson paces. "What is it in your genetic makeup — what is preserving this baby?" Her tone says Naina is being stubborn, refusing to provide critical information. "All the specialists I've referred you to, all the psychotherapists . . . I can't think what to do next."

Naina opens her mouth. Dr. Johnson breaks in. "I won't

override your wishes, Naina. Unless I think the child is at risk — amazing that all the tests show no danger there. Just amazing. Well, if it's not hurting you or hurting the baby, I suppose there's no harm. Two can live as cheaply as one. But upon my word, it's a strange phenomenon!"

Naina pulls her heels from the stirrups and rises from vinyl padding. Dr. Johnson leaves her alone to dress.

In the reception room, Naina folds the legs of her salwar about her calves and jams her stockinged feet into moon boots. She struggles into her coat, draws the scratchy wool of her scarf across her neck as if she were adjusting a dupatta across her shoulders. Dupattas are passé in India now, her cousin-sister Sunita says, but Daddyji insisted she wear one growing up in Malton; the scarf has become a substitute dupatta.

Every time, it's no different. The weight of her belly pressing against maternity underwear, the baby's pull on the placenta coiled within her. She waits at the bus stop for a while, till her nose feels frozen; then she trudges to the subway, emerges three blocks from the boulangerie.

André, the landlord, is coming down the staircase, a tray of petits pains levitating over his head as he descends to meet her. "Want one?"

"No. Merci, André." His apron leaves flour streaks on her coat as he brushes past.

The day Stanford moved out, André didn't offer her petits pains. "You could lose a little weight, a young woman like you. Get a haircut, buy some sexy clothes at the Eaton Centre. One date with a jeune homme, you'll forget all about Monsieur Stanford. I'll talk to Valerie, she'll know a few good guys." He meant to be comforting. When reporters besieged the boulangerie, André said, “They’re good customers.” But when they came snooping for Naina, he met them stone-faced, arms folded across his chest, on this very staircase — “No trespassing, mes amis.”

Busy in her loft studio, Valerie, André’s wife, never found Naina a few good guys but instead counselled her in brief appearances on the landing, holding hands mottled with clay out from her denim smock. “Ça ne fait rien, Naina, mon amie! Some things, they take years. This one I work on now — a lifetime. I try and I try, mais . . . it resists me. Maybe I resist it.” Valerie’s sculpture is realist, the figures so lifelike that when a caretaker statue she sculpted was exhibited at the Art Gallery of Ontario, people stopped to ask it directions.

Mothering, *Baby Care*, *Working Mother* — magazines besiege Naina’s door. She doesn’t remember subscribing; money is not for spending on subscriptions, money is for saving. But the magazines still arrive. Do their senders somehow know she hasn’t delivered yet?

Delivered.

She has delivered so many other things in her thirty-five years, why can she not deliver the girl? Delivering is giving, from the sender to the receiver, the woman who delivers just the conduit. One job she had, soon after Stanford left, was delivering parcels. She discarded her bright salwar kameez for the drab brown slacks and shirt of a UPS uniform. Perched high above cars in her cab, long hair wound into a tight bun and hidden away under the cap. Till the dispatcher said he couldn’t understand her accent on her call-ins, and she might as well forget it because it wasn’t his fault she heard Ramana when he’d said Ramada.

Naina turns the key, flicks the light switch. Not much here, but something to call her own. A lumpy Murphy bed, its two legs permanently lowered to the parquet floor, a desk and chair she and Stanford bought together from a junk dealer on Spadina, books piled on a low-legged piri from the family home in Malton.

A yeasty smell rises around her from the boulangerie below.

She lowers her weight to the seat in the bay window that bulges over Edgewood Street, not bothering to raise the blinds.

The ache again, at the small of her back.

When I know who sent you, baby, then I'll know to whom I must deliver you. But till then, you stay with me, achcha?

Sunita — "call me Sue" — is svelte in a sage green polo-neck tunic and black tights. Arriving as emissary from her aunt, Naina's mother, like a finger extended outdoors to test a chill wind, she is the only one who still comes to see Naina from the family. She has nothing to gain, Naina reminds herself, nothing whatsoever, by driving all the way east and spending several toonies to park her white BMW in the parking lot across the street.

Nothing to gain but satisfaction.

"Why don't you tell your Daddyji sorry — buss! That's all it takes. One little word and you can be back ek dum, no problem."

But this is the problem.

"I have done nothing wrong," says Naina. "All I committed was love. There is too little of it, so I felt it. Enough for all of us."

"Love, shove." Sunita's laugh could peel the dingy blue paint from the walls. "What happened to your gora guy now? Not that I'm saying you did anything wrong, mind you — you were just young and foolish. All I'm saying is now you should say sorry. Then we can all meet together — no more of this, 'I can't tell anyone I'm going to see Naina, but everyone knows and gives me secret messages for her.' So I'm just asking, does it hurt you to say it, or what?"

"No," says Naina. "Saying sorry would not hurt my flesh. It would not break a bone. It will not make me bleed. It will not kill me, that is true. But, Sunita, I am *not* sorry. It's important to me to mean what I say."

"Call me Sue," Sunita says automatically. "But I ask you, what is the harm in *saying* it? What does it cost you? Just to please everyone." A frustrated click of the tongue. "You really have no sense, Naina. Fourteen years! Even Ram returned home after fourteen years exile."

"He was a god, he was a king — men can return home once they do what they have to do."

"Such funny ways you see things, Naina. All this women's libber talk, see where it brought you?" Sue's hand rising to her nose ring jingles a wristful of twenty-two-carat gold bangles. "Lose a little weight," she advises kindly, three-inch heels clopping to the apartment door. "Otherwise, even if you make up, how will Uncle and Aunty find you a match? They'll have to find a widower or even a divorced fellow now, but still you have a chance. Then you can have children just like mine. Think what I'm saying — one little word."

The baby shifts appreciatively as Sunita leaves. A tiny fist punches suddenly, stretching Naina's lost waist. She strokes it, crooning, "Chanda mama dur ho . . ."

In the evening, Naina puts on her hat, mittens and coat and climbs on the 509 streetcar. Downtown, she and the baby within rise in a carpeted cell to the top of a tinted glass skyscraper. There she bends and straightens, emptying garbage cans and sorting paper from plastic to ready it for rebirth. She wipes a rag gently around the computer brooding in suspended mode in the corner of each vacant cubicle. The roar of her vacuum fills empty hallways, sucking up dirt. She straps on golden yellow kneepads to kneel and polish the expanse of wood floors in corporate meeting rooms.

The white fluorescence hums, "Good money, good money."

That's what André said when he gave her the card. "It's good money." Said it kindly, having printed off three late-fee notices in a row to slip beneath her door. Naina looked at the card, heart falling, realizing she was being given an option the family would find even less to their liking; the family is not of that caste of people who clean for others.

But André was being kind, and he did not know the family or its deep disgust for people who clean. And so Naina looked past the family and called the number on the card.

"It's just temporary," she told the baby. "Till you are ready to come into the world."

Emptying trash, she wonders at what point in the past four or five years had the cleaning become permanent? Become an important job that deserves a dedicated army instead of a crew or two? She can aspire higher with her college degree — anyone in the family would. But she's used to this now, it gives her mind space as her hands move, and no one demands she wear a dress or pants or hide her long black hair under a khaki cap.

It's important work that must be done each night to offset the white-collar crimes of the day.

Stanford wore a white collar, even in those days, when they were just students. And a suit. To class. They met at a Mmuffin stand and her love reached out by itself, extended beyond the family to enfold him, when he admitted to feeling as foreign in Toronto as she did. It took months for her to understand that he felt foreign because of "all these people from other countries coming to Canada, taking over all we've built." It was Stanford who rented the apartment above the boulangerie, winking at André as he rolled out his bearskin rug, set his poufy chair before his stereo. Rented it because he said it made him feel like a thief every time he had to park a block away from her home so Daddyji wouldn't find out she was dating a gora.

Daddyji found out, of course. Found out when her belly began growing. Her mother told Daddyji, "This is Canada, these things happen."

"But not to my daughter," raged Daddyji. "Have you taught her no better?"

Then Naina saw her mother's face close, close to Naina like the door her father slammed in her face.

After graduation, Stanford took his stereo, his poufy chair and his bearskin rug and moved to Seattle, gambling on a free-trade future without encumbrances. "Mistakes happen," he said. "You take responsibility, you move on. I'll send you money when the child comes."

He never did, for the child has never been delivered.

He probably thinks Naina got rid of it. Stanford, proud wearer of the yuppie label every day of the eighties, reads the *Wall Street Journal,* not the *National Enquirer* or the *Journal of Medical Research.*

Who sent you, baby? Where shall I deliver you?

Naina spends her mornings with her swollen feet up on the radiator, watching snow sail down on Edgewood Street, imagining tropical breezes. "You're so smart, baby. No reason to come out into this weather." She pats her stomach as a ring quakes the cordless phone.

"That woman I told you about?" Dr. Johnson sounds surprised. "She called again. She still thinks she can help you. She's so insistent, Naina, I think you should see her. I'll tell her she must come here. It can't do any harm. It may address the psychological effect this is having on you."

"I'm fine, I don't need to see anyone."

"Naina, listen to me! We've tried everything else for your case."

"I'm not a case."

"Well, you will be a case if this continues. How's next Friday?"

"Bad."

"Naina, I'm trying to help. We don't know what effect your decision to allow nature to take its course may have on the baby. There could be brain damage after this long, there could be personality problems."

"I still say — why are you not listening? — I still say, when my baby is ready, she will come."

"All right, let's look at it your way — don't you want to know, Naina? Don't you want to know what she's waiting for? Why she's waiting so long? This Dr. Chi says she can help us understand that."

Naina said, "'Maybe."

"Next Friday, then. Be here at ten."

Baby, talk to me. Only to me. Tell me where you come from. Say where I must deliver you.

"Hypnosis isn't covered by the Ontario Health Insurance Plan. You'll need to pay in advance — oh, we can worry about that later." A well-kept petite woman of about forty-five, the doctor is jovial, not earnest; Stanford used to say all Chinese people are earnest.

But then Stanford didn't know very many Chinese people. Stanford didn't know Dr. Chi.

Dr. Chi is the first doctor Naina has ever talked to who has not made her repeat her entire medical history. It could be she read it before she met Naina, the simplest explanation but the least likely. It feels as if Dr. Chi just *knows;* she has not asked Naina a single stupid question. For instance, whether her decision not to allow a knife near her belly is occasioned by vanity or by — delicate pause — her Hindu religion? Dr. Chi has asked her to lie down, not on the vinyl-padded table with her heels in the stirrups, but on a couch in Dr. Johnson's consulting room.

"I think you must ask the baby why she refuses to be delivered." Dr. Chi flicks a stray lock of straight black hair from her eyes; Naina catches a whiff of camphor. Tiger Balm.

"She does not come because she is not ready" — her standard explanation.

"And we could ask her, if she were delivered by Caesarean section, would she die?"

"Why should she answer you?" Naina asks, a little jealous.

"No reason, no reason — quite right. No, she will speak through you." Dr. Chi pauses, rubs her hands though the room is warm and the snow is outside, falling fast.

"You will use me to ask my baby to speak?"

"Yes, yes, of course. How else can it be done?" She pats Naina's arm, gives her a buddhi-filled smile. "Lie still, now, lie still. Allow yourself to relax," says Dr. Chi.

Allow myself?

The couch is soft beneath Naina's shoulders. The baby's weight settles above her. A cobweb hangs where walls and white ceiling meet. Naina holds her belly, rubs it soothingly, closes her eyes. Dr. Chi's Tiger Balm scent grows stronger.

"You are back where you were born, far from Canada. There's no snow outside . . . It's warm, even hot. Getting hotter. The heat is so strong it sears your eyeballs, you remember that kind of heat? Yes . . . Allow yourself to feel your eyes become heavy . . . getting heavier. Smell the fragrance of dust. Can you feel a nice breeze cooling your skin?"

"Yes."

"Allow your limbs to feel heavier and heavier . . . You're going deeper into yourself." Dr. Chi's voice flattens. "You are looking within your womb. There, in the dark . . . you see her yet? Yes?

See if you can move toward her. Ah, you are there? Ask her the questions you have in your heart . . ."

Naina can see her, very small, comma-shaped, brown-skinned, black-haired. She opens her arms.

Do you know me, baby? I am your mother.

I know you. I have known you a long time.

Why do you wait within me? Wait so long? Make me carry you everywhere?

I wait because you are not ready to receive me.

I thought you waited because you were not ready to come to me.

You were wrong.

I am ready, baby. What can I promise you that will bring you to birth?

Tell me you will love me into being. Tell me you will not be afraid.

That would be untrue, baby.

Then tell me you will live with your fear and your doubt and, even so, bring me to light.

Why have you chosen me for your birthing?

Kismat, the luck of the draw.

Who sends you to me?

The unknown.

Will you come by the knife or will you come without?

I will come when you are open wide and deep as a well.

To whom shall I deliver you, baby?

To life, to the world.

What if I fail you, baby?

You do not fail me if you try your best.

I will try.

Dr. Chi's smile is above her.

"Oh, your bindi is smudged," she says kindly. "It was weeping."

The prescription Dr. Chi writes for Naina is for a broth of chicken, laced with ginger juice and brandy, to be washed down nightly with red date tea.

Naina's baby is born in October on Diwali day, the day Ram came home from exile. Few diyas burn on the windowsills of homes, and there are no sparklers; few celebrate this festival in Toronto. After her second gestation, she comes quietly, from an unwitnessed, private labour. Labour that is joy, joy that is labour. There is no one but Naina to staunch the blood, clean the child, cut the cord and offer the gods her thanks.

All my thanks, heartfelt thanks.

And in the morning, Naina opens her door to Valerie, who cries, "Cherie, I finished it, come and see . . . oh, la la! What have we here?"

The bay window encircles Naina as she resumes her seat, the baby at her breast.

"Ah, your bébé and mine, they came together! I have work all night as if a beam had opened between myself and le bon dieu."

"I too worked all night," says Naina, smiling radiantly. "I'll come up and visit yours soon."

When Valerie is gone, Naina lifts the cordless phone.

It's time she told the family; she'll call Sunita — really shock her this time. Time to find Stanford and surprise him, tell him what she's done without his help. Time to register the hybrid little being in her arms.

Rendezvous

Hel-lo, Jimmy! Jimmy McKuen!

It's me, Enrico. How does this place call itself Greek and let you Irish in? Let you sit at their lunch counter, they'll let anyone in. You sure you're allowed this side of town? Good to see you, amigo — been one helluva long time.

You're looking good, but that corduroy coat of yours looks like it's from the Salvation Army. Feel mine — it's that new microfibre. And where'd you get that shirt, buddy? Looks like the one you had on the last time I saw you. Hey, doesn't cost much to be in style these days, but you gotta be aware. What's in, what's out, you know. Oh, and your hair — how come you still have so much of it? If I had my shears, I'd texturize it a little. Right here, above your ear.

Okay, I'll sit down a minute.

By the way, you'd know something that's been bothering me all day. What was the name of Gene Autry's horse? Trigger? Nah, it's about your memory, Jimmy. It just came to me — Champion, that was his name.

Yeah, coffee. I don't know — my god, do I have to decide this fast? Decaf, I guess. What's your name? Carlos, huh? Man, you are so Mexican.

I ain't his kind of Mexican, Jimmy, I was always kinda laid back. This one's so nervous, he's ambidextrous with that coffee.

Speaking of coffee, you know my son? Met him? In and out of problems — aren't we all! The latest one is coffee. He's buying it from a company called Bad Ass, what a name! They sold him a sixteen thousand dollar roaster, like he's going to roast that much coffee. He says it's the biggest commodity in the world after oil. All those kids lining up to order grandeys and double latteys — you say anything in French it sounds better, know that? You want a little class, just get out your English-French dictionary — it's all there, that's the key to class, my man.

And romance. You know it, Jimmy, even you got your Irish tongue around voolay-voo kooshay ahvec mwa, you know that one, eh? Bet you've used that one a few times — not in court, I'm sure, but extra-curricular. Am I right or wrong?

No, I never was in France, Korea was my war. You too, huh? Still writing wills and filing incorporations? Small claims and traffic stuff? Well, someone's gotta deal with that stuff.

Oh, let me see, I was last in Mexico in . . . remember my '57 T-bird? Turquoise, with the porthole windows? I used to store the top in the summer. Took me three months to drive down to Acapulco. Saw all the relatives. They thought I walked on water, still had donkeys and sticks in those days. Offered me their daughters. At that time, I liked every girl, let me tell ya. I had Norwegians, Germans, Greeks, even Italians. I never left any out, loved all my honeys, but I never did many Mexicans. I was too scared of the fathers.

Be still my heart, if it isn't the lovely Tula! Where have you been all my life, my darlin'?

No sense of humour, eh?

What're you having, Jimmy? Just coffee and a cruller? Hey, it's almost lunchtime.

Okay, Tula. Spinach omelette. No toast, no hash browns.

I found my own gene therapy, Jimmy: no carbs. Now I'm aware, it's so easy. I want to go out with my boots on, with feet, you see. So half of me is gone. I have a closet full of forty-fours and I'm down to thirty-four.

Women these days, even French doesn't work on them. Wish I knew what does work — when you're aware, everything is so easy.

Let me tell you about romancing women. I'd pull up outside Mercy High School in my '36 Ford with that rumble seat, you seen it? I glued the leopard skin to the dashboard myself. Skirts way down in those days, Jimmy. Way down, I swear, nearly to the ankle, and if I saw a kneecap I was so excited. They kept them pretty well covered in the forties, you know, Jimmy. Ah, you're too young, you only remember the fifties. Remember when the microminis came in in the sixties? Oh my god, I nearly died. And Elvis, how they wouldn't show him from the waist down? Those Evangelicals were saying that was terrible, but they can't put the genie back in the bottle now. I was ahead of the curve in the forties — now my kids call *me* old-fashioned. Now their friends look at me and say, I think my grandma went to your hair salon. And if you give them any advice about love — no one makes love like they do today, you know. No one can make love like these kids today. Oh my god, I'm old-fashioned now, but you know the kind of hairpin I am.

Thank you, my love. This omelette looks divine.

Grab me a napkin, there, would you, Jimmy? That woman is half in love with me, I swear.

Yeah, sure I was married. Twice. Once in Anchorage in '54 — the ratio there was five hundred to one, so marriage was the only way to find some warm loving. Second time — maybe you met Nance? You should have. What a woman.

Ah, it's a long story I should only tell to someone with an Emilio Zapata statue on the dashboard. Or Pancho Villa. They got along, you know, they had their own special interests like everyone else, but they got along.

All my friends were getting married, Jimmy — even you. Admit it. What year was it you got married to Arlene? I must have done it the year after, so 1965. I had to. Nance said marriage or the highway, and there comes a time when it's hard to resist a good housekeeper, you know? I said to her, You white women are all alike, but really, the ones coming out of college these days, hell, they're getting so many opinions a man doesn't know what's coming next. So I went and did it. Yes, I did.

I'm not going to say another word about my marriage, Jimmy. Just this. Nance was a fine wife, no doubt about that. I had so many honeys while she raised four kids. If I came home drunk, that woman would just let me sleep in the car, no matter what the weather. One night I was going home and I pulled over to take a nap. A flashlight shone through the window, I explained to the cop that I hadn't wanted to get sleepy driving. Ten feet from the curb? said the cop. He took me down to the station and called Nance. Nance said, Keep him — what'm I going to do with him? I'll pick him up in the morning. That's the way she was, see, a practical woman. So the cop came back and I'd been sitting there talking for an hour — to a fireman's coat and hat hanging on the wall. When I got home I told her, "Ay, you white women are all alike," and I tried to give her a kiss. She said, Keep your hands off the merchandise.

But I did that too many times, wore her out, you know. Now I'm on Nance's Ten Most Not-Wanted list, but she's got good reason. Takes years to wear out some women, and that Nance of mine stuck it out longer than most. You want to know why? Take one guess — don't bother, I'll tell you anyways. It's cause I'm more interesting than any of the young guys you see around these days. Oh, they'll be faithful and they'll be good providers to dull-witted women like Tula, but I ask you, do they have charm? Are they interesting? Can they make conversation with anything but their computers? Nah, Jimmy, you and I got it made in the conversation department. That's what I used to tell Nance, any time we fought. And she'd tell me I was way too good with words.

Conversation. For years I made my living by conversation. Like you, but not as serious — you were always so serious I used to say your middle name was Silence.

The Shampoo Shrink, that's what they called me. And they'd come saying, Oh, my wife just left me, or, I lost my job. And I'd sit 'em in my barber chair, and I'd pump the thing up till they were way off the ground, and then I'd tell 'em what I thought they should do and bring 'em back to earth again, cause that's really what they needed more than my haircuts. Oh, Jimmy, I got so many friends that way — guys and all my honeys too.

And do you know, that was the problem, I couldn't charge them! Over the years I collected so many friends I wasn't charging nearly anyone. Then Nance started checking the books to see if my honeys paid, and she said, Hey, stop with the talking and the flirty thing, just do their shampoos and styles. She was right, I couldn't pay the rent anymore with the number of paying customers I had left, so the salon went to pay its debts and I went personal.

Personal was good. I made house calls to rich guys, so they wouldn't be seen in public with curlers and bibs on, you know. CEOs, them guys who get golden parachutes and retirement plans even when their companies lose billions of dollars. Senators, doctors. Gave them some of my advice and got some. Rich men love telling how they got rich and how they go about keeping it, which is much harder, you know, Jimmy, a lot harder. Nance said I should have listened more and talked less, but you only go around once, and she was just mad because after thirty years of her work and some of mine, we didn't have nothing to show.

Yeah, sometimes I'd get loaded and say mean things. A silver tongue like mine usually comes with a black lining. Got so loaded one night, I fell asleep before I remembered to say the I-love-you's. Next morning there was a note on the door from a lawyer and I had all the space in the world for my clothes in our closet.

No, no more coffee. Slow down, boy, slow down. Got your Nikes moving like you're going to run in the Olympics. Don't crash the dishes, dammit, you're giving every Mexican a bad name. No one's going to call Homeland Security to catch you here.

Well, Jimmy these days I hang around, talk to young white guys like you. Black guys, gals — I'm not particular. Yesterday they said on the TV that if you're going to stand at a bus stop, stand with your back to the wall. Now, do I look like a pantywaist who'd stand like that? I said, I'm from Mexico, I don't need to be worried about my black brothers, the ones who gotta be afraid are people like you Jimmy, look at you, white as white gets, even your eyebrows.

Course, my eyebrows are white too now.

Speaking of TV, am I tired of car chases and shoot-em-ups. Oh, listen to their great dialogue, A man's gotta do what a man's gotta do. What do you think they mean by that? I mean, I'd like to ask Arnold that, say Hey, Schwarzi-negger, what did you *mean*? He doesn't know — I swear he paid for acting school just to get himself a wooden face. Forget TV, we gotta get out like this more, talk to people. And women.

I tried some bars, but romance is pretty confusing these days, Jimmy. Remember when gay meant happy? How 'bout Gaelic? That must be rough on you, Jimmy, you can't even say Gaelic any more, not that you might, seeing as you don't speak it, but I mean you should be able to say gay-lick, you know? Last month I went to some bar where they had all tall girls, and I tried to make out all night, and when I was leaving this one with big eyelashes says to her girlfriend, Forget him, the bitch is straight. Turns out her name was Rodney.

Now I'm at this restaurant that wants to be fine dining. New York style in the Midwest, and at New York prices — it's a lotta hooey! I wear a boutonniere and usher ladies to their tables while the young men tip the valet parkers. If you ever see my Nance, tell her I wear white gloves and pour the best champagne. Tell her I still have a few clients, but there's no one I call honey.

Oh yeah, you've never met her. But if you do, you can't miss her, she's still a looker.

Anyways, since Nance left me I've got time. A lot of time. So I've been writing — started about a year ago, going down to the lakeshore with my spiral notebook and dictionary. You know you just take a word, add it to another, and you never know where you end up.

Here's my new card. See the cupid? I make some bucks from young guys. They're like you always were, Jimmy — got no vo-cab-yoo-lary of romance. Here's a for instance: Last week, I was down at the beach and I finished a poem for next Valentine's Day — sure it's half a year away, but I keep in practice. I called it "Rendezvous," that's French for meeting someone you love again. I must've been missing Nance that day — my eyes were smarting. I get that way sometimes, whenever I get wondering if she ever thinks of me.

There was a young lifeguard sitting up on his high chair in his county uniform. Red shorts and all the sunscreen we never knew to wear at his age. I said, Here, give this to your honey. You got a honey? He said yes. I told him, Remember this: she's gotta believe in romance, she's gotta believe romance is everything, because the first minute your honey stops believing that, you've lost her.

Don't you wish someone had given us that kind of advice? You know, when we were his age? Maybe someone told you a secret no one told me — that's how come you've still got Arlene.

The lifeguard wasn't Mexican, but I could tell he was a good sorta guy, you know, like I was at his age. But he didn't understand what I was getting at. Probably won't for another twenty years. I gave him the poem anyways, and I said, No charge, because I really mean it.

No, no, no more coffee, amigo.

Tula, I love you too, my darling.

Thanks for picking up the tab, Jimmy. See you around in another twenty or thirty years. Give sweet Arlene a kiss on her lips, say it's from me. Tell her she's got to believe in romance. Got to believe in love. Stay off the carbs, now — it's real easy, once you're aware.

Won't do you no good, though. You can bet your Irish ass, this Mexican's going to be around a whole lot longer than you. And when I'm done, I got me a spot picked out under a willow in Lake Park where the girls go jogging — not too many Mexicans got their ashes spilled around Lake Park, you know. They don't like Mexicans around there.

But just think of it, I'll be laying there, looking up skirts, laughing.

Hey there, Jimmy!

Sure, I'll sit down a minute. I'm on my break. I got a whole fifteen minutes.

I was avoiding your eye, Jimmy, cause of Enrico talking to you. He a friend of yours?

Okay, I'll tell you something I won't tell many others. I don't like him. Leaves me his dirty poems as tips, makes me mad with his guy jokes. Comes in here crying about how his Nance left him, but he's still got no respect for women. Makes a big mess and calls me over like I'm going to clean up instead of Carlos.

But you're not like him. I told my ma about that time when you took me for a ride on your Harley last summer and we went over the Hoan Bridge clocking ninety. I said, That man's got some pep in him yet, he's not just some boring two-bit attorney.

Yeah, well, ma said, Don't get no ideas, Tula. That guy's married. I said, I ain't getting any ideas — we're friends. Aren't we? Besides, you're way too old for me. Safe as condoms, ha, ha!

And you don't laugh when I say I've got dreams. That Enrico, he don't think anyone's got dreams except himself. Keeps telling me I should cut my hair this way or that. Says he'd like to cut it for me. Offered to come to my home — said he was a personal hairdresser. He just wants to get in my pants. He's got balls, I'll give him that. A few years ago, all kinds of guys wanted to get in my pants, but a woman gets burned a few times, well, she gets ovaries.

Which reminds me, did you try the eggs Benedict today? No? I made the sauce, and it came out real smooth. It's not much, I know. But it's something.

My dreams are fantastic, Jimmy. And none of them are about you.

But I'll tell you, they ain't always going to be dreams. No way. I'm going to be a sculptor. How about that? Tula, walking in the footsteps of Myron and Polyclitus. And you know why I'm going to be like them, Jimmy? It's because I can see people from the inside and outside at the same time. That's thinking like a sculptor, right?

I borrowed this book out of the library, real thick, with glossy pictures, all about famous statues. Do you know what they thought was beauty in classical sculpture? They said it's when each part depends on the other to create harmony.

And that's how they came up with the idea of democracy.

No shit, I read it. Didn't they teach you that in law school? You want democracy, you gotta go back to greasy old Greece before galactabourikos and spanakopita. Maybe even before the Olympics.

But the Greeks got it wrong, too, they ignored the slaves and the women — everyone who had to run things and clean up after them. It wasn't beautiful, because it was out of balance, see?

But what can you expect from a bunch of old men?

Anyway, I wasn't interested in all the Caesars and Italian guys. I wanted to look at the statues of women — you know, like Liberty. Wanted to know where she came from. You heard of a place called Colmar, in France — you ever been there in your travels? Well, one of these days, I'm going there. Because that's where she was made. That's where Bertoldi had his workshop. Yep. He made her in France and shipped her all the way here. And you know what else? She's got two things, one in each hand. I bet you know one, but tell me the other.

Gotcha — you can't think what it is, right?

Okay, I'll tell you. It's called a tablet. Not the pill kind of tablet. A tablet like a slate or a plaque. Liberty is holding it like a book. And you know what's written on it? Think, try to see it.

No, it's not the Ten Commandments.

I'll tell you. It says July 4, 1776, in Roman numerals. Now what do you suppose the sculptor meant by that? D'you suppose he meant anything by that? Or do you think it's there cause that arm had to be there and he had to do something with it? What do you think?

I guess they didn't teach you symbolism in law school. Well, now that I read this book, I know all about symbolism. That tablet is about living under the rule of law. Awesome, that some Frenchie could think of that but nobody these days knows that, not that crowd in Washington, Bush and Cheney and that slimeball Karl Rove. They don't think laws apply to them, only to people like me. It's depressing, some days.

Yeah? A big attorney like you? What d'you have to be depressed about? So you're not as good-looking as you used to be, but you ain't worried about where your next meal is coming from.

Don't give me no sob story about how your wife don't understand you. Arlene — right? — she still at the VA hospital? Physical therapy for Gulf War Syndrome and Iraq amputees, well, someone's got to do it. I don't hear much about those vets. Every time I look up at that TV in the corner — between tables, of course — I see some guy who says he murdered that little girl JonBenét Ramsey and someone else singing on American Idol.

Hey, didn't Arlene make you buy that old twelve-apartment building on 17th Street? Yeah, you told me you renovated every apartment, just the two of you. Seems to me your Arlene has more sense in her pinky than a lot of men.

I got a friend who has business sense like that, she makes wedding cakes, says I should come help her. Says sculptors were just making cake molds, using plaster and metal in place of cake batter. And they probably learned it from watching their wives make cakes. Did they have cakes when Myron was around, Jimmy? Maybe you can look it up on the internet and tell me.

Well, what's it for then, if it doesn't have that kind of info?

To find me? I'll be damned. Who'd want to find me? Oh, when I get to be a famous sculptor.

Well, I don't have no bank account, so I wouldn't use it to check my money. I don't have no stocks or bonds, so I wouldn't need it for that. Air tickets? What's the use of me checking air ticket prices? You gotta have money to fly, buddy!

I could check it to get a different job. I could check the paper for that. Oh, in a different city. Yeah. But I have to be close to my gran's. I stop in and check on her every day, before and after work, do her laundry. If I got a job far away, who'd do that for her? She only speaks Greek, you see, so my mom and I are the ones who talk for her.

Course, if I go to school, I'll need a second job so I can pay the tuition. Maybe I'll go decorate cakes after all. It wouldn't be much, but it would be something.

I could find a student loan on the net, huh? That how you got to be a lawyer — with student loans? How many years did you spend paying them off? Oh, we don't get nothing like the GI Bill these days, and I'm shit-scared of debt, buddy. Know how much your credit cards are costing you? Student loan would damn near be like that. That's what you learn when you're the daughter of Greek immigrants. My folks didn't raise no dummy. Pythagorus didn't have no debt, did he? Euclid didn't have no debt. That's because they had slaves. Didn't have to work themselves, didn't have to pay no minimum wage — that's how they got to be philosophers. The internet can tell you that.

Ever hear of a guy called Sassafras? No, not Sassafras, I mean Sisyphus. My dad is always talking about him. Said Sisyphus got himself in trouble with his boss, and the boss put him to rolling a humungous boulder up a steep hill. And then just as he rolled that thing nearly to the top, it would roll back down. And he'd run after it all the way down to the bottom and have to start all over again. I would have quit. Maybe he couldn't.

Oh yes, I can relate to Sisyphus. Sometimes I don't want to get out of bed in the morning, cause I'm real tired and my feet ache. And then I think hey, someone's waiting for his coffee at table seven, and the guy who always sits at nine likes his eggs over easy and not runny, and who'll look after them if I don't? And that gets me moving quick. So I wonder if Sisyphus felt like that every morning. I wonder who he got up for.

Hey, Jimmy, did Sisyphus get minimum wage? What about health care? My dad said they didn't have things like that in Greece, that's why he left. So they couldn't have had it in Sisyphus's day. But they'd have to give him time off to sleep, eat and crap, right? My dad's been wrong about a lot of things, so when you get a chance, you ask the net for me. But maybe the answer will be in Greek and I couldn't read it.

You couldn't either? Well, you could have fooled me, but not my gran.

Oh, yeah, I could do a second shift right here. Yeah, old man Petropoulos, he's my dad, he'd put me to work like a shot if I let him. In the kitchen, serving coffee, busing tables like Carlos, but I say no way. I'm Greek, not Mexican. I got my pride. Carlos says I'm stuck up like my dad, that's what he says. He says it's money, that's all that matters. But how would it look if I was in college and some students stopped in here and saw me busing tables? I'd have to be in acting school for that to be cool.

So what do you think, Jimmy? What are my chances? Slim, or none? Think Tula could be a sculptor? I like molding things. Giving them a lift so they look alive. Like my customers after coffee. It's not much, but it's something. Ask the net — it's all there, isn't it?

Okay, maybe it's not the Delphic Oracle.

My dad told me they kept those priestesses behind the scenes, like waitresses. They always gave advice from Apollo, but didn't anyone ever wonder what advice a priestess would have given if she was asked what *she* thought? Or what she would have said if she wasn't always doped up and stoned? Anyway, she was always giving them riddles so they'd have to come back and ask some more questions — isn't the net like that? I guess if I ever go back to school, I'll ask it everything.

Hey, you tried the breakfast burrito special last week, right? Carlos showed me how to make it. He says we should put some Mexican dishes on our menu. I told him don't tell Dad it's Mexican till he tries it.

You know my dad? Guy with the bushy eyebrows? He's always hanging around in his wheelchair — you can't get him to go home. The summer he bought this place — he was big and strong and striding around back then — he brought me along for my education, though I shoulda been in school, and we sat in the car every day for a week. Just sitting across the street from the door. The heat was choking, but Dad handed me a wet towel and we sat there watching. He wrote down how many people were walking by, how many walked in, how many cars and how many buses drove by in an hour.

When that man gets an idea, it's like a piece of gum stuck in your hair.

Like a few weekends ago. He got the idea he wanted to see Millennium Park, but of course he can't drive no more. I heard him asking our pastor if he could drive him to Chicago sometime, but the pastor's real busy. So I offered to go with him Monday when we're closed here. I always wanted to go on a train, and we got up real early to ride the Hiawatha, and all the way, he didn't shout or swear at me once.

Do you know you don't have to phone for a cab in Chicago? They have so many, the cabbies line up outside the station, waiting. I sure as hell didn't know that. Felt like a queen. And the cabbie, a dark foreign guy, put the wheelchair in the trunk for me and got Dad inside. And he was so gentle with Dad, I was amazed. I never realized there are folks who don't speak American who care about older people — I mean, let's face it, here's a guy who can't walk. He said his father was old too and needed a wheelchair, but wheelchairs were too expensive to buy wherever he came from — I forget where. Imagine that, a country where you can't afford a wheelchair.

Not that it's cheap here, I gotta say.

I don't know how that cabbie found his way, but he scooted up and around those streets and down Wabash Street under the el like he was born there. And then he pulled up on Michigan Avenue and there, right in front of my face, was Millennium Park, with the Pritzker Pavilion shining way in the back. We got out and I counted out a whole day's worth of tips in singles into his hand. And he bowed with his hands together like he was praying, or like I was royalty.

Oh, you should have seen us, Dad sailing along past the lampposts in his wheelchair and me behind, and the sun shining down on us. Felt like payday. I looked up at the names of all the founders carved into the limestone pillars and wondered just how did these guys make so much fucking money? Did they screw lots and lots of people, and for how much? But then Dad started racing a park attendant on a lawn mower, and I had to run behind him.

Later, I pushed him over to see Cloud Gate — that's the steel sculpture right by the open-air theatre. The sign said its sculptor came all the way from India — no shit. It has two hundred and sixty shiny plates, but you can't see a single seam. Looks like a huge doughnut. We walked underneath, into the navel — Dad called it the omphalos. I wondered if I'd ever make anything as simple and beautiful.

On the way home, I told Dad what I felt. He said I should try frying doughnuts and selling them, what use are doughnuts made of steel? That man — can't fight with other men like he used to, so he's gotta pick on me. Only pays me when he has the money.

Hey Jimmy, did you try the new coffee? I switched our brand to Hazelnut Cream when we came back — Dad hasn't noticed yet. Tastes better, huh? Yeah, it's not much, but it's something.

Oh, sure, I thought of getting married in my twenties. Did some serious shacking up with a Greek guy for quite a while, till I finally got tired of doing his dishes and laundry. Dad said he wasn't good enough for me, but he said that about all my boyfriends. Then the guys didn't come around no more. Now he says I'm Hestia — centre of the earth, without consort. Bullshit! I think he just needs me to take care of him and my mom and Gran. A husband would be one more person to feed and clean for, and where would I find a guy who'd share me with my family? I've got girlfriends who say their husbands are jealous of their kids. So I just have dates.

No thanks, Carlos, I don't need no coffee. Jimmy, you want your usual now? Tomato-feta salad, rosa marina soup and a roll? I'll put your order in in a minute.

You know, I thought of going to Greece for a bit, just before the Olympics. But then me and my mom and Gran saved up and got a ticket for Dad to go — he was still walking then, just slow. And he came back saying Greece was too much like America now, not like it used to be. Well, which place is still like it used to be after thirty years? I think he just wanted to feel he made the right decision coming to America. I'm glad we got him to fly when we did — it wasn't much, but it was something. He'd be too scared to fly now, what with his MS and the terrorists and all. Says the government's got info on everyone — unless we speak in Arabic.

They've got all kinds of info on me, Jimmy.

Okay, call it data, just like your bank and your firm have all kinds of stuff on you. And Homeland Security has Carlos in their computers. We're all data now, Jimmy. You, me, Carlos. I don't know how they do it, but eventually I figure they'll come for the women first, like in Salem. Dad says they did that in Europe before anyone could stop them — he says they did that for centuries. Lose Roe vs Wade and it'll take us the next five centuries to get our rights back.

Ain't a lawyer that doesn't know that one. I don't know any other cases, but even I know that one. They want it to be history, so I figure it must be something women need. What does your Arlene think? Is she like the Washington wives who want to ban abortion till they need one for their daughters? Naw, I bet she's a regular nice woman or she wouldn't have married you. Plus she's almost a nurse, so she oughta know.

Let you in on a secret, Jimmy? I had an abortion. And you

know what, I chose to have it. I walked in there and I said, here — take it out. I ain't bringing no kid into this world. Not till women like me get a better shake. I have girlfriends who are married and might as well be single moms for all the help they get. And getting pregnant is no reason to get married. It's bad for girls, and bad for boys too, when they see their mamas and sisters treated any old how. The guys in Washington could give us daycare, for a start. But if I had a kid and took her to daycare, who'd be working there? Women, right? You don't see a lot of men in daycare.

Carlos, give Mr. McKuen here some more coffee. Thank you.

I never told my dad how I used Roe vs Wade, all those years ago. He would have thought it meant different ways to cross a river, ha ha. They don't go for that in Greece, you see. He'd have knocked me on my butt. Wouldn't have talked to me for a year. But I did tell him if I got married I wouldn't be like all these suburbia cuties, making their daddies pay for their weddings. I said if I ever got married I'd send out the invitations myself, buy my own wedding gown and walk down the aisle myself. He said I shoulda been a boy. He said he couldn't wait to give me away. I said, Give away? Do I belong to you? I belong to me. Why would I let you give me away? Then he got really pissed and didn't talk to me for weeks.

But now he's glad cause he didn't have to pay for no wedding. Not even a kid.

Like the new menu, Jimmy? I worked on it. Figured I could make a bit of the world more beautiful. See the green and maroon border? I did that.

Not much, I know. But it's something.

Gotta go, Jimmy — need a smoke and pee before I put my hairnet on again. I'll put in your order. And the Greek custard afterwards? Sure.

Say hello to your wife for me. And next time you come, ride that Harley. I'll take a break and we can rocket over the Hoan again.

Hola, Mr. Jimmy. Coffee? I make it fresh. New hazelnut flavour.

Good salad, yes. Best tomatoes, yes? They have nice smell, yes? Vine ripe. From Mexico, like me.

When I was little boy only this high, my grandfather he used to grow tomatoes. And we all — my father, my brothers — worked on the Contreras farm. Those days, the land, she was alive. And in the evenings, I remember how they talked about the best queso rellenos we ever ate, the most wonderful escabeche we ever tasted, and who grew the hottest habaneros. I still remember, not like that Mr. Enrico. He's Mexican outside, gringo inside.

No, the farm is gone, but still I have its name, Contreras, like my grandfather. He sold it, and we went to work for an American company. My grandfather, my father, my brothers. One time my boss said the company paid much money for research about tomato seeds, and I said, You could pay some of that money to my grandfather.

Ha, ha! My boss laughed, you laugh, I laugh. Maybe lawyers like you should make a law like that, but you're a wills and contracts guy.

You know why I like you? Always you order the tomato salad with feta cheese, and I say to myself, Here's a big man who cares how tomatoes taste, how they smell. Because always he comes here, where we only buy tomatoes from Mexico. And sometimes you order spaghetti, but always with the marinara sauce. And last week you ordered the breakfast burrito with double salsa. Did you see I put extra sour cream with it? Yes? Of course.

Mr. Petropoulos didn't notice. He's good man. He doesn't have cameras everywhere, like in grocery stores.

These are so good tomatoes, yes? When I was young we had

so many kinds. But now this tomato on your plate, he tastes the same as the tomato on his and his and hers.

You know why? Because of fertilizers. You give fertilizers to the earth, it's like giving hormones to a cow or a woman. So this tomato grows faster and stronger than the tomatoes when I was small. Can you find one black spot? No, not one. The spots are on the hands of the sprayers — women like my wife, my Rosa.

You know, it is five years that you and I know each other. Twice a week you come here, you sit at the counter and read your paper and open letters. You come for Tula's smile, my coffee, our tomatoes. One day, you left a big tip — a twenty dollar bill! And you said, Merry Christmas! For Carlos. So Tula gave me all of it. I sent it to Rosa the very next day and I said, It's from mi amigo, Mr. Jimmy McKuen, a very great lawyer.

So you know what she did? See — Rosa sent this invitation, to our daughter's quinceañera. It's for you and your wife, Tula says her name is Arlene.

See here is written, To Mr. and Mrs. James and Arlene McKuen.

Open it! Open it!

You see here it says, Princesa de Precious Moments and Mis Quince Años. That means fifteenth birthday. And here her name, Ingrid Contreras.

Yes, she invites you. You come to Merida — to our barrio. They call it the White City because it's very clean. All white buildings.

Rosa knows you, I tell her all about you. Rosa, I said, I have one friend in America who is not Mexican. He's white, white, like an over-sprayed tomato. He has no cracks, no scars, no blemishes. He's tall, big. Much taller than me. I said, He is Irish, and you know they had the English same as we had the Conquistadors. But I think maybe the British were more like Americans, yes?

I said, Mr. McKuen's family ran here from Ireland because all the potatoes died. His Irish people, they were starving, I saw it on my TV. He never speaks of it, but it's nothing to be ashamed of. You never told me, but I understand.

Rosa, she understands, she says, Oh, sometimes when I get so tired, I wish all the tomatoes would rot, but now I hear about Mr. McKuen's family, I will never wish that any more.

Rosa works, sometimes in a greenhouse, sometimes on the land. Not in Merida, no. She goes in a truck two hours. She plucks the shoots, ties the vines to hold them up, picks the tomatoes, yes, by hand. From seven-thirty in the morning till two-thirty in the afternoon. Forty pails a day for twenty-eight pesos. Five dollars, maybe less.

She's very gentle, very quick like I am with the coffee and the dishes, so sometimes she makes more. I used to work on the same farm, driving a tractor, taking the tomatoes to the plant. That's how we met.

What happened? Oh, you mean why did I leave?

Tula says if you talk to a lawyer, it's like talking to your priest. So I can tell you why I left, my friend. No one can make you tell them what I say, right, Mr. Jimmy? Not even the Homeland Security — right?

Okay, so one day my boss says to me, Women are best. They come to work on time, they come every day, they don't get drunk, they don't steal. I don't have to teach them how to plant and care for seedlings. They are patient. Their fingers pick and pack better. They keep the count better. When they put stickers on the tomatoes, they are never crooked.

I say, Men are good too. We look after your machines. We clean and plow the land with tractors. We dig holes for stakes. We mix and spray insect killer, weed killer. Look how strong are my muscles from carrying boxes from the field to the plant. One day I will be a production manager.

But my boss, he acts like he don't hear me good. He says, Carlos, you know the best thing ever happened to you and me? Betty Friedan.

I say, Who is this Betty Friedan?

An old woman in Al Norte who says women are equal to men, women can do every job men do. She taught this to women in a book, and now any time a woman doesn't do as much as a man, you just have to whisper that she is not as good as a man, and she will work three times as fast.

And he laughed.

I say to him, Maybe you are right, boss man. Because I didn't want him to fire Rosa, but after that, when I think of what he said, I start burning inside, I don't want my Rosa working three times as hard as me. Our Ingrid was four years old then, and we had two more, even younger. When I get my pay that week, I go home and tell Rosa, Tomorrow I'm going to al otro lado. You tell him I left you, I'm gone, you don't know where. Tell him you hate me so he will keep you working. I'll send money as soon as I can, and maybe one day you don't have to work here.

Rosa says, Carlos, los Americanos, they want our tomatoes, not our people. For you they say come here, come here with one hand and go away, go away with the other.

But I tell her, A gringo company made people like me, so America should help me. I'm export quality. I believe in capitalism. I work hard.

It's dangerous. And you can't miss Ingrid's Primera Comunión, she say.

I say, No danger, I have a friend. And I will find work, I will send money home. We will save. Ingrid, she is so small, but she's smart like you — she will understand.

This way, I finally persuaded Rosa. She gave me all the money she saved for us, and I paid it to a man — ah, you have heard many stories like mine. But my story, it's not like any other man's story.

You want to know how I came? I became a tomato. Sí, a tomato!

For a little while, I worked in a grocery store — I can still say all the PLU numbers of the vegetables I rang up. But even that — I was working like a machine. Hello, how are you, paper or plastic, have a nice day.

Then I worked in McDonalds, temporary, three years. Then one day I see Help Wanted in Mr. Petropoulos's window. I look. And there behind the sign, Mr. Petropoulos in his wheelchair. He is shouting and shaking his fist at someone. I say to myself, That is a real boss!

That night, I say to Rosa, I will work for Mr. Petropoulos. He needs my help. He's in a wheelchair, but he doesn't let anyone push him around. I think he can understand people who just need a little help sometimes. And I can tell you, for these five years, Mr. Petropoulos, he never pays me by check or takes any taxes. He says to me, Carlos, anything I pay you is not counted for Social Security, so until you are a legal resident, it is not right for you to pay for mine. And he never tells me what to say or how to say it. Now when Rosa calls me late at night, I don't say to her, May I take your order, please? I'm sure Mr. Petropoulos will give me more time off than I need to attend my daughter's quinceañera, because I never take extra vacation before. No, not even one day.

No, I don't need to ask him — I know. He is good man.

I know you're thinking, Carlos isn't coming back. Or maybe you're wondering how will I get back. I show you. Same way I got back the last four years.

Here is my Notice of Removal — safe in my wallet. See what it says? Look carefully — see the cross in the box here, beside where it says Permission to Stay Granted. They gave me this after my last deportation hearing — yes, many years to get it.

It's a little faded. It got wet last week when I was feeding the ducks by the lake. I was pulling bread from my pocket, my wallet fell in the water, I had to jump in to find it. But you can read it. Anyone can see the cross, if they look carefully like you.

Okay, I make a copy.

So what do you say? You'll come to the party, yes?

Yes, it's a beautiful invitation and no, no, do not thank me, my friend. I missed my Ingrid's Primera Comunión, so I say at her quinceañera she will be like Cinderella and Snow White and Princess Jasmine and Pocahontas. I even sent Rosa a wand with sequins in it. You will see, we will present it to Ingrid as her sceptre.

Yes, it's hard for you to leave your clients, but Mrs. Arlene, she will like you to take leave, right? It's easy to get there. From here you go up and in four hours you are in Cancún. Americans like Cancún, she will like Cancún. Cancún to Merida — just one bus ride. So. You come to the party. Afterwards, I take you to the temples at Chichén Itzá. Have you seen El Castillo there? It's big pyramid, with four sides and ninety-one stairs on each side. And every step, it is one day in the year, so three hundred and sixty-four stairs, and with the top, three hundred and sixty-five! For Mayans, every little thing — even a moving shadow — it means something much bigger.

Of course you have money. You are the biggest tipper. Always I see it. One small plane ride to Mexico? One or two hours of work is all — that's cheap for you.

Oh, you think I invite you because I want to ask for money? You think this is how I ask you for money? Mr. Jimmy, if I need your money, I ask you. No. I ask only friendship.

You must come for the quinceañera. You must see Chichén Itzá. And tell Mrs. Arlene: after the party, I'll rent a car — air conditioned! — and take you to Pisté with my whole family. Say she must bring her swimming suit, so she can swim in a cenote! Have you ever done that? You will feel the water — so cool after the sunshine — and you will look up and see just a little blue circle of sky. And birds will be flying in, and when we laugh, it will echo.

I will call Rosa tonight. I will say you are thinking about the celebration. In my country, we never say no to a friend. Now I get back to work. You tell me next time you come.

Hasta pronto, Mr. Jimmy.

Fletcher

A growl rises into Fletcher's throat the moment the Sunday bullhorn sounds. He jumps off Colette's bed before she can yell, "No!"

"Repent! Repent, ya sinners!" roars the voice of the Apocalypse Man.

Fletch barks and skitters downstairs. In a second his claws are scraping at the metal strip he has almost torn from the base of the front door.

"Come to Jesus and be saved! Stop sinning! The end is NEAR!"

Fletcher knows just what's on the other side of that door — a rusty black Pontiac station wagon covered in dripping white graffiti, with a dead Christmas tree and a sandwich board tied to its roof. And he knows who is making the half-circle turn in the cul-de-sac in the godmobile, pounding his message at the living with a fervour to wake the dead. The wall between Colette's home and the adjoining vacant apartment trembles.

He has only a minute while Colette places her bookmark between the pages of *Guide to Landlords' Rights and Responsibilities* and pads down to swat him.

The honour of all Lhasas is at stake; he starts yapping his head off. His first and only owner, Colette's grandmother, would say the Apocalypse Man provokes him. Colette scoops him up and scratches behind his ears.

Very soothing.

Fletch refuses to be soothed. He will continue barking till the Apocalypse Man goes away. The guy is a lot worse than the mailman.

Colette struggles to hold Fletcher and scratch behind his ears. She gets him to wriggle outwards, so he isn't clawing into her nightie. He probably thinks the house is his, having lived here with Grandmère, then Colette's mom and now Colette.

Except for mailmen, Fletch is very discriminating about the people he detests. Colette too distrusts the beatified look in the Apocalypse Man's eyes. What does he do, eat hash brownies for breakfast? Colette had one in the eighties that made her sick for days; she hasn't had one since.

The Apocalypse Man is a small annoyance, even if he gets under Fletch's fur. Colette's home in this subdivision is way nicer than her old bachelor apartment downtown. Her French-Canadian grandparents built the house years ago. Few people they knew still live here — too expensive. But Colette can't find many condos where a peppy little dog would be welcome, and she's sentimental about him.

Fletch's bangs are falling over his eyes. He's so cute when he's angry.

Grandmère treated him like a grandson. Played him audio books, public radio and classical music. On Sundays when Colette would come to visit her, she'd be sitting in the kitchen, reading the newspaper to her puppy. Poor little guy was probably forced to watch hours and hours of Chicago Public Television, the History Channel, Discovery and National Geographic.

Grandmère's house is still in good shape, an asset Colette dangles before Tim. A dowry, Grandmère would have called it.

Colette's mom once said, "You need to make it worthwhile for a guy to take a plain Jane." Always so frank. Mom was convinced that Colette wasn't trying hard enough to date, find a man, get married. As she got sicker, she often said to Colette, "Live here when I'm gone and rent out the other half."

Colette would give this house and the world to hear her mother say that again.

Fletcher would give the same to smell his mother again — he tries not to dwell on that. He does dwell on the fact that the house includes an adjoining apartment above the two garages. Plenty of room for him and a live-in girlfriend, if Colette would ever consider his needs and let him invite one.

No one builds homes designed like that today. Anyone who buys it will have to tear it down and rebuild it in compliance with a zillion new regulations. And if she'd inherited from anyone else, Colette would have sold the place. But she keeps it, and Fletcher.

Fletch fawns all over her for that.

He might even stop barking, just to make her happy. But now she's scooting all over the kitchen with her forearm pressing against his delicate stomach. He's sailing over linoleum — whoa — she opened the refrigerator. Nearly knocked out his eye. Oh the fragrance, the fragrance! But he's not even salivating; his paws itch for solid ground.

The morning after Colette moved in — summer of '98 — she cried out that she saw her neighbour pissing on her newly planted flowerbed. Fletch rushed downstairs, only to find the man holding a hose at fly level, watering her flowers. Cedar Gables is that kind of helpful community.

The new generation of neighbours all agree it's "really neat" to be living here. Colette often says, while watching suffering people in third-world countries on TV, that such camaraderie exists only in America. But Fletcher knows how hard you need to wag your tail when all you've got before you is an empty bowl.

Where is his bowl? Colette's swinging him around, she's looking for it too. He's barking, so maybe she'll find it behind the bag of dog food — and please put him down.

He misses Grandmère, and not only because she was kind. The quantity and quality of food scraps has slipped to an all-time low: Colette usually zaps a Weight Watcher Smart One or heats up Campbell's soup.

Actually, he's barking because he's been worrying. What if Colette marries Tim? What if she sells Grandmère's home, the house he's protected since he was a pup? But Colette has lived at Cedar Gables for three years now, and Tim, who reserves finesse for the business of business, has come no closer to proposing marriage. A house like this one might have been incentive enough for a man a few years ago, but with stocks skyrocketing over the nineties . . . well . . .

What if she does marry Tim and Tim doesn't want Fletcher? Colette might give Fletcher away to the pound. It's too early to think. Besides, a bowl of milk has appeared before him, and oh boy, is he hoarse.

Colette watches Fletcher trying to bark and lap at the same time. She won't let the Apocalypse Man annoy her today. "You'll never guess what I did, Fletch."

At Land's End last night, over soup, while waiting for the every-Saturday prime rib and mashed potatoes, Colette told Tim that after years as his paralegal assistant and girlfriend, she was going to find a guy who could transition from fiancé to husband in something less than seven years. She was about to add, "a professional kind of guy, someone who can see himself saying I do without fifty-plus clauses and subclauses in a pre-marital agreement, and true, maybe I can't find such a wonder, but it's worth a try" when she saw Tim had splashed clam chowder over the hundred-dollar Brooks Brothers tie she'd recorded as a business expense only the day before.

Which was the kind of shock Colette hoped for. "You should have seen him, Fletch. His face turned even redder than usual. He asked if I was planning to quit the firm. Now, I ask you, why would he think the girlfriend and administrative assistant positions were coterminous?"

Fletcher looks up from his bowl, cocks his head and whines, as if considering.

"If I quit, Tim will never find a case or a file or be on time for a single appointment. And you know what — I care about that. And if I don't see Tim ever again, who else is there? You, a couple of girlfriends from high school, maybe. So I said, I don't know. I might quit. I'm going to rent out the apartment. Been meaning to do that ever since I moved in.

"So he says, 'How 'bout I give you a raise' — like he was going full steam into negotiation mode — 'effective immediately?'"

Colette squeezes down on a can opener, the can's lid splits to reveal the dog food inside. She spoons it into Fletch's bowl and recalls, as she had the night before, the scripted office days of the past years. The dinner and movie nights (with Tim usually too cheap to spring for popcorn) when she'd paid for her own tickets, the one clinging night per week if work allowed, and her growing despair that the land of Happily-Ever-After would ever grant her a visa. She recalls the ever-spreading rumps of girlfriends who have worked fewer years than she in Tim's firm, the screen-hours of real estate cases she has plowed through on *Westlaw*, the deals, the shareholder meeting minutes, the limited partnership documents, the investment brochures, the financing plans entered at seventy to eighty words per minute. Invoices mailed and collected, checks deposited, the many times she'd kept her mouth shut about certain clients who paid with cash.

"And you know what I thought, Fletch? I thought, You're darn right you should pay for all that, so I said, Thank you."

"And you know what he did, Fletch? He left his usual three-buck tip for the Liberian waiter, telling him, 'See you next Saturday.' And he meant both of us, in spite of all I'd said. Tim just can't imagine Saturday nights at Land's End without me. That's sweet. Endearing, don't you think?"

"Repent! Repent!" the bullhorn blasts faintly as the godmobile retreats till next Sunday. Colette pats Fletcher's hackles down.

If she doesn't do something, anything, and soon, the end of the world might come and find her at Land's End Inn every Saturday night with Tim and the prime rib and mashed potatoes. Still living alone with only a Lhasa apso for company. That *would* be something to repent.

Fletcher wouldn't call Tim endearing — he's infuriating.

Rrrrff! A man who thinks he can buy Loyalty.

Why did Colette have to accept that raise? Now Tim is going to believe he owns her again. Same way Colette's mom thought she owned Fletch, just because she fed him.

If Fletcher had been under the table, he'd have bitten Tim's ankles, chewed him to bloody bits and spat him out. Too bad

Americans don't learn a thing or two from the French — like allowing dogs in restaurants.

Fletch would look after Colette — he promised Grandmère — even though he'd prefer Yoriko, a poodle who flirted with him on Sundays when Grandmère had left him tied to her church fence. Maybe they could take in another old lady like Grandmère. Why bother with Tim?

Colette says some women still need men. Or maybe they just need husbands, unlike Gloria Steinem's generation. Perhaps, genetic mutation being what it is, there are by now fish who need bicycles and Lhasas who need snowboards. Maybe it's just that she has so many years invested in Tim. That's it — she's in-habit with him, and getting close to forty.

A few days ago, Fletcher tugged the personals page from the newspaper and trotted it over, hinting she should advertise there. At his third attempt, she did look at it. But she said she'd heard too many horror stories around the office and much repentance about Personals in the paper and on the net.

"Too in-your-face obvious," is what she said.

Colette stays home from work for the Open House, and Fletcher goes after the mailman. This time he has the satisfaction of ripping the mailman's pants. Which causes the mailman to swear, while calling Colette "lady."

It's high noon and there's been only one call for an appointment to see the adjoining unit; Colette apologizes to the mailman, smacks Fletcher's butt, then lets him take her for a walk.

The incident, she says as Fletch snuffles grass, has discombobulated her. Will the mailman sue? She says she should have asked if he was bleeding. She says if Fletcher does that again, the police could make her lock him up or get rid of him.

Fletch grovels and whines, but right this minute he doesn't care. He finds the right grass to settle his stomach. *The hell with the mailman — must have fed me a piece of junk mail.*

Where are they? Here's a path they haven't taken before.

Fletch peeks into the model home adjoining a developer's office. Overstuffed sofas and corded window "treatments." A normative tale hovers just out of reach, challenging all who enter to live it: the unstated presence of a spouse and two-point-two children.

He can see Yoriko and himself living here too. He hasn't made her any promises, though.

The scent of chocolate chip cookies wafts past; Fletcher pulls Colette inside.

A man in a bowling shirt stands beside a high-heeled, brightly scarved and gilt-brooched broker, asking for the same interior decor as the model, scaled down for a bachelor.

Bowling shirt. Not Colette's type. And he must have eaten all the cookies; Fletcher can't find a crumb. He leads Colette outside again.

Halfway across the park, Fletcher spots Yoriko. Colette, angled like a leaning pen, follows his straining, sniffing form.

"Fletch the letch," she says.

When he gets close enough to take in a whiff of Yoriko's poodle perfume, Fletcher struts past as if she's any other dog. Yoriko's master restrains her. She's suffering, Fletch can tell. She's pining for him.

An hour later, Fletcher's legs are ready to fall off, and he's lagging as far behind Colette as his leash allows. She comes panting around the corner and back to the cul-de-sac, four minutes late for the rental appointment. She stops; Fletch stops. He blinks at the sight of a sleek black limousine parked at her front door. Not a stretch limo, but a limo all the same.

Oh no! Tim has come around. He's making up. This is the beginning of his proposal.

Nah. Tim wouldn't rent a limousine to take Colette out. He wouldn't try to surprise her — he knows zilch about surprise. Flowers, maybe. And there'd never be an apology or proposal to go with, so — a limo? Black. Tim would have chosen white. Colette stands there. Fletch is half expecting those tinted windows to drop, Mafia-style. It takes him lots of scraping at the ground to pull her up to the limo and around it.

A man in a leather bomber jacket leans against the gleaming black body, looking up at Grandmère's two-storey house with an appraising eye. Fletcher goes for his ankles just to sniff him out. His throat closes immediately as Colette yanks him away.

She nearly choked him! Fletch whines. His growls were merely informational, approving, friendly.

"Martin Roseman." The guy offers her a handshake. Tall, hairline slightly receding at the temples, wavy hair, tanned. Fletcher can tell Colette's thinking: moustache à la Tom Selleck. Tom Selleck in the eighties, that is, playing Magnum P.I.

"You must be Colette. We have an appointment?" says the tenant.

Prospective tenant. As Grandmère used to say, "Slow down, Fletcher."

"Yeah, sorry I got delayed." Colette juggles her keys and the leash. Martin's socks smell of just-cut grass and pond water — pleasing. Fletch jumps up to his knee. He even allows Martin to ruffle his pooch-cut.

. . .

"I used to work for the nuclear weapons industry," says Martin. He pronounces it "noocyular," Fletcher notes. Not Colette's type. And he's Jewish. Which, even in fantasy matchmaking, is like being non-Lhasa apso — less acceptable. But cross-breed loving isn't impossible, considering himself and Yoriko.

Slightly more muscular than actors she admires on TV. Maybe he is her type.

The house tour takes a few minutes, and then Martin inspects the garage to see if it's long enough for the limo. When he noses it in, its sleek blackness lifts the gloom. "Roseman Limousine Service" and a cell phone number mar its gleaming sides. Fletch would bet Colette is hoping her neighbours get a good long stare before the door slides down.

They stand talking in the garage, and when Colette asks pleasantly about his family, he shrugs. "They don't need me, I don't need them. Moved out as soon as I could, as far away as I could without leaving the country."

Jewish families on TV are always so close, almost stuck together.

"Brothers, sisters, uncles, aunts, cousins?" asks Colette.

None of the above, he says. A bit like Colette.

Colette stands there, and Fletcher senses her trying to remember the checklist in *Guide to Landlords' Rights and Responsibilities.* He is just about ready to go fetch her the book when she asks, does Martin have many visitors?

"A few," he says. Then, his face half-turned away, he squares his shoulders beneath the brown leather and says, "My partner will be here sometimes."

"Your business partner . . . ?" she nods at the limo.

"Domestic partner," he enunciates clearly, slowly, allowing no mistake.

"Oh," says she, leaning a few degrees back.

Who would have guessed? I can never tell with dogs either.

. . .

If Martin and his partner had shown up together, well. . .

You might say Martin is up front and honest. But Colette isn't prepared. Nothing like this in the *Guide*. No ready-made social procedure.

Colette hasn't met a gay man in her thirty-seven years. They don't hang around Tim or his law office — not that she knows of, anyhow. And guys with names like Roseman don't hang out there except for business.

Colette sets her chin just like her grandmother. She did say she was going to change something, anything.

She can deal with this. Sure she can. Grandmère was very open-minded; Colette should be too. She might have to keep it a secret from Tim, but there's no way out. The book said no discrimination on the basis of age, sex, race. Did it say sexuality? Gayness? Anyhow, she can't excuse herself to run upstairs and check, not with Martin standing there, still half-turned away.

"I see." Her voice comes out faint. "Does your, uh, partner live nearby?"

Each muscle in his shoulders tenses, as if he's anticipating her rejection.

"Rochester, New York."

Far enough away. New Yorkers don't come visiting the fly-over states.

She mutters, "Okay." Very casual. She pat-pats Fletcher on the back as if patting her own.

Accepting gayness is so New York or California, she might forget where she is — in a subdivision in the heart of the Bible belt. It's her French-Canadian side; Tim would have shown this man the door right away.

Colette touches Martin's arm lightly. "If you're all right with the rent, you can move in the first of next month."

. . .

A week later, Martin has sponge-painted the half-bath white on blue, transforming the tiny room to a tiled raft floating through sky. He has doggie treats ready for Fletcher, and they aren't the ones that look like other dogs, so Fletcher doesn't feel like a cannibal as he scarfs them down. Then Martin leads Colette and Fletcher through his new home with a solicitousness, a politeness Tim would never show.

It's respect. You could even call it gentleness, in light of what the only alternative radio station in town would call his "sexual preference."

Dark, brooding abstract art on the walls — none featuring naked men or body parts, Fletcher notes — healthy ferns and palms in every corner. Nothing too floral, no lace.

The sight of Martin's queen-size bed knocks Fletcher to a crouch: leopard-print sheets are folded over a pitch-black down comforter.

A cat lover. Well, nobody's perfect.

Colette is standing with her palms turned up, as if testing the weight of the atmosphere.

"I feel completely safe here," she says.

Yeah, I bet you do, thinks Fletcher. Hasn't he heard about all the men who've led her to their bedrooms over the years, many of whom mentioned their interior decor or art collections as a pretext to get her in the sack?

The best ones are either gay or taken — or turn out to be cat lovers.

In the living room, a white leather sectional sofa cordons off a sports-bar-size TV. The kitchen's dining space features a smoked-glass tabletop on a scrolled wrought-iron base. There's even a rose silk flower arrangement at the centre.

Fletch curls up on the sofa, testing it. Colette shoos him off.

The fragrance of thyme, sage and rosemary rises from a rack by the stove; how Fletcher misses the smell of Grandmère's cooking. Actually, cuisine. Far removed from the salt, pepper and parsley flakes Colette grabs on rare occasions when it occurs to her to enliven a can of soup. Martin's windowsill overlooking the shared front lawn is lined with flavoured oils; the corresponding sill in Colette's kitchen holds one never-opened tin recipe box from Grandmère. When he goes to the fridge at her standard request for Diet Coke, Fletcher sees there's no beer but glimpses a bottle of Moët & Chandon.

Once, on Grandmère's eightieth birthday, Fletch stole a sip. Well, more than one. Missed half the party.

What's Martin doing here? He's capable of more than living in Grandmère's old house, renting instead of owning, running a one-man limousine service. Fletcher can feel he's nursing a festering sore. He'll move away soon, that's for sure. Meanwhile, he's more fun than Tim.

Colette opens a closet and reaches in. Unthinkingly, she starts to tidy a jumble of old photo envelopes tossed on a shelf. Then stops herself with an embarrassed laugh.

But Martin doesn't join her. In an instant stripped of social pretence, his sadness enters Fletch. Even Colette catches an expression of sheer desolation in his eyes. For no reason.

Denying that look is easiest. Polite. Colette feels that too.

She gives another half-laugh. "I'm a control freak, I know."

What a confessional tone — somewhere between an Oprah guest and a member of Weight Watchers.

"You are," he says. She was trespassing, but he could have protested — one of Colette's girlfriends would have. Maybe gay guys don't react *exactly* like women; Fletcher hasn't met enough of them to compare.

At the end of the tour, Martin invites Colette to dinner soon, once the kitchen is repainted. A courtesy invitation, thinks Fletch.

Say yes! Those treats were the best.

Colette accepts. Then she says, "Will your partner be in town? It would be nice to meet him."

"No." But his voice has coloured with gratitude that she asked. Fletcher can feel her admiration for her own magnanimity spreading like a tutu around her. Martin adds, "He's gone backpacking around the world for a few months; he has things to work out."

Colette's shoulders relax, drop an inch. "I'd love to travel," she says.

She won't travel much if she lets Tim think he owns her. Once upon a time he must have liked to travel; foreign countries offered him backdrops he could brag about, backdrops for photos of himself. Now he's bought Photoshop, loaded his hard drive with clip art and pastes himself anywhere he wants.

"Hey," she says, as if suddenly inspired, "mind if I bring a guest?"

"Other than Fletcher? Sure." He picks up Fletcher.

Fletch glares into Colette's brown eyes. They're so hard and opaque he has to look away.

The next day, when Colette returns from work, she tells Fletcher she's invited Tim to meet her "new boyfriend," counting on his curiosity, knowing he will accept. She did add they were "just friends," with a simper and a flutter of eyelashes Fletch has seen many times, many ways on TV. Disturbing Tim's complacency was so simple, so safe, so easy to effect, she says. A little jealousy . . . she's been too available. She is thirty-seven, too old to invest another two or more years in a new relationship.

That Sunday, the Apocalypse Man takes his turn around the cul-de-sac, shouting "Repent! Repent!" Fletcher goes ballistic again. But Colette doesn't budge. She has stuffed her ears with earplugs.

She's thinking, plotting, scheming.

. . .

Martin has thoughtfully provided Fletcher with a bowl of Kibbles and his very own cushion in the corner. Chin resting on his paws, Fletch watches Colette surveying Tim and Martin over the rim of her third glass of Merlot — good thing she doesn't need to drive home. The wine is helping her relax, keeping whatever plan she has going. Fletcher stays alert because he watched a program on Discovery once about dinner being the most dangerous of human rituals. He can't remember the whole thing, something about humans being as vulnerable as he is while eating but armed with knives. Tim keeps thrusting his knife into the stir fry vegetables. He's sprinkled them with soy sauce and cut everything on his plate into smaller, unattractive morsels.

And he doesn't toss Fletch one scrap.

Colette has manoeuvred the seating into a triangle with herself at the apex, Tim's U of Chicago sweatshirt and Martin's black turtleneck facing off across the table.

Tim gets his preliminary small talk over. Then, "You get that limousine around here? How many miles to the gallon?"

Fletch gives a small rrrrff, just to interrupt him. Martin tosses him a piece of chicken.

"How much do you charge from here to O'Hare?" Tim is interrogating Martin as if he were a hostile witness. Martin counters with nutshell answers, as if he's heard the questions many times before.

Tim the predictable.

"Do you get lots of wedding parties?" Colette interposes, offering everyone a chance to change the subject. Tim's got one chance at redemption. He can repay all Colette's loyalty right now and claim her back. He should say, I was thinking you could do ours someday, or, We've got one coming up for you, don't we, Colette?

The lines scroll on Fletch's teleprompter through the moment in which Tim misses his cue.

Well, Colette did tell Tim that Martin was her new boyfriend — but that guy! He's taking her seriously. Even though he didn't when she broke up with him at Land's End. Can't he tell Martin is gay? Maybe he thinks Colette doesn't know, and he's waiting for her to find out.

What a scumbag. Fletcher wants to taste his blood.

Martin answers Colette. "Quite a few wedding parties — that's why I'm not around much on weekends."

"But Martin heard our Apocalypse Man before he left Sunday morning." Colette is smiling, but Fletcher can feel her fighting the urge to hold her dinner knife somewhere near Tim's jugular. Make him pop the question now. No whereases, no notwithstandings.

He goes over and noses her leg, but it pushes him aside. She's describing the weekly doom and gloom visitation.

Fletch jumps up on the couch where he can see and hear better. Nobody orders him off.

Tim interrupts, "Wackos'll go on believing anything, even after Y2K arrived and nothing happened." He assumes a good-ole-boy tone, as if he's from Texas. "End of the world — ha! I didn't worry about computers packing up, I worried about the Ayatollah types."

Martin says, "It wasn't the end of their millennium."

"Yeah," said Tim, "but they knew it was ours. True believers, those Moslem fundamentalists. All so sure of themselves."

He's looking real sure of himself, too. "Can't even get on the same calendar with the rest of the world." Now he's stuffing himself — he can't resist Martin's cuisine.

Colette raises her glass to eye level and gazes at Tim through a ruby red lens.

Martin says to Tim, "Makes you wonder what we've been doing to cause so much hatred, doesn't it?"

"Oh, we haven't done anything they wouldn't do to the tenth power in our position," says Tim, bristling. "If the ragheads were on top, you think they wouldn't blow up more than the World Trade Center? They think they're going straight to heaven when they blow themselves up. I say lock 'em all up and sterilize them."

Tim expects Martin to nod in agreement — he thinks everyone agrees with him. Fletch never has, but no one pays him any attention.

"Lock who up?" says Martin, leaning forward. "All Arab-Americans?"

A tiny smile tugs at Colette's lips. She wants Martin to fight Tim, like Fletcher would fight for her or Yoriko.

"Nah, just the foreigners," says Tim.

"That's how the Nazis began, with just the foreign Jews. Gradually, they turned fear to hatred."

"I'm not afraid of anyone." Tim is backtracking as if a swastika is rising in a thought balloon over his head. "But," he says with passion beyond provocation, "anyone who can't speak English should be sent home."

"You sound like you hate lots of people who are already at home, and a lot of other people in the world who aren't doing anything wrong, unless you count existing," Martin says evenly. "Is there anyone you love?"

A question Tim probably has never been asked and to which Fletch knows Colette wants him to respond, Yeah, Colette. I love Colette. But he doesn't say anything.

Her expression says, It was on the tip of his tongue. He was willing to say it — he just can't get it out.

Fletcher doesn't think so.

"Sure — I love my family," is what Tim finally blurts. "My mom, dad, sister."

"And they love you?"

"Sure. Of course. They have to — they're family."

"Don't think it works that way," said Martin. "Sometimes you can hate what you've created. Especially if it turns out different from your expectations, from what you wanted. Fathers can hate their own children, sometimes. Mothers too."

Fletch rests his head on his paws. So long as he gets fed, brushed, walked and petted, what does he care? He snoozes.

When he opens his eyes, Tim is still being his usual self. Martin is still objecting, but he looks as if his stir fry is decomposing in his mouth. Fletcher gives him a bark just to say, Tim's like the Apocalypse Man, blowing into his bullhorn. There's only a graffiti-splattered station wagon and a dried out Christmas tree to tell them apart.

But Martin doesn't understand Fletch. He leans back, and that look of desolation Fletcher saw the day of the apartment tour crosses his face. "Sometimes I think we humans deserve to be annihilated, like that Sunday morning preacher says, for what we do to one another for profit or love or religion."

The scent of his anger mixes with frustration, pain beyond words. Fletcher goes over and rubs against his shins.

"I don't believe in any God who'd destroy his own creation," Colette says.

Fletcher takes Tim's shoelaces in his front teeth; he pulls them loose. He steals back to his vantage point and tries to look innocent.

"But," she continues, pert and bright, as if reading off a Trivial Pursuit card, "do you believe divine intervention is possible?"

Tim consults his Rolex, the Divine being a judge whose jurisdiction he acknowledges only on Sundays. "Don't need the Lord's intervention," he says. "What we need is for government to get the hell out of business's way. Bush has the right ideas — a hundred and thirty-five trillion in tax relief."

"For the rich, yes," says Martin.

"For the small businessman, Roseman. People like you in the limo business."

Fletch rolls his eyes and feels his ears droop. It's the usual liberal-conservative stalemate.

"It will take more than divine intervention." Martin speaks with passion, as if talking about something he deems anything but trivial. "Things don't get better. You think, now we're in the twenty-first century, people will finally realize we're all equally human, despite our differences, and then along comes one more guy to remind you just how wrong you are."

"Any wine left?" Colette interrupts the men's staring match. Tim reaches for the bottle. Colette holds her glass out to Martin, raising it slightly.

A homemade cherry pie is served — Fletch drools and whines. Nobody cares.

Veins stand out on Tim's forehead. Fletcher would bet he's calculating the income differential between himself and Martin. He can see Tim chewing on the idea that Colette might prefer Martin's lower net worth to his own.

Not the Colette Tim thought he knew so well — uh-uh.

Afterwards, Martin walks Colette and Tim out by way of the garage. A helium tank in the corner stands ready to puff up pink and powder blue balloons. Just Married signs in varying sizes rest against the wall, white tulle and ribbon sachets of rice stand on shelves. Ribbons of all widths stick their coloured tongues out at Tim for not thinking marriage. Fletch sticks his tongue out too because he's darn happy Tim is messing up. Whatever happens, Tim must never think he owns Colette, or Fletcher.

Colette smiles sweetly as she says goodbye to Tim but doesn't yell at Fletch for spraying pee on the hubcap of his Lexus. She takes Martin's arm to walk back to the house. Tim will notice that as he drives away. Well, at least subliminally.

Martin pulls his arm away at her front door. "You," he says, "have been using me all evening."

"Using you? Why would you think that?"

Martin looks down at Colette and Fletcher with a terrible bleakness on his face. "You've cooked up a cool scenario for Tim and all you want from me is silence, right? My complicity, right?"

Colette laughs uncertainly. "What are you talking about?"

She's so transparent.

"You want that man, that's your problem. You can have him. He's a piece of work. I didn't say anything tonight because you were my guest, he was my guest too. But from now on, just leave me out of it, okay? Don't need any more complications in my life."

Colette opens her door a crack, lets Fletcher in and stands in the doorway.

"Okay," she says. "Next time, I'll invite you, and you bring your partner."

"Oh, sure! And you'll invite jealous Tim to be cured, right?"

She's see-through. Born in a glass factory.

"It won't work, unfortunately. E-mail from Nepal today — my partner says we should, um, separate. Things to work out, he says."

For Colette, Nepal is just someplace without Jacuzzis or minibars, and Fletcher can tell she didn't think they had e-mail. As for the rest, she doesn't know how to react. "I'm sorry," she says at last, in a neutral tone she uses with her girlfriends when they split with a guy. "Were you together long?"

"Twenty years. And I fought my loving parents two years before that, just to be with him."

He was looking away.

"Tim and I were together seven years," says Colette, as if searching for a parallel.

"And you're desperate for a wedding. I understand. Public acknowledgment, right? Two becoming one."

Same as Fletch wanting Yoriko for a live-in girlfriend, getting tired of stealth encounters behind park bushes.

"When I want to be analyzed, Mr. Know-all, I'll see a therapist," says Colette with a laugh. "Thank you for a really neat evening. Fletch, are you in?" And, over her shoulder, "Good night."

Going upstairs, Colette tells Fletcher that the last time she'd played one guy off against another was in college — a delicate, tedious business. Those college boys had been as predictable as Tim, never coming out well in a political test. Martin, on the other hand — not as predictable.

She falls asleep without reading a page. Lights on, clothes on, without brushing or flossing or applying her Retinol cream, three glasses of wine being more than she's had in ages.

Fletch wonders if gays can be reformed; he would sure prefer living with Martin than with Tim. But he remembers Grandmère reading him a piece from some paper Tim would call radical — probably *The New York Times* — that said they can't. Too bad. And Martin is good at weddings. Might be even better at planning his own.

Fletcher doesn't think reforming Martin is part of Colette's game plan, anyway. Which went fairly well for her tonight. But it appears Martin isn't going to play along, so there's no way she can go any further.

All right! Yeah!

Fletch's nose twitches. He licks it, then makes his last nightly round of the house. If Yoriko were here, he'd give her one big slurpy kiss and snuggle up to her all night.

Fletcher finds a nice spot and curls up at Colette's feet.

Fletch is in Colette's dream, barking from a great distance, though his little yapping head is right by her nose. She tries to reach up and push him away but her hands refuse to come with her arms. Light jabs her eyes as Fletcher pulls away her blanket and wrestles it to the ground. He will smother himself. Colette struggles to raise herself on one elbow. She reaches down — hard floor rises to meet her and a sharp pain notifies her she is awake. Fletch disentangles himself from the blanket like a triumphant Houdini and leaps at her again, the whites of his little eyes very close.

"Stop it!" says a woolly voice something like her own. He tugs at her, growling. He must have to pee badly . . . Well, better this than messing the rug.

At the top of the stairs her legs suddenly refuse to carry her. Too much to drink . . .

Colette sits down. Her feet look tiny from this distance. Walls warping, colours blending, everything, she muses admiringly, turning very abstract, one colour beginning to predominate: black.

One corner of her nightie pulling — it's caught in Fletch's teeth. Colette drags herself up against the banister, holds on tightly all the way down.

Bowls of Alpo and water come into focus, still full — he can't be hungry. And he's almost ripped off the metal strip at the base of the front door. "Bad dog!"

No sound comes out. His barking is hammering in her skull. A wave of nausea — this is no hangover.

Is she being punished for all the Sundays she's missed church, for too many missionaries turned away from her door, too many refused donations to Father Flanagan's Boy's Camp, St. Rita's Rescue Mission, Save the Children? She should have heeded the

Apocalypse Man, the end is near, but he'd been wrong about it coming last New Year's Eve . . .

Kitchen tipping and tilting around her. An eon to drag herself to the phone near the stove. Where's the nine, the one and the one? Oh no, oh no! She's passing out; this must be death.

Where's God? Jesus, save me!

The ambulance siren is louder than the Apocalypse Man's bullhorn, and the things she is saying! The things she can laugh at! And the next minute she is crying for the only mammal who loves her in the whole world. Where is Fletcher? Without him she has no one.

Someone is holding her around the waist and peeling her fingers off the front door. A scream, her scream, "Fletcher!" The seasoned professional voice talking into the radio belongs to the burly black man beside her. "Seventy-two calling . . . We're ten-nineteen. Convulsions, passing out." He growls something ornery but resigned about being summoned at four in the morning, says it looks like a drug OD to him. Colette tries to say she hasn't taken any drugs, only a few glasses of wine, but she can't. He listens, then forces a tube into her mouth, and she can't make a coherent sound.

A jolt; the ambulance begins to move.

Bright overhead lights in Colette's eyes. She clutches the breathing tube on her chest with both hands in case someone tries to put it back.

"Fletch! Fletch?"

"Try not to worry about your dog," says a coat-shaped man

who has risen between her and the lights. "Try not to identify so closely with his needs."

A man who looks like Tim springs up at Colette's bedside, blustering to the man in white about suing the lot of them — has to be Tim. His face close to hers, he strokes her hair.

He says, a long way off, "The phone rang and all I heard was barking. I thought, oh shit, that pampered little mutt must have hit the speed dial. I waited for you to shut him up, but when that didn't happen, I got this bad feeling: I should have checked out that wise-ass Martin."

He was worried about her. He is still worried; Colette drinks in his anxiety.

"Anyway I got out of bed, got in the Lex and zoomed over. Found that stupid little animal of yours lying there barely breathing, flat as a pancake with his nose to the base of the front door. Then I found you. On the floor, clutching the phone.

"I called the paramedics, and by the time they came, I had followed the smell and the engine sound, opened the garage door, and there was that no-good new boyfriend of yours, power-locked into the limousine with the engine running. The fumes must have drifted into the ventilator and up to your bedroom. And I guess we won't be hearing from him again. Anyway, so the medics realized you weren't ODed on drugs.

"Then I came back to the dog and he was so small and weak and not yapping or peeing or undoing my shoelaces any more, just looking up at me with those brown teary eyes. I wanted to leave him to fend for his goddamned little self for a change. But he'd done the best he could — shit, even if he hadn't, I just couldn't leave him to die . . . Colette! Hey, Colette!"

The walls begin a vertiginous slide, all the surfaces colliding in cubist shards and opening to nowhere. She falls fast, spiralling off into infinity.

. . .

Prongs rasp against the soft membrane in Colette's nose as she bobs near consciousness, Gurney wheels vibrate beneath her shoulder blades. Strong gentle hands. Another siren screeching vaguely. A stranger's tight voice. "Step on it, man — five minutes and she's a goner. Move, move!"

Running and shouting, down a hall past a sign marked Emergency — Triage. The gurney halts before the heavy door to an acrylic cylinder. Colette slides in on chrome tracks, swallowed feet first by the machine. A sound like a refrigerator door closing, sealing shut at her head. She will remember a brass mouth tube expanding her throat, silent air pressing for an instant on her eardrums, and the eerie echo of her interior pinging its message to the universe — *please please let me live.*

I am, I am. I want to be.

Pressure climbs to three atmospheres on the exterior gauge. Colette comes to, breathing in fire. She lies motionless, sweaty-hot. Unreachable woman-pharaoh mummified live in her sarcophagus. Tim's face at her side. Through the intercom, "Colette! Don't quit on me. I need you! Hey, you want to be married, Colette, we'll do it. I promise! I'll even live with that goddamn dog. C'mon, live!" And as her eyes open wide, he repeats it, nodding vigorously.

He said "married."

Each cell jolts, gasps, takes in air.

The garage door screeches and thunders, rolling up over Fletcher's head. The limousine is gone, the scent of death lingers. He leads Colette in, trots into Martin's wing.

Fletch has been feeling awful ever since he got back from the vet. As if he had peed everywhere. He didn't keep his promise to Grandmère and protect Colette enough. He should have woken earlier, barked louder.

On the speaker phone, because Colette was stirring water into soup, he heard Martin's partner explain to Colette, "I don't — that is, can't — keep any of Martin's stuff, you know."

He was with Martin twenty years and then left him. Does his kind of loyalty deserve a reward? Martin didn't think so. Colette said his will left everything he owned to charities. "Didn't leave his partner a frigging cent, just left him all the work."

Martin's partner wrote a formal letter requesting a key as executor of Martin's estate; Colette sent him one. He packed most of Martin's personal possessions, anything suitcases could carry, and sent them to the parents who had been ashamed of Martin. Now they've got something to be ashamed of — Tim printed a newspaper article from a net archive and read it out loud to Colette, savouring the words: "charged with embezzlement in New York state." The charities, he said, are going to have to hire someone like him.

"Robin Hood," said Colette to Fletch, but only after Tim left.

Now, in the dining room, Fletch sees Martin like a holographic image. He's ladling stir-fried vegetables over noodles. He's rippling all the brown drooping ferns and palms as Fletch passes. Fletch's nose twitches with his spoor in each room. The bedroom closet is open, Martin's clothes are gone. The leopard-print linen has been stripped from his bed, only the comforter remains.

I should never have trusted a cat person. Never.

Colette sits down on the bed and holds Fletcher. She says there must be a story if only for herself. She says he was friendless, an outcast. Maybe the terror of existence grew larger than he could withstand. Maybe he checked out rather than checking himself in for therapy, counselling, self-remaking.

She says this, but she's describing herself, what she might have done in his circumstances. Any story she's going to tell can only approximate reality. It'll be a fabrication more fabricated than any she's constructed before. Its plausibility will rest on the silence of the dead and her own fear that there, but for some neglected intervening deity, might have gone her still-breathing self.

Fletch thinks she shouldn't dig too deeply to explain Martin's death. She'd only be using him again, as a prop in another story.

She rubs his head, pushes bangs away from his eyes and says, "Tim wants me to sell the place before the wedding. The real estate lady from the Model Home has already called this morning."

Fletch growls and chews her hand a bit to say, This is so unfair. What about his job, his job to protect Grandmère's home?

She ignores Fletcher and continues. This house, she says, is where her life was almost taken, then given back. It deserves better. And it's so full of memories. Of Grandmère, her parents. "Besides, selling a house where someone just committed suicide is so difficult. I'll rent it out."

Fletcher wags his tail till he thinks it's going to fall off.

Colette lies down on Martin's black comforter and pulls him close. "Oh, Fletcher, Martin had no one to cry for his last moments in the limousine."

Martin was Fletcher's hope too. At least for a while. Now he's gone, Tim's going to think he owns Fletcher. And Colette.

Fletch licks away Colette's tears. It's been a while since she's cried for anyone other than herself. Then she says, "We're going to be moving, Fletch."

Yoriko! Fletcher feels all of him drooping, not only his ears.

At least Colette said *we're* moving. No plans to give Fletch away to the pound.

Tim did save Fletch's life, so Fletch figures he owes him Loyalty for a few years.

Oh shit! Tim won't appreciate him.

Fletcher's lip curls. Tim better not mess with him or Colette — Fletch's ancestors were wolves. His pedigree traces all the way back to the lion-dogs who guarded the Emperor's palace in Lhasa.

Can anyone predict what a man will do? Fletch doesn't want to remember how his hackles rose but he couldn't move to bite Tim. How he nearly passed out with fear that Tim would just leave him there on the floor. And he doesn't want to remember his tears of relief when Tim picked him up off that floor so someone could rush him to the vet. He who hadn't cried since he was taken from his mother.

Colette is going on: could she have helped Martin? Was it something Tim said? Was her using Martin against Tim the last straw?

Self-recrimination descends, then lifts. "No, we can only help ourselves. People do what they're going to do."

What's the big deal about having the power of speech if Martin couldn't talk to someone who'd understand? Fletch didn't have speech and even *he* had figured Martin was in unbearable pain.

If he could speak, he'd tell Yoriko: *Forgive me! I'm glad there were no promises between us.*

Circling the cul-de-sac outside, the Apocalypse bullhorn flays the Sunday air. "Repent! Repent!" Fletcher lifts his head from Colette's shoulder, gives a growl and a whine, but is unwilling to engage in a genuine altercation today.

"No more games, no more plans," says Colette. "This one nearly cost me my life."

But when her friends ask how she led Tim, of all men, to the altar, will she give Fletcher any credit for waking her up, or nearly dying with her, or mention Loyalty?

No. She'll put it down to divine intervention. Tim, she will say, couldn't have persuaded her any other way.

The View from the Mountain

I met Ted Grand soon after he came to Costa Rica and built the Buena Vista. He didn't know of me then, but I knew of him — every day during the construction of the hotel, I sat on my veranda in the morning, nursed my first bottle of Imperial and squinted to gauge his progress. The Buena Vista's walls capped a peak three miles away, at first grey, soon white. Trust a gringo, I thought, to buy that view, with all the lights of San José twinkling in the valley below. A man was beaten to death by the local bosses and found picked clean by crows right where Ted Grand was building. Trust a gringo not to care that he was building on blood-soaked land. I refused to go see the hotel.

Ted wouldn't remember the day we met. I still do — my annual day of sadness. All my days were days of sadness then, but that day was the worst, the anniversary of the fire. The night before, I went through tequila, guao, Heineken, Pilsen and whatever else was in my cupboards to prepare myself. But Madelina and Carmen were before me. My little Carmen, only six years old. Screaming, crying. A bout of dengue seemed to be upon me. In the morning, I soaked a towel in ice water, went out to the veranda, sat down in my wicker chair and put the towel over my eyes.

I heard Jesús' Isuzu stop on the road below, but I didn't budge.

He came in without knocking, the folds of his pelican neck wobbling, his shirt flapping about his paunch. He stuck his big nose into a cupboard in my kitchen, removed a steel bowl, returned to the twin aluminium vats sitting in the flatbed of his truck and ladled out enough milk to last me a week. He talked the whole time, as he always did, and some words got through the buzzing and screaming in my head.

The gringo of Buena Vista, said Jesús Martínez, needed someone to look after his garden. Wanted someone who could care for ten coffee trees.

"Listen to me, señor Wilson Gonzales." His sombrero creaked and I knew he was tipping it back the way he did when he was serious. "The man who gets that job at the hotel can have all the coffee. Can you believe — he doesn't want it."

"What for are you telling me?" I mumbled. "I drink a lot of coffee, but I never took care of coffee trees."

"What for —?" Jesús shook my shoulder. "If my son was old enough, I'd make him go talk to señor Grand, tell him he knows all about coffee. Tell him looking after coffee trees is what his father and grandfather knew in their cradles. But my son is too young, and he doesn't speak English like you. So I tell you, mi amigo."

I lifted a corner of my towel and thanked Jesús for his tender concern and suggested he was wasting his time and gas.

"You're drinking more than milk — an educated man like you." Jesús, like my long-gone mother, would be silent only when he had finished saying what he planned to say. "And señor Grand might need a man who can cook too. He should get a new wife. I hear his old one left him the very day the hotel was completed. Went to Florida with the man who sold señor Grand the chandeliers."

"I always said I'd never go up that hill. A man was killed there." I took the towel off my eyes and wiped it over my face.

"Yes, he was killed. And he died. A man died there and there and there." Jesús pointed at the hill, the valley and the road dotted with crosses between them. "Everywhere you look, a man has died. Men keep dying, and what does it matter where they died or how? We all die." He spat to emphasize his irrefutable logic.

I groaned.

"Even I, Jesús, will someday die, and I won't be back to save you if you don't save yourself right now."

Having delivered his prescription, Jesús pulled his sombrero forward again and crunched away to swing into his cab.

What did Jesús know? He was just one of my many creditors, that's why he wished me a long life and prosperity enough to pay his bills. And he didn't charge interest like the others. Eyes closed behind my wet bandage, I took mental inventory of my creditors. All would agree with Jesús. It took all day, but the thought finally pushed me from my wicker chair so I could drag my alcohol-soaked body up the hill.

As I made my way into the hotel, I ignored what Jesús said. It should matter that someone dies, even a stranger. Death should matter so Madelina and Carmen's would matter.

I can never tell an American's age, because so many tourists have had plastic surgery, even men. Ted's face seemed older than mine, and his hair was sparse and turning grey, but his spine was more erect. The new hotel was spacious and airy. A "bow-teek" hotel, Ted called it, as he showed me around. Each of its twenty rooms had a balcony with a view of the valley. Each would be uniquely decorated, each would have a name — "the Bird Room . . . the Conquistador Room . . . the Monsoon Suite."

Ted said Costa Rica attracted his investment with a large middle class, democracy, no military, no oligarchy.

"I do not know what it is like to live in an oligarchy," I said, "but we now have a military. It lives in los Estados — the USA, yes? When the president of Nicaragua said he wanted to drop a bomb on our president, what did our president do? He picked up the phone and called Mr. Reagan. And Mr. Reagan sent troops to Nicaragua."

I was only joking, but Ted didn't laugh.

"Out of friendship, because we are just like los Estados," I added hastily. "A democracy."

"Don't count on that, Wilson," said Ted. "It's all about interests. There's no friendship, only interests."

I thought of my friends, even Jesús. I could not have survived the years since the fire without them. They had no reason to help me. I said — not to Ted, because I didn't wish to offend him, but to myself — that I hoped I never thought like him.

Ted had built himself a white stucco villa beside the hotel. Modern, with a few Spanish arches and flourishes. He took me to see it the next morning. I felt comfortable inside, though it was not quite finished and had little furniture.

"I hired a Costa Rican architect," said Ted, when I mentioned it. I warmed to him immediately — which gringo would hire a Costa Rican architect? We went out to look at the coffee trees and I assured him I would look after them. He said I could keep the coffee. I protested we would share it. We shook hands when I left.

"Wilson," he said, quoting some great American poet, "I think this is the start of a beautiful friendship."

Jesús was pleased that I'd followed his advice but warned, "Señor Grand is here for la pura vida, but give him a little more of the pure life and maybe he'll go home. He could sell the hotel as soon as it's finished the way he wants it, you know."

In the next few days, I drove Ted to the SuperMaas so he could buy peanut butter; he didn't blink at paying 1150 colons.

He bought coffee for 2530, an avocado, an onion and a tomato for 1500. He didn't ask how I could afford to eat. Perhaps he knew what we all knew: to buy anything at the SuperMaas, anything packaged, you must work for gringos or be in the tourist business.

Driving home, I translated a street sign for him: "Despacio — eslowly."

He corrected me: "Slowly."

When we stopped, he bought a *USA Today* from an expat-run van service, and from then on he read a few stories aloud to me every day. That's how my English got better.

And for once Jesús' fortunetelling was wrong. First, Ted didn't sell the hotel. And second, we opened.

Ted put me in charge of the ground staff, then the inside staff. I hired willing women — not too pretty, but happy at heart — and put attractive, sensible Consuela in charge, though she was the youngest. I forgot all about the dead man, just like everyone else, being too busy even to take one drink or lie around like a sloth anymore. I paid Jesús back, with a substantial tip for passing on information, and even more important, I began paying my other creditors back as well.

In October I harvested the coffee cherries from the trees. I brought the sacks of cherries to my own veranda, and Jesús helped me pack them carefully into his Isuzu. I sent him to a factory in Heredia for the best wet processing and roasting. The coffee returned, now dressed in silver bags, each with a generously flourished "Arias" label — Oscar Arias Sánchez had just won the Nobel Peace Prize. Its aroma turned heads in the hotel. And in April, I hired younger men than Jesús and supervised the planting of more trees down the side of Ted's hill.

One day, just after I set up a huge satellite dish for his TV, he said, "Wilson, let's take a drive." So I took him in his new SUV and we drove through the mountains. I pointed out teak, mahogany, Brazilian cherry, bocote and purple heart where I could. At Rio Tarcoles we stopped in the middle of the bridge to gaze at the crocodiles. Ted didn't admire the scaly brown shapes nosing the shore — fifteen on one side of the bridge, ten on the other. He said they were animals that ate other animals.

"You like vegetarian animals only, my friend? Horses, cows?"

"Yeah, I was in the service. I had enough of killing," he said.

Does killing or dying in war matter more or less than a death from accident? Again I was thinking of the fire. The fire killed, but I blamed myself. I should have come home earlier, should have had some sixth sense as a husband and a father. We strolled over to the other end of the bridge, where palms rustled like a whisper of Madelina's best dress. I became Ted's tour guide as we entered a store, identifying packets of rellenos, dried bananas, cashews and coconut cookies. Behind pyramids of watermelons and mangoes, a little girl laughed — I heard my Carmen.

When you have lost the little girl you created with the only woman you have ever loved, when you have failed your family and disappointed yourself, it takes someone like Ted to make you believe it is possible to create again.

And create we did. A hotel with a bar, a restaurant, an organization. In 1993, we opened a tiny grocery store in the hotel and Ted taught me to stock Skippy low-fat peanut butter, Entenmann's doughnuts, and SP-45 with Aloe sunscreen. The Buena Vista offered internet service with a cup of Arias in 1996, before anyone else in Costa Rica had an internet café. And Ted taught me to hang paintings by local artists above the computers and call them primitive art.

He took a buying trip to Florida and returned with more chandeliers. While I stood on a stepladder, installing them in the lobby, he handed up tools and the delicate globes, telling me how he visited his ex-wife and forgave her. I went home and told Jesús the next day how much I admired that when I can't even forgive myself.

Hurricane Mitch did a little damage in 1998, and I would have just renovated the hotel to look the way it used to, but Ted said destruction is an opportunity for change. He moved things around in the dining areas, redesigned the kitchen, redecorated the bar. Change, he said, sends a signal to customers that we are growing, not standing still.

"It tells people you're with it."

I wasn't easy to convince. Most of our customers came once in their lives and then went somewhere else. But Ted said, "Change is like music, felt but not seen."

Even so, I saw no reason to tear out a perfectly good swimming pool and talked him into simply repaving ours with blue floral ceramic tile. And after my days of hard work installing the tiles, Consuela told me the bright tiles uplifted the whole garden.

Some changes I liked immediately: he decreed the Buena Vista would play no more Kenny G. That music had been playing in every bar, restaurant and hotel non-stop since 1993. He said people might like to listen to Costa Rican salsa and mambo, and I told him he was becoming one of us after all.

I didn't tell Ted the salsa and mambo reminded me of Madelina — we used to dance. He had never asked me anything about my past or told me anything about his. Whenever I asked, he said the past wasn't important. Yet he called me brother.

"Individuality, that's what we need, Wilson," he said. "Distinction. We don't want to be like the cookie-cutter resorts, bringing in hundreds of people on charters and storing them in high-rise hotels, turning them over like meat on a grill and sending them back tanned on both sides."

Individuality, I learned, was available to those who could

afford it. I was shocked and apologetic each time Ted printed out a new season rate card. Ted had to spend a lot of time teaching me not to stutter when I said *only* $175 per night, *only* $185 per night, *only* $200 per night.

Every time something broke down, Ted asked, "Don't you have anyone who can fix that?"

"Nobody," I would say. "Okay, maybe my cousin . . ." and I'd call. Soon I had every Gonzales working for Ted at Buena Vista. Slowly and "eslowly," relatives I had pushed away in my grief came back into my life.

The clock over my stove moved forward, circled three hundred and sixty degrees three hundred and sixty-five times in a flash, then another and another. Ted and I moved in lockstep into the new century. I couldn't remember what forty and fifty felt like. I only realized Ted was on the other side of sixty when he told me he needed a hearing aid.

I was in the gift shop helping a couple from New York make up their minds — modelling a sombrero one minute and spinning folk tales about hand-carved parrots the next. They had to catch a plane, so I had arranged for my cousin to take them to the airport.

But just as I was packaging the parrots, Ted came in. In a very professional tone, he informed the couple that he had just heard no planes would be flying to New York City that day. He said he just saw New York on CNN and . . . and . . . his face caved. Amazement hit me like a thump across my chest: Ted was holding in tears.

I juggled rooms and accommodated the New York couple and a number of others for extra nights while we sorted out rumours from news. The net, the TV, *The Tico Times*, *La Naçión*, *Al Día*, *La Republica* and *USA Today* offered an intermingled dose of both. Bit by bit we learned a crime had been committed in New York by nineteen men, and the death count was growing. The New York couple kept saying this was just like Pearl Harbor. I think they really believed some other country had attacked los Estados. The death count passed a thousand, then two thousand, then three thousand, and then I watched President Bush II say he was on a crusade; he too thought the country was under attack.

Now I regretted installing the satellite dish. Suddenly Ted was not with us at the Buena Vista anymore, except for collecting his money every evening. He bought a small TV and made me install it behind the reception desk so if he was there he could watch the sad and angry norteamericanos on CNN and FOX News all day long. If I was on duty, I watched it too, and I felt the same sadness of the families. I too wanted all those deaths to matter. There were donations, there was talk of insurance — norteamericanos seemed much more valuable than my Madelina or Carmen ever were. I watched so many wearing or waving flags, but only for los Estados, though CNN said people of many countries died in the towers.

One day, two days . . . it became five days since Ted made morning rounds with the housekeeping staff. Then I began doing it for him so he would have time to cheer that man Bush. And he was still cheering a month later when that man Bush dropped bombs on people in Afghanistan. So Ted hadn't had enough of killing after all.

Late one evening, I was watching a CNN special report on bioterrorism after an anthrax scare in Washington when I heard shouting and crying. I rushed around the reception desk into the hall to find Ted standing over a cowering maid as if he meant to rip her apart. No, not a maid — Consuela, my most efficient housekeeping supervisor. Consuela, who had been with us since our grand opening. The heat of Ted's anger hit me though I was standing three feet away.

"Ted!"

He turned to me, and I saw the face of a man I did not know. "Wilson, don't you protect her. The clumsy bitch was about to break one of the globes on the chandelier."

Not a shard of glass on the floor, all the globes intact and in fixed orbit above.

"Which one has she broken?" I said reasonably, hoping to calm him.

Consuela's hands covered her face; she was weeping.

"None yet, but she was going to."

Dark tear-filled eyes met mine in mute appeal.

"Ted, Consuela has been dusting and cleaning this chandelier for years."

"You too, Wilson. You and your whole family . . . I know all of you . . . going to cheat me."

Insult churned in my belly. "Yes, you do know us, Ted." I knew I should be respectful but my voice climbed away.

I heard myself almost shout, "Ted, we are your friends, not your enemies!"

A gleam came to Ted's eye, a gleam I didn't like at all.

But he did turn away from Consuela.

He strode back to the reception desk, but instead of going behind it, he stood arrested before the TV. Retired generals debated pre-emptive strikes. "Motherfucking bastards," said Ted. I thought he was swearing at CNN. "Bastards! Nuke the lot. I'll sign up again. Do it myself."

His face — like a cold sun.

I came up behind him. "Do you remember the first time you saw the crocodiles?"

"What crocodiles?"

It was many years ago, but if he chose not to remember the crocodiles, he would not remember what he had said. So what use was discussion? I went back to Consuela.

Her shoulders were fragile under my clasp. She looked up at me, confused. Teardrops on her lashes like dew on petals. I led her to the garden gazebo, and we sat bathed in the sweet scent of flame vines. The evening view from the mountain, the carpet of lights spread below, calmed us both. I wiped her tears and apologized for Ted.

Normally, Ted would have invited me next door to his home for a nightcap after the last guests left the bar. He'd usually have a little Courvoisier in a snifter. I always had a Pepsi, because if I took anything stronger, I might keep drinking, and I knew it. But this night I would not yearn for what had flown.

I stopped at Jesús' shack on my way home to my cabin in the valley and told him what happened. And I admitted I had wanted . . . yes, I wanted very much to kiss Consuela and make sure no one made her cry ever again.

Jesús reappeared the next morning. "Señor Wilson," he said, "I delivered the milk to Buena Vista and I tell you the gringo has gone mad. He says maybe I have poison in my milk. He said, Milk — *venenoso!* I told him, The cows are tethered in my yard and I milk them morning and night. Where from would there be poison?"

"He has anthrax on his mind," I said. "He's annoyed even with me. Things will calm down."

But they didn't. I was working with two labourers on the hillside below Ted's home, picking crimson coffee cherries, when Ted swaggered over and pointed at the burlap bags hanging at our waists. He told me to load them all onto the hotel truck. Our agreement was over at his whim, with no mention of payment to the labourers — or me. Embarrassed, I turned to the labourers, translated what Ted had said, added an apology on Ted's behalf and paid them myself. Maybe Ted's shares in some big American companies — Enron or Worldcom — had fallen. But then I saw on TV that Ted's president had also decided he was not bound by previous agreements — larger ones, international ones.

Ted was just following a bad example; he would return to normal when his president did.

Jesús said a good friend would leave Ted Grand alone because that's what Ted wanted. "You yourself were like that only a few years ago."

"You didn't leave me alone."

Ted's anger and suffering wouldn't leave me alone. I could not be his "brother" any more. I hoped I was still his friend, but I remembered him saying there are no friends, only interests. Did I have any right to call myself more than an employee? Servant, perhaps? I sat on my veranda that evening as the sun faded over the rainforest and the cicadas pulsed sí, sí, sí all around, while my blood pulsed no, no, no.

My Suzuki Samurai was all beaten up and rusting out, and my cabin was little better than Jesús' shack, its only claim to beauty being a shrine I built to the Virgin from half a concrete pipe. Actually it was a shrine to Madelina and Carmen.

I talked to the Virgin now — I told her I had neglected my own life in favour of the gringo's. I made him my centre. The hotel was my life because it was important to him. But all Ted cared about now was cheering his country's troops through the liberation of Iraq. Fool, fool! What did I have for myself if he went away? I hadn't even saved very much.

During Holy Week everything was closed in Alajuela and no alcohol was being sold anywhere. I drove Ted to the coast, his air-conditioned van sealed against the humid warmth — slower than usual, as everyone had the same idea. We drove in silence, as if neither of us could think of anything to say. I longed to blow foam from a chilled mug of Heineken. Coffee trees flowered in surrounding farms; I opened my window a crack to get a whiff of their fragrance. Woods of teak and mahogany flowed past.

Madelina and I used to take Carmen to the coast every Easter. One time I drew two concentric circles in the sand. We each caught a hermit crab, placed them in the inner circle and blew. Madelina's crab moved first, and went far from the centre — and better still, out of its shell. I think she won.

It didn't matter who won.

Afterwards, we warned Carmen about the poisonous manzanillo trees by the beach, and she listened solemnly, then ran into the Pacific, shouting her glee.

This day, the drive did Ted some good — he closed his eyes most of the way. I wondered if running the hotel was becoming too much for him. I resolved to help him more.

Jesús brought his new monkey Luisa, and she swung from my rafters, her funny white face hanging below her long curly tail as if righting our upside-down world. She reached for peanuts, and I confided to her, though really to Jesús, "It's cancer. It's eating señor Grand from inside."

"In the brain?" said Jesús.

"No, in his spleen."

"If it was in his brain, it might explain his behaviour," said Jesús. "But the spleen — that excuses anger and pain, but not injustice."

"I went to see him in the hospital," I said. "He complains of insatiable hunger and unquenchable thirst. They have told him he can go home because they can do no more for him."

"So of course he called you to come bring him back to Buena Vista?"

I nodded. "Ted said he has been through difficult times before. And he has resources I never had."

"You're comparing your loss to his illness," said Jesús. "But each loss, each trouble is itself. Right now he's not here with us. In his head, he's in los Estados, in New York."

I had to agree. Ted was only following what had happened or was happening in los Estados, and he seemed to believe no people ever, anywhere, at any time, had suffered as great a tragedy as norteamericanos. Could I blame him? All he ever read was *USA Today*. And the many stories he read me to improve my English featured only norteamericanos. No norteamericano, no story. As if the rest of the world was inhabited by non-persons and monkeys. And he never heard my story or had any point of comparison because he never asked.

I should have asked more questions, I should have tried to find that thing in his past that was eating him now.

"Is it good that his head is in the United States?" I wondered out loud.

Jesús nodded. "Sí, sí, it's good. If his body was also there, not only his mind, he'd have to pay a lot more for doctors."

"He has extra expat coverage. Six months free hospital in los Estados."

But Jesús' compassion had fallen low. "Señor Grand has everything he needs. He lives in fear and anger anyway. But, amigo, why do you look so anxious?"

"Should I go with Ted to los Estados? I mean, when he goes for treatment?"

Jesús said, "Señor Wilson, I will say to you what I would say if you were my son: don't go. Mr. Bush's Injustice Department would stop you at the border. And now they take people who want to stay a long time in los Estados and put them in camps and prisons. We wouldn't even know you were gone, we wouldn't know how to find you."

I thought about this. I thought about never seeing Consuela again. Then I thought about the employees of the hotel — some of them my relatives — who all relied on me now. I thought about how many years I might have left and the things I still wanted to experience. I decided I did not wish to disappear.

But Ted once called me brother. What should a brother do?

Eventually, I didn't go because Ted didn't ask for my help. He believed he could do everything by himself: be angry alone, fight cancer alone. And he still needed a caretaker to run his hotel and send money to the hospital up north.

Ted left Costa Rica on a night the monsoon decided it must arrive. Torrents hammered the roof and pounded the broad leaves of trees. Titi monkeys swung downhill before us as I drove his van to the San José airport.

It wasn't exactly goodbye, but I didn't sleep much that night. A clay-coloured robin woke me with its drunken *dudududu*. After Jesús delivered my milk, I got in my Suzuki and drove to the coast. The rain lifted early in the morning, and I eventually noticed I was in Manuel Antonio. In the Parque Naçional, I sat facing the beach, my back to the smooth trunk of a Naked Indian tree that had sloughed off its bark.

On the path behind me, a park guide had set up her telescope on a tripod. "Some species have adapted so well they can't survive any place else," she chirped for a group of tourists. White-maned waves reared and tossed on the shore. Turquoise water, shady palms. In the distance a smooth hard island rose from the water, a lighthouse at its peak.

This was what Ted saw: the postcard he had crawled into for a while. Maybe he could only be blown so far from his origin. Maybe he feared that if he crossed into the next circle of the world, he would lose his American shell.

. . .

Ted went into remission a few times but never completely recovered. His cancer claimed him one day in a hospice in los Estados. My sorrow at this death of a friend and brother shouldn't have been so vague, so much like the sorrow I once felt for the man beaten to death at the top of the Buena Vista hill. His death should have mattered more than the death of that stranger.

But one-way caring has become difficult for me.

The same year Ted died, Consuela and I agreed to care for each other. She did me the honour of marrying me. Jesús brought his only son to play the guitar, and our friends and relatives danced the salsa with us at our wedding. Soon after, Jesús moved closer to Irazú, the smouldering volcano — his family said he was needed there. More opportunity for his son, he said. More swinging-trees for Luisa. He comes to see me when he needs a favour for someone — that's as it should be.

Now Consuela and I operate the Buena Vista, take salaries and send profits to its new owner, Ted's nephew in Portland, Oregon. The hotel gives travellers so much joy that it has made Ted's life matter. And the view from the mountain continues to bring joy to its guests: people from los Estados and the rest of us.

We Are Not in Pakistan

It's the first week of September, and leaves are already beginning to fall along the black strip of bike path where Kathleen walks with her grandmother. The foliage is still thick and green, hiding the granite block walls of the canyon on either side. Above the retaining walls, buildings seem to grip the ground and teeter as if they've backed up as far as they can.

Kathleen's footsteps echo in the earth-smelling cool as they pass beneath Lafayette Street. Cars swish above on the over-pass. Beyond the steel trusses of the bridge, the sky is a uniform blue, ragged where it meets the treetops.

"If this were Pakistan, Kathleen," Grandma says, "whole families would be living under that bridge, would have been living there for years and years."

Kathleen knows that. If it wasn't for Grandma Miriam and Grandpa Terry and their old house, she and Mom might be living under some bridge.

Grandma's dress sways about her tall lumpy figure. She has a faraway look; maybe she doesn't realize she has really rubbed it in again.

Kathleen is passing through the wedge of shade jutting from the Prospect Avenue bridge. Tires howl and ping on the steel mesh surface. Past the bridge, a rusty remnant of track runs parallel to the path.

"See the narrow-gauge?" Kohl-ringed eyes turn to Kathleen. "A train used to deliver coal to factories along this path." Grandma's eyebrows rise under her hatband. "Years before Grandpa and I came to live here, I'm sure. See how straight it is here. And how very, very gradually it turns up ahead."

Her tone — like she's talking to a five-year-old: Kathleen draws away.

She can't imagine a toy railroad. She can imagine the hard nose of a glacier that once covered this whole area, plowed this U-shaped channel into the western shore of Lake Michigan.

The glacier's back today, a massive ice block at the base of her tummy.

New faces, a new high school.

Grass borders the bike path, fresh and green on Grandma's side. Kathleen takes the brown side, where joggers have beaten the path pale. Far enough away from Grandma, off the road. Kathleen and her backpack. Backpack full of wrong stuff. Old stuff, retro stuff. From back-to-school shopping with Grandma. On Grandma's budget, not Dad's.

No laptop, no cell phone. Every kid gets a laptop and a cell phone except Kathleen.

Insects sing and whistle in the humid grass.

"We're so fortunate," Grandma breathes, "that Riverside High is so close. And isn't this a lovely shortcut? Thank the Good Lord."

Kathleen's nerves twang. Grandma's silver crucifix shines at her neck. Her Good Lord meddles in everything, even the location of high schools.

"I could have walked there myself," Kathleen says. "I could have taken the bus."

"Yes, but Grandma doesn't like you to go to school alone," Grandma says, as if speaking of a stranger.

"If I had a bicycle, I could ride to school." Kathleen injects venom into her voice.

"And if I had a horse," Grandma chirps, "all my wishes could ride."

Kathleen trudges faster, closer to the undergrowth. Only wood beams hold this section of the hillside back, keeping earth from avalanching over the path. Houses with peaked roofs peer down at her through the branches. A dog barks above.

A narrow path slants upwards. A street name is stencilled on the asphalt in bright gold: Farwell Avenue. Another path slants up: North Avenue.

A cyclone fence. A rundown old garage.

Kathleen plans to say goodbye when she gets to Newhall Street. She doesn't want Grandma walking her to the school building.

Grandma Miriam and "her world."

Third world.

If Kathleen's family were normal, her parents wouldn't have jumped from quarrels about whose turn it was to do laundry or control the stupid remote to shouting matches. And over what? The CIA's funding the Taliban ("didn't" said Dad, "did" said Mom), whether General Musharraff was President Bush's puppet ("is," said Mom, "is not" said Dad), whether the US ought to act unilaterally or wait for the UN ("shouldn't," said Mom, "should" said Dad). And the final brawl about whether there ever were any weapons of mass destruction in Iraq, and did that suspicion justify killing thousands of Iraqi civilians.

Without Grandma's world hanging its stinking sandals about her family's necks, Kathleen's mom wouldn't have been born in Pakistan or have a name like Safia. And Mom wouldn't have jabbered in Urdu every Sunday on the phone with Grandma. Mom wouldn't have "needed" Pakistani food all the time, so Dad wouldn't have complained endlessly about heartburn. And Kathleen would still be with her old school friends in Eau Claire.

Without Grandma Miriam, Kathleen wouldn't have long black hair and a too-prominent "Pakistani nose." And she wouldn't get so mocha-toned in summer that her skin got out of sync with her hazel eyes.

"Weird-looking," she overheard her last teacher say. "Probably Hispanic."

A bike approaches; Grandma veers left over the dividing yellow line.

"Keep right, Grandma," says Kathleen. "We are not in Pakistan." Even Dorothy knew when she wasn't in Kansas any more.

Grandma stoops over flowers. "Allah!" she says.

"They're just daisies, Grandma." People at school will think she's Muslim.

"No, see these blue prairie flowers beside the daisies. I never know their names." Black eyes shine and crinkle.

Kathleen scuffs along, the scent of grass and morning moving past her. The glacier is getting bigger, stabbing icicles between her ribs.

The other girls won't have come to a new city. They won't have moved into an attic bedroom at their grandparents' house. They will have best friends already, will have been in twos since first grade. They will already have boyfriends — all the cool guys will be taken. And they won't be wearing last year's fashions.

Grandma's fault. Tankinis, tank-tops and spaghetti straps were not allowed. Nor were bare midriffs. Hipster jeans were forbidden. And no Nikes, absolutely no Nikes.

"Nike has sweatshops," Grandma said during the back-to-school sales, as she removed a pair of shoes from Kathleen's shopping cart.

"You have carpets made by children in Lahore."

"How else should children learn their family's trade?" she said. "Those aren't sweatshops nowadays, not since the government took them over."

"Socialism," said Kathleen, just to make her mad.

"Regulation for the better," said Grandma.

"Bet there's a class in carpet weaving — want me to sign up?"

"Lord forgive you for teasing Grandma," she said.

Now cyclists on a tandem bike whiz by, an American flag stirring gently behind them. A jogger huffs and pumps past. Gold letters stencilled on the path: Newhall.

"Thanks, Grandma, I'll go from here."

"Nonsense." Her hat cocks toward Kathleen. "I should meet your teacher, introduce myself."

Kathleen kicks a heel across the lettering. "Oh, no, Mom's introduced herself already. Really, I'll be fine. My teacher is probably very busy — first day and all."

Grandma looks thwarted but ready for another try.

"And Grandpa Terry's alone," Kathleen adds adroitly.

Grandma tilts her wrist to read the time. "I'll pick you up this afternoon. Meet me right here, darling."

"I'll come home myself." Kathleen sounds firm and even, like her father giving instructions at one of his construction projects.

"Kathleen," says Grandma, "in my world, we don't allow young girls to walk home alone."

She didn't say "you," she said "young girls."

Inside, Kathleen's glacier clenches and expands. "I'm glad we don't live in your world," she says, plumping her cheeks into sulk mode. Ignoring her grandmother's outstretched arms, she sprints up the incline to the brown brick school buildings. At the top she glances back to the bike path.

Grandma Miriam is waving her hat. "Three-thirty!" she yells, and points at her watch.

. . .

"How was school?"

"Okay," says Kathleen, shifting the clinging weight of her backpack.

But school had been better than okay. Kathleen had popped out in front during the summer, and boys noticed her, buzzing about like flies. She acted as if she didn't need them — that helped too. She signed up for guitar lessons, foiling Grandma's wish for her to learn piano. Kathleen and another newbie, Jodie, a Chilean-American kid from Minneapolis, got together in the cafeteria.

Thanks to Jodie, Kathleen had fared better than other new kids; one girl with dark eyes and a nose like her own sat through lunch all alone. You'd think by now she'd have figured out that even if you're wearing jeans, a white scarf tucked behind your ears and brought forward to cover them up screams "Muslim" so loud people can hear it a mile away. Nope, the girl was totally out of it.

Grandma rests her hand on Kathleen's head. "Coming toward me just now, you looked exactly like a little girl in Pakistan. Did anyone ask where you got the lovely shape of your eyes, your silky black hair?"

"Yeah. I told them my dad's Black Irish."

A second's pause. "So he is, darling. But there's a lot of me in you."

"I don't look like a girl in Pakistan," says Kathleen. "All of them wear those black things."

"Burkhas? On TV you mean. CNN loves showing women in burkhas. But I didn't see many burkhas in Lahore when I was growing up."

A woman encased in black tights rollerblades by. She pivots on one skate, faces back, gives a graceful wave. Grandma Miriam waves back.

"We were so cosmopolitan, then, darling. It's so different now because of the fundies in the rural areas."

Fundies. She thinks she's being naughty because it rhymes with undies.

"For instance near Peshawar," Grandma continues. "What you'd call farm country. So parochial they are — you know, just like Americans who haven't travelled. But my friends say, what if you didn't have the mosques? Would Musharraff or any other president give the homeless welfare? And who would take care of war refugees, orphans? At least the fundies give them food."

Her friends say. Her Pakistani friends. Mom says you never know who might be listening these days. If she were here, she'd shush Grandma from going on and on about Pakistan.

". . . Women take their burkhas off in private, you know. And I wish you could see how lovely they are, how *fab*ulous their jewellery is, how ornate are their clothes."

Kathleen takes an over-the-shoulder glance. A few other kids are walking home — alone. No one she recognizes from class. A couple of women jog behind strollers. A few cyclists are leaning around a curve ahead.

A splash of colour flutters past, a butterfly. One flutter of its wing can affect what happens far away in Pakistan. But a butterfly in Pakistan can't affect much in America.

"If you love Pakistan so much, Grandma, why did you leave?"

Silence. Kathleen steals a look.

Grandma is so old. Kathleen is going to get famous and die young.

Can't she just answer? Anyone watching will think she doesn't speak English.

At the top of Lafayette Hill, Grandma has to stop and catch her breath. Lake Michigan brims before them, Eden blue.

"Our family," says Grandma Miriam, so low Kathleen can't be sure she hears. "We had to leave. Slowly, gradually, each of us realized we had no future there. I went first by marrying your grandpa, but then my brother and sister came away too. People in Pakistan didn't want us, Kathleen. We're Christians."

Kathleen has never heard this from her mom, though Mom lived in Pakistan when she was little. Maybe she was too little to remember. Grandpa's Christian and he lived in Pakistan for years, but he's never mentioned anyone being mean to him. But then, Grandpa Terry's hair was natural blond before it got whiter than anyone else's. And you can't get a word out of him during football season and it's always football season. And he doesn't remember a lot of things. And even if he did, he wouldn't remember things the way Grandma does.

Kathleen believes her grandmother. Because her dad said quarrelling and hatred are all you can expect of Third World people.

By six each morning, when Kathleen comes downstairs, Miriam has woken up Safia, picked up her husband's dirty socks, tidied Safia's clothes, books, papers and mail. She has also done a couple of loads of laundry, washed the dishes in the porcelain sink, dried them with her embroidered dish towel, made Taj Mahal tea with cardamon and brewed coffee.

"I hate tea and coffee," says Kathleen. "Got any OJ?" She opens the fridge but doesn't find any. This has happened every day since Kathleen and Mom unpacked their bags, but Grandma doesn't buy orange juice. What would it cost — a dollar? Two?

At six-fifteen, Miriam climbs the stairs to nag and chivvy Safia so she won't be late, the airport is a forty-minute drive. "It shouldn't be so hard for her to wake up," she says. "I keep asking, Why do you have to sign up for so many hours of overtime? All she says is "'Time-and-a-half, Amiji, time-and-a-half.'"

Kathleen thinks Safia works way out at the airport and signs up for hours of overtime so she doesn't have to talk to her.

Every second day, Grandma Miriam bakes cranberry bread for Grandpa. And in the past week, she has been walking Kathleen to school and meeting her afterwards. Grandma and Grandpa don't have a car for Kathleen to borrow. Which means that unless she rides the bus forty-five minutes to Jodie's house, she will end up staying home in the evenings. Which means she will have to swallow things with funny names like alloo cholas and eggplant bhartha, all served over an endless supply of cumin-scented rice.

Kathleen is desperate for hamburger, pizza or a single mouthful of Uncle Ben's. She skips class a couple of times to walk over to the nearest McDonalds, but she has to eke out the twenty dollars Grandma gives Grandpa Terry every week so he can present it to Kathleen. In her world, Grandma says, it's the men who give allowances to the women in their families. "But," she says with a conspiratorial giggle, "we women have to make endless allowances for men."

We women — huh!

Today is Sunday. Grandma sits in her customary corner of the couch, which she has draped with orangey-red "priceless" jamavar shawls to hide the holes in its upholstery. "Did you find a job, yet, darling?" says Grandma.

"Nope."

Two days after school opened, Jodie found a waitress job at George Webb's diner, and lots of other kids have found burger-flipper jobs after school to escape their families, but Kathleen doesn't seem to get offers for anything but babysitting.

I have no patience with kids — they're brainless.

So Miriam settles down with the phone on her lap and begins phoning her friends and relatives, beginning with her sister in Calgary, her brother in Houston who may be "voluntarily departed" any day now to Lahore, and Sadruddin in New York (whom Kathleen has never met), who's almost like a relative.

Then she runs her finger down her list of friends. There's Anser Mahmood, who volunteered to go with the INS officers when they promised he'd be home the next day since he only had an expired visa. He spent the next four months in solitary at the Detention Center in Brooklyn and hasn't been the same since. "No point calling him."

"And Aisha," says Grandma. "No point calling her. The Immigration chaps arrested her husband Tosueef — anthrax possession, can you imagine — then they came back and searched his home. Aisha was taken away to the local jail and strip-searched. All for possession of a bottle of garam masala. Garam masala!" Grandma laughs. "I cook with it every day. They brought her before a judge, and no wonder she asked to be deported. Some vultures will probably take their beautiful home and all their new furniture." She turns her pencil over and erases the name.

There's Shokeria Yagi who was abroad with her three sons and came home to find her husband had been taken away. There's Jalil Mirza to whom Grandma sent some money that got him and his two sons out of a Detention Center, but he's now stuck in a Red Cross shelter with his whole family. They're waiting their turn along with eight hundred others applying to Canada for asylum. Grandma erases their names.

Kathleen goes up to her room and turns on Eminem at full blast, but Grandma still racks up long distance bills calling Mohammad Akbar, who sold his 7-Eleven store on Devon Avenue in Chicago and moved to Winnipeg last year, Professor Nayeem, who changed his name to Gonzalez months ago to avoid domestic registration, and Habeeba in Schaumberg, Illinois, who manages the carwash since her husband was deported.

Kathleen comes downstairs wearing a Britney Spears tank top and shorts. Grandma is so set on telling her that everyone says she should "go into computers" that she doesn't curl up her nose immediately. She's convinced that Kathleen has to know "all about computers." A checker's job at a grocery, Sadruddin Uncle has said, will do it, teach Kathleen all about computers.

Grandma knows shit about computers. She can't even do e-mail.

"Your friends wouldn't know shit about computers if they weren't listed in the National Crime Info database," says Kathleen, who wouldn't know about the database herself if Safia didn't keep bringing it up.

"Don't swear, Kathleen. There's no shame in that. All our names are on someone's silly list. Safia says they're only in the important ones, Galileo, CAPPS, IBIS."

"Those are databases, not lists."

"List, database, list — same thing. All I'm saying is: find out if you're good at computers. I was always accurate at typing — slow, but accurate. And when Safia took her test for the airlines, they told her she went sixty words per minute. I tell you, you'll be *fab*ulous at it."

Kathleen uses computers every day in school. She will now give up trying to find a real after-school job to make sure she doesn't learn more about them.

Before school on September 11, now called Annual Patriot Day, Kathleen, her mother and Miriam watch the Secretary of State — Safia calls him Rummy — speak at Arlington cemetery about the triumph of Freedom over Tyranny.

"And to us to whom the task of justice has been sent from on high . . ." intones the chaplain. Grandma calls him the mullah. He ends with "God bless America."

Kathleen's trying to figure out what to do with herself.

She was all ready for a Saturday at Octoberfest with Safia, when Safia was called in to work. She left muttering angrily — not about the work, or that her plans with Kathleen were cancelled, but about "an eighty-seven billion dollar blank check made out to the likes of Halliburton."

"Come sit here! On the sofa." Grandma pats and smoothes her shawls.

"Sofa?" says Kathleen.

"Couch, then, couch! Sit beside me on the couch."

Grandma Miriam kicks off her sequined slippers and sits cross-legged, hands clasped around what has to be her tenth cup of Taj Mahal this morning. Grandpa Terry leans forward, duct-taped glasses only a foot away from the green and gold movements of a Packers rerun. His newspaper has fallen beside him.

"What do you want to study, Kathleen?" Grandma asks in her brightest, warmest voice. "So many opportunities I never had. Are you going to take computers?"

Like it's easy as Parcheesi. Ludo, Grandma called it. Claimed it was ancient, invented near Lahore.

Okay, Kathleen will play along for a bit. But no computers.

"Haven't decided," she mumbles. "Maybe psychology, maybe advertising."

"Wonderful choices! For one you need to be interested in other people, and for the second you need to find some enthusiasm. Not that I've seen much of either in you lately." She stops, then says, "You might need a just-in-case plan, darling."

Kathleen doesn't flinch, only seethes as if she'd swallowed live coals.

Dad hasn't sent a check this month and there's no just-in-case plan. Grandma's fault — she never liked him. If she had been nicer to him, maybe Dad and his lily-pale orangutan-haired girlfriend wouldn't be off on a cruise through the Panama Canal. And Grandma's treating Mom like a baby, picking up after her, cooking her favourite meals. These days, Grandma's even stopped her morning nagging and chivvying — she's been letting Mom sleep late or leave early as she pleases.

No wonder Mom won't take Kathleen home. Won't even look for an apartment.

"If you decide what course you want in college, Kat, you can work backwards to decide the classes you should take now."

Hate-glow spreads and blazes within Kathleen. No one calls her Kat but Dad.

"Don't know why you're talking about college. Like there's any way I'm going to make it to college on twenty dollars a week."

"The Good Lord will see to it you go to college."

"Like the Good Lord really cares," says Kathleen.

"The Good Lord forgives, Kathleen. I pray every day that he gives me strength to do the same."

Kathleen sets her lips. She looks past her grandmother. Through the window behind the couch, bright leaves swirl and dance before a cooling wind.

A grunt or two. That's all Kathleen allows herself on the daily walks to and from school. Today, heading home, Grandma Miriam is prattling on about the bunches of tiny berries tinted pale yellow and cherry red. Berries so beautiful are almost surely poisonous.

"Not poisonous at all," says Kathleen, and pulls off three. Into her mouth they go. She rolls them against the inside of her cheek.

"Oh!" Grandma's hand goes to her mouth. She thinks Kathleen has swallowed them.

"If I need help, I'll call 911 when we get home," says Kathleen. "I can do that — we're not in Pakistan."

Kathleen walks ahead for a while and manages to spit the berries out without her grandmother noticing.

When Grandma figures the berry poison danger is past, she says in her chitchatty way, "One day you'll wish you'd asked me more questions about my parents and about when I was small."

Heard all about it. Grandma's mother was Catholic, born in Iran, Grandma's father was an Anglo, a mixed breed left behind when the British washed their hands of India and Pakistan. He saw Grandma's mother at the Lahore Gymkhana Club and converted from Anglican to Catholic so he could marry her. Grandma got born, grew up in Lahore, a city in India that somehow got itself moved to Pakistan. She became an "air hostess" for BOAC, an airline that doesn't even exist anymore, and she met Grandpa when he was a Marine guard stationed at the American Embassy. At a "do," where they danced like Fred Astaire and Ginger Rogers. And they got permission from Grandpa's CO to get married. And then they had a baby — did they have to call her Safia? — and then they travelled as Grandpa Terry got stationed in different countries. And Kathleen's mom grew up to work in the airline business too, except that she's still only in ticketing because, she says, nowadays Pakistan-born employees need not apply to be crew members.

". . . and about my life in Lahore and all my travels."

"Uh-huh," says Kathleen. "Like I'd care."

For once Grandma Miriam falls silent. She pulls out her handkerchief, dabs her eyes.

Kathleen keeps walking.

Grandma is sniffing.

Kathleen is savagely glad. She can't remember how it feels not to be angry.

. . .

Next morning, Kathleen comes downstairs in her pyjamas.

No water boiling on the stove in the kitchen. No Grandma bustling around in her scuzzy old apron.

Kathleen yawns. She dreamed of Dad last night. He was showing the orangutan-haired woman around the house, Kathleen's old house. He was standing in Kathleen's room by her old toy box. The toy box opened and that woman leaned over and looked inside, and then she threw back her head and laughed. Kathleen shakes her head and flexes her neck, trying to get rid of the sound.

Grandpa Terry is sitting in his chair in the living room, in the dark, newspaper folded on his knees.

"Is Grandma still asleep?"

"I don't know. Maybe she went to the store for milk."

"It's six a.m. The store isn't open yet."

"She saw Safia off to work," he says. "Said Safia had to leave early." He looks around, pats his pockets.

"Is something missing?"

"Can't find my watch."

"Don't worry," says Kathleen, imitating Grandma. "It'll show up. Did she take her jacket?"

"Of course she took her jacket — she's always cold." He sounds peeved. Grandma says he gets "crotchety" if she doesn't feed him.

"Make some coffee," he says.

"Didn't she do that yet?"

Kathleen looks for coffee in all the cupboards but comes up with only a dusty jar of instant.

Why on earth does Grandma need to hide all the spoons — is it some ritual from Pakistan? Grandpa will have to use a fork.

"I'm hungry," says Grandpa. "Make some cream of rice."

Kathleen wants to tell him to make it himself, but he's semiblind and forgetful and her grandfather, so she can't. She figures out how to turn on the stove and when a blue flame finally blossoms, sticks a saucepan and Grandpa's cream of rice on it.

"Make it thick," he shouts from the living room.

Kathleen tries to remember the times she has half-watched Grandma make it.

"Why don't you get a microwave," she says, as she stirs and stirs.

"When you get rich, you can buy us one." Grandpa guffaws into his false teeth.

Kathleen puts a bowl of cream of rice and a fork on the kitchen table. Grandpa shuffles in till he bangs against the table and takes his seat.

"There's no milk," he says.

"You're welcome, Grandpa," Kathleen mutters into the cold that greets her inside the fridge. Where is the milk?

Grandma went out to buy coffee and milk. Maybe she went for a walk before she went to buy milk. Maybe she couldn't sleep. Yeah, that's it. She went for a walk before she went to buy milk. Maybe she fell in Lake Michigan — happens in winter when perfect idiots walk out on cardboard-thin ice. Could happen in fall too, with the currents and all.

Fine, she's dead. Now there won't be anyone to scold Kathleen. There won't be anyone really Pakistani-looking in her family any more.

Kathleen finds a tiny jug of milk in the back. She pours half the milk over Grandpa's cream of rice and places the jug back in the cold interior. She runs upstairs, wriggles out of her pyjamas and into a sweatshirt and jeans. Turns on rap music louder than loud, just because she can.

No, Grandma is not dead. She can't be. Maybe she just left Grandpa. No — what did Grandpa do to Grandma, anyway? Did he ever order her not to eat Pakistani food? Does he drink and watch CNN non-stop till three in the morning? Did he ever take a bimbo on a cruise to Panama? So he has false teeth — Grandma never said she minded. People her mom and dad's age get divorced, not Grandma Miriam and Grandpa. They're like salt and pepper, peanut butter and jelly, Mary-Kate and Ashley. Well, maybe not Mary-Kate and Ashley.

Grandma went to the store to buy milk. And coffee. And the store didn't have any skim milk, which is all Grandpa drinks, so she must have gone to another store.

Kathleen turns off the music and goes into the bathroom. She brushes her teeth till her gums tingle. She runs the water at a trickle so she can hear the front door opening when Grandma comes in with the milk and coffee.

She doesn't come.

Kathleen drags on her socks, ties the laces of her sneakers.

Grandma'll be really mad if I'm late for school.

She thumps downstairs. Grandpa is sitting in the living room in the dark again, the paper still folded on his lap. His magnifier lies on it, and he is just staring. She turns on the light beside him and, before leaving, says, "Don't worry. She'll be back soon."

She doesn't know if he heard her. If she were married to him, she'd dump him. But Grandma . . .

On her way to school, Kathleen kicks stones along the bike path, looking over her shoulder in case Grandma is following. In algebra class, she comes out of a daydream to find the teacher talking about simultaneous equations you can solve only by adding them together or switching sides. That glacier is back at the base of her stomach.

What if Grandma has left Kathleen?

Fine. She can be that way. I don't care.

. . .

At lunchtime, Kathleen slides her cafeteria tray over the rails behind Jodie's.

"What's up?" says Jodie, helping herself to a strawberry yogurt.

"Not much." Kathleen takes the same so she doesn't need to decide. "I think I lost my grandma." That sounded pretty stupid.

"No kidding." Jodie leads the way to a table. "Didn't know she was sick. When's the funeral?"

"No, I mean we can't find her. She wasn't at home this morning. She didn't walk me to school."

"And you think she got lost?"

"No, she's lived in this area since before I was born. I don't know. She could be a missing person."

Kathleen keeps her back to the Muslim girl as she gives Jodie the details.

"Have you made flyers, you know, like people make for lost cats?"

"No, no yet." Kathleen pictures Grandma's face on a milk carton. With hat or without? She should have checked her hats.

"Did you call 911?"

"No. I mean, not yet."

"Aren't you going to?"

"Sure."

"They have canine search teams," Jodie says. "I saw them on TV. But hey, maybe she's been kidnapped."

"No, Grandpa's not rich."

"I know — she went for a walk by the lake. People fall in sometimes."

That's not what Kathleen is imagining. Kathleen is imagining Grandma boarding a plane to Pakistan right now with her brother, both "voluntary departures." Hadn't Kathleen said, "If you like Pakistan so much, why did you leave?" Grandma might be on her way home to Lahore — Kathleen can't go find her in Lahore.

But wait, didn't she say people in Lahore didn't want her or her family?

Jodie lends Kathleen her cell phone to call Grandpa.

"No," says Grandpa. "She hasn't come home. And I'm pretty sure she's taken my watch."

"Taken your watch? She has her own."

"Well if *she* didn't steal it, either Safia did or you did. Or someone else did."

"I didn't steal your watch, Grandpa. Bet you anything I can find it for you. Did you find a note?"

"No. Did you?"

"I haven't looked for one."

"Well, why do you think I should look for one?"

"Right," says Kathleen. "Okay, thanks, Grandpa."

Kathleen flips the cell phone closed and hands it back to Jodie. Leaving her tray, she runs to her locker. She yanks her backpack out and turns it upside down. Books thud, coins ping on the floor, her makeup kit pops open, powder spills all over. There will be a note. It will be in a lavender envelope. She will use her key to Grandma's house to slit it open. There will be a picture of blue prairie flowers on a card. She will see Grandma's tidy writing: "I'm tired of your rudeness," it will read, "tired of being your unpaid servant, of picking up after you, running after you. You bore me because you're always bored. I'm tired of telling you nicely. So I am on strike."

But there is no note. Kathleen puts all the stuff back, returns to the cafeteria, borrows Jodie's phone again and calls Grandpa. "Maybe she's on strike or something. What do you think?"

"Yeah, could be a wildcat strike," says Grandpa. "But she'd do some yelling first."

"Did you have an argument?"

"Nah," says Grandpa. "Maybe. I don't remember. It's hard for me to remember. But I never argue with that woman. Never. She's a good cook. But you know those Eastern women. So nice and sweet when they first get here. But then, oh boy, watch out once they get a few American ideas."

"She doesn't have nearly enough American ideas, Grandpa."

"Uh-huh. Well, let her strike all day. Maybe I'll lose a little weight."

Kathleen hangs up. Maybe Grandma was right about Grandpa Terry being in the early stages of Alzheimer's.

If her mom were lost, Kathleen would want someone to tell her, so she calls Safia at work. Tells her all the Twilight Zone parts — didn't walk me to school, didn't tell grandpa, and no note — but doesn't say how she's feeling because she doesn't know what to feel. "Mom, what do you think?"

"Hmmm," says Safia. Then she doesn't say anything. Kathleen can feel her wishing Kathleen spoke even pidgin-Urdu. "Can't talk right now," she says eventually.

Jodie is making slashing gestures. "Guitar class," she mouths.

"All right, Mom. Call me. You have Jodie's number? Call me on her cell if you hear from Grandma."

It's chilly on the bike path after school. For no reason but the menace of shadows, Kathleen remembers she's a girl and alone.

Grandma will be home by now, she figures. She picks some blue flowers. She will ask Grandma what kind of flowers Grandma had in her home in Lahore.

The house is dark except for the floor lamp Kathleen turned on that morning. It shines right on Grandpa's face — hasn't he moved all day?

"Make some coffee," he says, when he realizes she's in the house.

Kathleen makes him a cup of instant.

"What's for dinner?" he says.

"I don't know," says Kathleen. "Grandma'll be home soon. You can ask her."

She goes up to her room and puts on a camisole and miniskirt that shows more leg than Grandma can handle — make her feel guilty for leaving as soon as she walks in.

When she is back downstairs, Grandpa says, "Make us some dinner."

"Why do I have to make it?" Kathleen sounds whiny and middle-school-girlish even to herself.

But Grandpa has switched on the Packers; he doesn't answer.

Kathleen finds a box of macaroni and cheese and some butter. And the milk left in the jug. And a sausage. She burns the side of her thumb on the saucepan but eventually there is macaroni with sausage for dinner. Afterwards, Grandpa doesn't put his plate in the sink, much less offer to help clean up. He goes back to the TV.

Kathleen goes out to the convenience store, buys skim milk and coffee. She asks the Lebanese guy at the counter if Grandma Miriam came in today — this morning — anytime? He says, "Yesterday, not today," and gives her a Tootsie Roll with her change, so she knows he knows Grandma.

Cheerful voices of sports commentators greet her as she opens the front door. But no Grandma.

Kathleen sinks down on the staircase, knees to her chest, waiting for Safia to come home.

Grandma Miriam doesn't come home that night. Kathleen and Safia turn the house upside down but cannot find her purse, passport, the address book that usually sits by the phone, or a note.

No hats are missing. Safia searches Grandma's desk but cannot find her check book. Kathleen scans Grandma's shelves: Urdu poetry, English poetry — all English Victorian poets. Not a single American writer, not even Twain. *The Baghdad Museum Guide to Mesopotamian Art*, an English-Urdu Bible translation, and an Urdu-English dictionary are the scruffiest. Cookbooks and more cookbooks. A stack of audiotapes, no CDs. Kathleen rummages through to-do lists, knitting needles and stacks of handwritten letters in Grandma's drawers, one of them full of dog-eared crossed-off address books going back to 1982.

After dinner at the end of the second day, no one can sleep; they all put on their pyjamas and slippers and stay up waiting. Even Kathleen is drinking Taj Mahal, and she keeps forgetting about acting bored and nonchalant. Grandpa Terry tells the story of the American Embassy do where he first met Grandma. Safia tells how Grandma Miriam used to teach English to an Israeli general. Then everyone falls quiet.

Safia says, "Okay, guys, one day, two days — but this is the second night." She gives a huge sob and grabs for Kleenex. She says she knows — not thinks, but knows — what happened. She pads into the kitchen in her pink fluffy slippers and pulls out all the drawers. She pulls the lid from the largest tin, sniffs and holds it out to Kathleen.

"Turmeric?" she says. Kathleen looks at the yellow powder. "This is a three-year supply!"

"It's for Grandpa," says Kathleen. "Against Alzheimer's."

"He doesn't have Alzheimer's," says Safia, and snaps the lid over the mouth of the tin.

She arranges four half-full tins of garam masala on the kitchen table. Then she finds three bottles more. She examines them — different brands, some Pakistani, some Indian, some home-made. "But how many tins and bottles of garam masala did Amiji have to begin with?" she frets.

"C'mon, Mom," Kathleen says, taking Safia's arm. "Maybe we can't find her passport because it expired and she was getting a new one. Maybe she's away somewhere writing a new address book. We need to call 911. The cops will know what to do."

"You crazy?" says Safia, shaking her off. "We might as well phone Homeland Security. The cops are in cahoots with them anyway. Don't I see it at the airport? They don't look at the expiration dates on passports. They're looking at Place of Birth. Mine says Pakistan. If they take me away too, who'll look after you?"

"Nobody's going to take *you* away," says Grandpa from the kitchen doorway. "And don't worry. If they do, I'll look after Kathleen."

Safia snorts and flaps her hand at him. "I'm just saying we have to be careful. Remember that woman right here — no, in the suburbs somewhere — what was her name? The Immigration guys barged in while she was in the shower, and next thing she knew she was on her way back to Somalia, leaving her husband and children behind."

"Yeah, but she must have been illegal," says Kathleen.

"Have you any idea how difficult it is to stay legal? It's damn near impossible. Lose a job that brought you here or get laid off before you have enough money saved for the trip home and two months later you're illegal. Take nine credits instead of twelve on a student visa and you can be deported. And now they just take away your passport and you're stateless. Can't prove you're from anywhere."

"How'm I supposed to know?"

"You're overreacting," says Grandpa. "Miriam is legal and staying legal. She's married to me. But maybe someone in the military thinks she's a sleeper."

"She never sleeps past six o'clock," says Kathleen. "And even if she did, why should the military care?"

"A sleeper," says Grandpa, "is someone who lives here a long time and gets activated by orders from somewhere overseas. A terrorist."

"My grandma?"

"Always told her she should become a citizen," says Grandpa. "But that's one stubborn lady. Didn't want anyone to think she'd married me to get an American passport."

Safia wipes her eyes and says Grandpa might have to cook for himself now, like Habeeba looking after that car wash all by herself.

"Why? Can't you cook?" says Grandpa, and stomps back to the living room.

That was mean.

Not meaner than Kathleen was to Grandma. Kathleen made Grandma cry.

"Maybe he does have Alzheimer's," says Safia. She flops into a chair at the kitchen table. "She could be wearing an orange jumpsuit along with the 9/11 detainees and the Afghan POWs at Guantánamo, and we wouldn't know. She'd be like that guy Ali Raza. He couldn't afford a lawyer, and they wouldn't get him one, but they told him he'd be in jail for twenty years if he didn't sign his deportation papers. So — poof! He's gone. Where is he? Who knows?"

"Aw, c'mon, Mom. Why don't we call Dad and ask him what to do?"

"No. My Amiji could be in solitary, without bail, without trial, or in shackles. They could move her from jail to jail across the country and your Dad would say, Oh, the government must have information, something we don't know about her."

"That's not true," says Kathleen, although she feels it is.

At school, Jodie had said Kathleen might never find out where her grandma is — that is what happened to her relatives in Chile a few years ago. Things like that happen everywhere, to innocent people all over the world. All the time.

Kathleen told Jodie, “We’re not in Chile. And we are not in Pakistan.”

By five o’clock the next morning, Kathleen doesn’t feel anywhere. Grandpa turns on the TV, but even the local news is about how the UN should take responsibility for Iraq now that the US has liberated it. Not a word about Grandma.

“Liberated!” Mom clicks it off.

Kathleen goes upstairs to pee.

She pumps the lotion soap and scrubs her face. Then she has to wash it again; she didn’t know she was crying. She turns on a rap station. Softly, just to get herself mad again, rather than sad. Turns it off. Goes back downstairs into the kitchen, where Safia is making yet another pot of tea.

Kathleen opens the fridge. No OJ.

She closes the fridge.

“Mom,” says Kathleen. “Grandma doesn’t spend a dollar more than she has to. She’s probably staying with someone.”

“Most of her friends are Pakistanis, but I don’t really know them. Haven’t talked to them in ages.”

“Yeah, but they have names? And addresses? Look in the old address books.”

“Uh-huh, but they’re all known to the FBI. They didn’t even need to grab her latest address book.”

“So if we call any of them, the FBI could be listening to us?”

Mom nods, pours a mugful for Kathleen and adds milk. “Or Homeland Security. Or the CIA. They’re just waiting for us to call her friends.”

The mug is warm in Kathleen’s palms. The reflection of her face is tiny. It floats on the brown surface. She has never drunk so much tea in her life.

Then out of the blue, Mom says, “Connections.”

“What?”

“She’s Pakistani.”

"Yeah, so?"

"So she'll meet a Pakistani cabbie and twelve minutes later they will have figured out that they're long lost relations or even from the same city. They'll find someone in common."

"So?"

"I could call Aunty in Calgary and talk in Urdu. She could call Uncle in Houston, and he'd know how to reach Sadruddin in New York, and he could call one of her friends here in town . . ."

"Yeah." Kathleen wants to say please but can't get it out. "We've got to try."

At sunrise, Safia leaves a voice mail for her boss to say she's taking the day off work. She'll make the calls. "Go to school," she tells Kathleen.

In the cafeteria, the girl in the white scarf — hijab, Grandma Miriam would call it — is eating alone. Kathleen takes her spaghetti, leaves an empty chair between, sits down and tries to eat.

Worms and dirt.

Kathleen sniffs back tears, inhales a whiff of spices. The Muslim girl has brought her own food. Alloo cholas? Maybe eggplant bhartha?

"Hi there," says Kathleen. "Where are you from?"

"Fritsche Middle School." The girl sounds surprised, as if Kathleen is the first student at Riverside who's ever spoken to her. Magnet eyes ringed with kohl. Like Grandma's, but without the crinkles.

Kathleen takes a stab at her spaghetti. She rolls it over her fork and unrolls it again.

"But where are you really from?" The question Grandma hates blips from her mouth because she doesn't know how else to ask. Her cheeks grow warm.

"My family is from Iran," says the girl, drawing herself taller. "What about yours?"

"American," says Kathleen. "My grandma is from Pakistan."

The face set in the white scarf brightens. "Assalam Aleikum!"

What's the right response? Kathleen can't remember. "She's Christian," she says, to explain her ignorance.

"Oh."

This girl wouldn't know Grandma Miriam even if Grandma were Muslim, even if Grandma's mom did come from Iran. And why did Kathleen have to say Grandma's a foreigner?

The girl is looking at Kathleen as if expecting her to leave. But if Kathleen leaves now, everyone will go back to pretending they can't see the girl, though she's right in front of them.

Kathleen looks around. Jodie is standing, tray in hand, beside the salad bar. Jodie turns. She's looking right at Kathleen. Her gaze moves to the white scarf. A corner of Jodie's mouth pulls inward. Kathleen waves before Jodie can do the eye-roll, inviting — no, willing — Jodie to come over and join them.

"Everyone's connected to everyone," Kathleen tells the Muslim girl. "We just need to figure out how."

Night of the Leonids

Driving home from a gala dinner in Toronto, Tania reminds Philip to look up for meteors, look up tonight.

"Might be too cloudy." The first words he's spoken since they left the lights of downtown.

The black tongue of the road swallows the car into the illuminated circle of the headlights. He has driven an hour and a half west, to the village. Tania squints, searching. If she sees a mailbox marking a side road, she'll know it's another forty-five minutes ride through the forest. Spying it, she settles back in her seat.

Her gaze lingers on the dim line of his close-shaved jaw. She wouldn't mind the feel of his bicep beneath his sleeve. Or the feel of more than a bicep. Philip in a tux is a real turn-on.

Getting turned on ain't everything. And he'll say it's late and he's tired. He won't say he's pissed because I screwed up his award night.

No more mailboxes. If the car breaks down, there's no one for miles. A flash of yellow eyes could mean black bear. Tania watches all the way.

The Merc rolls around the driveway and stops. And Tania is out, a heel catching in her black velvet hem, sequins scattering to gravel. Inside, she hangs up her coat and drops her handbag on the demi-lune table. For a second, she is caught by her reflection in the hall mirror.

Who'da thunk she'd look like this? Thin brown eyebrows above glittery dark deep-set eyes, sharp cheekbones accentuated by hair drawn tight. Halter-top gown, neckline plunging between big boobs — she's still got what it takes.

Tania turns on the light in the kitchen. She crosses to the patio and slides the door back, humming "Figaro, Figaro . . ." a fragment the performer had sung passionately over the chatter of doctors and hospital administrators swirling wine in long-stemmed glasses, passing the butter curls and raspberry vinaigrette.

Those hospital guys. This house. A million kilometres from the Windsor apartment where she grew up — and she ain't thinkin' physical distance.

She's living some other woman's life.

"You sound crazy when you sing out loud," says Philip, coming up behind her. He hesitates, then says with effort, "I'm going to have a look through the telescope. Care to join me?"

Before Philip said "Care to join me in matrimony?" five years ago, Tania's life was going to be a dirt-track stock car race, obstacles and pitfalls everywhere. But Philip was ten years older, had a map, and seemed to have it all worked out. So Tania hopped into his bed to make sure all the troubles of women like Ma couldn't happen to her.

Ma, worn out, buying Lotto tickets, spending all her money at Casino Windsor. She could sell anything at craft fairs, and did — doll houses, spoon rings, china, wind chimes, ice cream, temporary tattoos, candy apples, tarot readings, hot dogs, feathered harlequin masks. She'd tried selling books for a while, but back then you had to know what was in the books to sell them, so books were about the only things Ma couldn't sell.

Tania could sell anything too; all it took was a pucker of her lips, a sidelong smirk at the camera, the angle of her pelvis tight against silky fabric. "Tania never has to raise her voice," Ma used to say. A flurry of camera shutters got her out of Windsor and into auto shows in Detroit. She exhibited long expanses of leg as the stages revolved and the cars offered their glossy flanks to men — mostly men — below. For a while Tania thought the crowds were admiring her as much as the cars.

Dr. Philip Trent was in the crowd one day when Tania was posing beside a sleek banana-yellow too-eco-friendly-to-ever-be-profitable model. Other men stood and gazed at the Lexuses, BMWs and Mercedes, and Tania scented a hunger already wistful, whipped and cowed. But there behind Philip stood the gargantuan maw of his hunger. Eighteen-year-old Tania understood in a flash that no adman would ever have to prod it; Philip would be a glad slave to it daily.

So she walked down the ramp in her zircon-studded red shoes, doing her best imitation of Madonna. "I'd like a ride home — would you mind driving?"

And the next week, when Philip called to say he was organizing a bachelor party for a friend in Windsor, she suggested he stop by to see her perform at Jason's Gentleman's Club. The guy she went with till he got picked up for ferrying drugs across the Ambassador Bridge had talked her into dancing there part-time — said it turned him on, watching the guys watch her. From the age of twelve, from the time of her first boyfriend, Tania's "fortay" was whatever her steady-du-jour wanted it to be. All she needed to know then was, What did Philip really want her to be?

Come to think of it, they hadn't done much talking.

And she's come a long way from Windsor — even gave up smoking Slims after she met Dr. Philip.

. . .

"Why must we look at Jupiter?" Tania stands on the patio, scanning the sky for the shooting flash of a meteor. A path at her feet, each stone grooved and molded to its neighbour's shape, leads from the patio to the dark hollow of the empty pool at the centre of the lawn.

"It's the biggest," says Philip. "It will fill the whole lens." The telescope has been pointing at the planet ever since it came out of the box. Philip put it together on the back patio, following each step in the manual with laser concentration.

He offers her a look.

She puts her eye to the lens and moves the scope slowly. Jupiter's just a big ball of hot air. She wants to see its satellites and maybe the Leonid meteor shower the CBC said could happen late tonight.

"Why do they keep revolving round it?"

"Which?"

"The moons."

"Gravity and inertia, Tania."

"Crap. They're just stuck in their orbits and can't figure out how to get someplace else in the universe."

"Don't say crap, Tania. It's still too cloudy."

"You've missed the news," she says as he goes indoors. But he strides upstairs, leaving her standing in the kitchen. In a few minutes, she hears the rush of a modem in his office, calling to another of its kind.

Philip reminded her a few weeks ago, as he did every time they drove past the university, that he took his viva voce there, in that building. With a whole bunch of guys like him.

"That one?" she pointed, pretending to have forgotten.

"No, that one. The newer one."

"The one with the old facade, I see it now," she said, quoting Philip because she knew he liked being quoted. Philip voted regularly "to ensure that interiors could be rearranged or redesigned, but the facades must be retained." He didn't notice the village growing ever quainter and cuter than its inhabitants, commuters to Mississauga and Toronto. Thirty-to-forty-something range, like him.

"You keep saying you'll get back to school some day," he chided, turning homewards.

She had told him she was on the verge of college but never said she'd have to get her Ontario Secondary School Certificate first.

"I should do what I know best," she said brightly as they sailed down the main street of the village in the Merc. "Look, there's that nice little restaurant that just opened. Maybe I could wait tables."

Philip's expression said over his or her very dead body.

"I'd need a car for school," she said. "And if I got a job. Any job. Unless you want me to get a job at Mississauga General and go to work with you."

"We can't afford two cars," he said. "And I wouldn't want you getting in an accident." She would have thought that remark was real sweet only a couple of years earlier, but since she can't go as far as a neighbour or the village without a car, it's not real sweet any more. Maybe he doesn't want her working at the hospital.

If he weren't so opposed to her driving, she might have proposed getting an office job, but her typing isn't good enough, and every job advertised had a computer that came with it.

She tried a different angle. "I could get a few shoots — might feel good to be in front of a camera again —"

Philip cut her off. "Ta-ni-aa." Turning her name into three syllables, each of them upbraiding.

Oh-oh, maybe she shouldn't have said "feel."

"Besides," he went on, "I've signed you up for a course."

"Hel-lo? Did you ask me?"

"Etiquette lessons. Two hours on Friday nights."

Surprise turned to wariness. Once Philip encouraged her to sign up for the Junior Women's League but then found so many things for her to clean at the last minute that she'd ended up missing the monthly meetings. Another time he suggested she volunteer as an organizer with the local book festival, but he could never get home in time for her to take the car to meetings.

"Etiquette lessons? Where does anyone get etiquette lessons?"

"At the university. A four-week extension course. Fifty dollars, that's all. You'll enjoy it."

"The hell I will."

He winced, and the back of her hand went to her lips. She knew he thought mentioning the price would make her attend — spare change to a guy raised in Toronto, fifty dollars not to be wasted, to Tania, lately of Windsor.

So last Friday night, Philip gave Tania the keys to his Merc. She drove off alone.

Instead of two hours at etiquette class, she drove the country roads, feeling only a gentle vibration as she sped along alone in her bubble. Five top-shelf finely calibrated stereo speakers exhaled some classical thing on CBC Two — a violin? a viola? Some piece she might have known the name of if she'd finished school. Lullaby-nice.

Someone should have given her directions — she wasn't sure who or whom. Someone should have said, This is what you can expect from the country-club set when you didn't graduate from private school and have difficulty with three-syllable words, when you've been making love to a pole, panting, arching your back like a cat in heat. Which is what the other doctors' wives were thinking, even if they never said it. Someone should have warned her, but you couldn't explain this to anyone without sounding like some poor dumb little whining rich girl, and who the hell'd believe it? Half the girls at Jason's would give their first-born — what's a D. and C. but a once-a-year routine for most of them anyway — to be in her low-heeled two-hundred-and-fifty-dollar Ferragamo pumps cruising the back roads of Ontario in her husband's Mercedes that very minute.

She drove and drove, timing her return to coincide with *The National*. She had her commentary about class all ready to spill, but luckily she didn't have to.

As the car keys clinked to the hall table, Philip was standing at the kitchen door holding the phone at arms length; he whispered theatrically, "Your mother." Then Ma's smoke-thickened Michigan drawl gave Tania the latest instalment of her car troubles, this week's list of bum checks, details of the newest telephone rip-off she hadn't fallen for and the multi-level marketing scam for which she had . . .

Half an hour later Ma asked, "How're ya then, Tania?" And as Tania searched for an answer that wouldn't make her sound like a platinum blond debutante, she signed off with, "That's real nice, dear. Gotta go."

Philip never asked her about the class. Then, or since. Maybe she should attend a couple of them — learn to say "that's wonderful" instead of "crap." And smile while saying it.

Standing near the screen door, Tania's thoughts spin with the laundry. She slides the door back, goes out on the patio. The fragrance of white alyssum rises around her. The Leonids must be falling out of the sky all around, unseen.

Something different could have happened tonight. Should have happened. Still could happen. But what?

There'll be a sign. Maybe a pattern will reveal itself.

Even to Philip, checking e-mail on his laptop upstairs and pretending he isn't pissed.

Let him simmer down.

Would Tania know if she sees a sign? Or a pattern? And how will she know what it means? She'd stopped asking Ma to do tarot readings for her sometime in her teens when Ma said you'd have to do tarot readings every minute to read all the signs and find all the patterns to really know what's coming.

It's when you think you know what's coming that you really don't. Dr. Philip Trent isn't the same guy she met six years ago. Today his needle and the drip sends patients into guilt-free darkness, then conjures them back to consciousness. But back then, he was Party Animal Extraordinaire, when not working toward a seat in what he then called the Canadian Anesthesiologists' Cartel — he'd call it something polite, like "Society," now he's part of it.

Anyway, the week after that car show, when he came to Jason's, there was Tania dressed in scarlet leather, the way he and all his "gentlemen" buddies wanted her to be. A few months later, he bought this house without her ever seeing it, sure she'd be so excited. And she was. She'd moved in and become Mrs. Philip Trent.

The perm went first, the hair dye changed from blond to auburn. Tania packed all her spike heels and the red leather corsets, the black leather shorts, the little-girl ruffles, the feather boas in a suitcase and drove them down to Windsor to Ma's low-rent apartment complex.

"Find someplace — here, put 'em in the tub," said Ma. "Those cost ya somethin' —"

"Never know if I'll be needing them again, eh?"

"I'll have a rummage sale one of these days."

"You are *not* to sell my things," Tania told her. "That would be really mean, like when you sold my dolls and my comic books. I'm leaving these things with you because I have no place else to put them, okay?"

But Ma held a rummage sale the very next weekend in a ramshackle shed that abutted the complex's parking lot. "Eighty-five bucks." Satisfaction gilded the smoked voice as Tania's how-could-you's blistered the phone line.

"Eighty-five dollars for all those beautiful shoes, for the boas, my g-strings, my black leather lace-up stays, everything? I could have given you eighty-five dollars . . ."

"Never took nothin' from no one, not even when your dad didn't pay his support."

But eighty-five dollars — that's all the props of her life in Windsor had been worth to Ma, hell, to anyone.

"You're on your own, kid." Ma's affection came in heavy doses of unvarnished reality. "Over eighteen — not my problem no more."

She was right, technically, except Tania hadn't felt ready to be eighteen yet. And she wasn't ready to be Mrs. Philip Trent. Didn't know what she was getting into.

Tania draws the door closed, shivering a little. She lifts the lid of the washer, digs inside and transfers the damp white mass of clean sheets to the dryer. Philip is just tired from working in surgery all day, and she's gotta try and understand. What does she know about zapping someone into "stasis," as he calls it, then bringing him right back?

At the dinner this evening, one of the doctors teased Philip about a patient who woke up in surgery and screamed at the sight of his exposed heart. Philip went pink. "It does happen sometimes. I did the best I could."

He went from pink to scarlet when she told that asshole to go fuck himself instead of picking on Philip. And maybe she should have said it with a smile like some other wives would have.

But she was thinking of the one time, the only time Philip told her how he felt. The time he talked about his dad dying. A five-year battle with bone cancer, from when Philip was ten. And Philip wasn't Dr. Philip then, so he couldn't do anything about his father's pain. He's had so much college since, he can't even say, I felt like shit, but he must've.

"Did you pray?" Tania had asked. Philip laughed, the way he laughed at Ma for lighting candles in church and praying to the BVM.

Why isn't Philip more curious about mystery? He once said he doesn't have a clue how any of his drugs — succinylcholine, sodium pentothol — work. He just knows they do. Like the guy who did that hypnotist act at Jason's for a while. All Philip needs to know is how to switch a mind off, switch it on.

He'd love to do the same with his wife. Probably wished he could switch her off tonight.

She spoons coffee into the well of the Braun and, as the steady brown stream begins, tiptoes downstairs to the basement for a pair of socks, a sweatshirt and sweat pants from the sports closet. She drops her evening gown to the kitchen floor. She listens for movement upstairs.

All quiet up there. She changes.

She wraps herself in her coat and a heavy blanket from the hall closet, unfolds a canvas deck chair on the patio and settles in, coffee cup warming cold fingers, to watch the night sky.

If she could, she'd switch her mind on and off herself. Go into what Philip calls the twilight space between sleep and brain death. Philip's probably asleep right now or she'd ask him: when you induce anesthesia, how do you make damn sure your patient's heart and lungs keep pulsing? And the rest of her organs, the involuntary ones? What about a patient's mind?

Would it keep chattering?

Tania's would chatter a whole pile of crap — even after etiquette lessons.

A year ago, Philip took her to a Queen Street office with cherry wood panelling and funeral parlour-style paintings to see a therapist he knew from his undergraduate days at Western. This was right after Tania had a screaming fit, shouting that he was killing her. That everything she thought was fun was either a no-no or too risky.

The therapist, a tall guy with glasses and an elbow-patched sweater that made him look older, began by asking where they met. From the way he said it, gazing at Tania's cleavage, she could tell he remembered her from the bachelor party.

"Talk about your expectations of marriage," he said, but Philip acted as if he didn't have any. All he wanted, he said, was to keep Tania safe, and he couldn't understand why she was so upset — he forbade her nothing.

"Nothing forbidden, eh?" said the therapist.

Tania sat mostly silent, the desk between her and the men. Like they were expecting to hear knocking and see the paintings tremble.

The therapist asked, "Do you plan to have children?"

Tania shook her head. She couldn't imagine looking after a child or children. Ma had taken her to the doctor for her first birth control prescription at fourteen, right when she got her first period — insurance in their neighbourhood — and taking it had become a ritual ever since.

But then she glanced over at Philip and thought, hey, if Philip wanted a baby, why not? She'd oblige. Taking kids to school or hockey games would require a second car.

"No," said Philip. "Before the epidural, it's like a limb amputation without anesthesia."

Tania could see the doctor thought she should feel touched by Philip's concern, but she wasn't. "Your ma must have gone through it," she said, "or you wouldn't be here."

Philip's ma wouldn't have done it natural — she's like Philip, and not just about pain. She won't even take a vacation to Jamaica or Cuba with her friends for fear she might see poor people, and certainly she'd never visited Tania's area of Windsor. She'd think it dirty, ugly, poor, run-down — no beautiful Toronto people.

Soon their fifty paid minutes were up.

As the therapist ushered them out, she felt two thick fingers inserting themselves into the back pocket of her jeans.

"How do you feel now?" Philip asked as they got in the car. Like the question hurt to ask.

"I feel nothing."

He nodded and patted her hand.

She drew a hundred-dollar bill wrapped around the therapist's business card out of her pocket and held it on her lap where he could see the card. And the money.

Philip glanced down at the card and the money on Tania's lap. Then his eyes returned to the road.

"No pain anywhere?"

Did Philip think his friend's obvious admiration of his wife — or his wife's boobs — was a compliment to his good taste? Did he think it was a joke? On whom?

Philip seemed to imagine that he had accomplished a gallant rescue in whisking her away from dancing at Jason's. And what did he expect in return? Her gradual retreat to his castle and the guarantee she would perform only for him and a select few.

Like in Saudi Arabia.

No big deal — Philip was like her old boyfriend, the one who'd gotten her into dancing at Jason's in the first place. Or maybe like one of those professors who'd stand and watch her dancing with that look that said, I'm only here for research.

She wouldn't have to go as far as before, but was it much different?

"No pain," she said firmly, staring ahead.

"I can't be responsible for making you happy, Tania." Philip set the cruise control. "You should really try to find happiness for yourself."

But damn right, Philip was responsible for making her happy. Every girl at Jason's dreamed of a guy like him, a Dr. Prince Charming who'd take her away, marry her, make her rich and happy . . . and then if she wasn't happy, he was, yeah, like, *responsible.*

Even so, by the time they got home, she got to thinking, okay, maybe he was right, and she would try and find happiness for herself, because Philip sure as hell wasn't going to do it for her.

They didn't go back to the therapist — not that she minded, but maybe Philip did mind about the card and the hundred-dollar bill.

And then Philip took over the shopping, which only made things worse. And it was impossible to complain that things were getting worse, even if there were someone to complain to, when he would call every afternoon at four to get her grocery list before leaving the hospital and end with his canned, "I love you."

Sometimes he picked up cat or dog food instead of her two daily Slimfast shakes, but usually he bought everything on her list. Tania no longer had any idea what things cost or what was available, and Philip never seemed to notice that she cooked the same seven dinners over and over.

Daily, she cleaned with the determination of a fifties housewife, took long walks and runs on the deserted country roads, came back and made dinner.

But when she told him she was jogging, Philip warned her about black bears. After that, Tania no longer jogged out of sight of the house.

Once he took her to a street festival in Toronto. And stayed with her every minute, pincer-grip on her elbow, steering firmly. And sometimes, like tonight, he took her to official dinners where he needed a wife beside him. Usually she stayed quiet and didn't screw up.

Tania's bottom is frozen to the lawn chair, despite her coat and blanket and the unseasonably mild night. Damp seeps into her shivering, still-waiting form. A semi-crushed Slims she had stashed in the kitchen drawer for emergencies dangles from her fingers. When she finishes, she stubs it out in the flowerbed, pulls on a pair of black gloves, and resumes her wait.

It's two-thirty when the Leonids arrive, sparking over the empty pool, lacerating the basalt bowl of the cold night sky, too swift for a telescope. Tania smells burning, but no, that can't be. She listens for an electrical crackling or the hiss of a storm, but there is no sound. She debates if she should wake Philip — a couple of years ago, she might have tried, invited him to watch this display of natural fireworks with her.

Never mind Philip.

There should be celestial music, music — a tiny laugh puffs from her nose — that Philip could dismiss as New Agey. Meteors have edged out the stars now, and still they fall. Her soul thrills. Waves of faint, fast-moving points, the meteors rise as if from a common origin, set the sky ablaze. Light streaks arc as they fall.

Their smoke trains linger through the cold night. The Leonids come from so far beyond, beyond anything she has ever seen, anything she has ever felt, sparking, falling, fizzing . . . what would it feel like to be one of them? Flying up — oh joy, joy — higher, higher, high as she can go. At the top top top of the curve she knows the terror-fall of the meteor, feels herself begin to fall fall fall toward the dark yawn of the pool, flying with one small fragment that has hurtled out of its assigned orbit, streaming particles of itself everywhere, screaming through the heavens with the ferocious pain, the burn and shock of entry as it comes down. Then another one, up up up . . .

Tania stands on tiptoe, now laughing out loud. Every sense is awake, every nerve afire, every synapse smoking. She holds up her hands as if to catch one as it showers its trail of stardust over the planet.

When the last of the smoke trains fades, Tania is trembling. She hasn't felt such joy in five years, in this someone-else's life.

Every moment, every moment should be lived like that. With that passion. Yeah! With intensity. Yeah! And awareness. Yeah! Like that! Live like you're on the path of a fireball.

Tania pulls her gloves off. She swings the telescope toward her and adjusts it to focus on the pool. The Movado cuffing her left wrist glows to equal the gold bracelet cuffing her right — each came in a Birks blue box, one for their third, the other for their fifth anniversary.

Happiness doesn't always come in a blue box.

If, impossibly, a fireball did crash in that dark pit, it would be lost till morning. CBC said that if you came upon a fragment, you'd miss it completely, think it an ordinary rock. That in the light of day, there would be nothing beautiful about a single Leonid particle.

Even meteors leave parts of themselves in places they don't want to be, run into pits they can't get out of. Even meteors can't go home the way they came. And look spent and ordinary in the morning.

But oh the beauty, the beauty along the way.

It's a sign. For her, for Ma, for Philip, even Philip's mom — the rise and fall of the meteors is a sign.

I gotta have pain. I gotta have fear, danger, terror, ugliness and ordinariness along with beauty and comfort and joy. Nothing beautiful and no joy happens without pain.

Mrs. Philip Trent has been standing very still on the patio for hours. She's wearing black gloves again. The coat she wears is open. The blanket is draped around her.

Tania wants to tell her if she does not go now, this minute, on the heels of this night, she will never leave.

If Mrs. Philip Trent stays now, she will never again feel a meteoric exhilaration nor the terror of despair. She will stay in this house, bounded by fear, till she feels nothing deeper than a gentle melancholy to be alleviated by Prozac.

Mrs. Trent will then progress to the age when living is a chore. The worst that will ever happen to her might be a washer breakdown. Perhaps sickness, later the irritable regrets of a well-medicated old age.

But Mrs. Philip Trent seems to have something left to do here. She is dropping her blanket on the patio and going into the kitchen. She is peeling off her black gloves. She is taking a very sharp knife from the drawer by the sink. Is that Mrs. Trent who is holding her arm out before her, Mrs. Trent opening the patio door? A dripping arm leads Mrs. Trent down the stone path, down the steps into the empty pool.

Perhaps Dr. Philip will find Mrs. Trent in a few hours, wake her with a princely kiss, bring her out of stasis, like a patient etherized upon his table.

Or perhaps he won't know how to switch her on again.

Tania zips her coat, closes and locks the patio door and returns to the kitchen. She stops briefly in the hall to lace on a pair of running shoes and pick up the keys and her handbag. Off come the gleaming Movado and the Birks bracelet. In a few minutes she's behind the wheel of Philip's Merc, swinging out of the driveway and away.

She hums out loud, Tracy Chapman, not opera. And so what if she sounds crazy — who cares! Just imagine Philip's face when he finds his car gone.

Red and pink streaks appear like burst vessels across corneal blue. The illumination from her headlights merges with the dawn.

This Raghead

Larry Reilly slides open his balcony door and takes a seat overlooking the lawn. Only a week since he unpacked his boxes in number 101. He doesn't miss the rake or shovel he left behind. The music teacher who bought his ranch home must have inherited money — Larry would never have paid as much. He's not going to miss climbing ladders to clean leaves from clogged rain gutters, descending basement stairs with the laundry or having to fix the furnace. At the yard sale, his grandpa's crank telephone brought in more than the computer his grandson Ronan gave him. And now Larry is content in his newly minted two-bedroom condo. His Social Security is automatically deposited every month, along with the company pension that has kept on trucking for eighteen years, since he was sixty.

Gertrude no longer disturbs him with her snoring — he has his own room and a new bed. It took a while, but Larry has brought Trudy the joy of a dishwasher at seventy-six, and a kitchen so open she can watch the TV in the living room as she cooks. And if she's not feeling up to cooking, he can escort her down to the dining room.

Larry never misses Mass each Sunday with Trudy. Unlike the kike in number 109 down the carpeted hall, or the Lutheran kraut in number 111. He's pretty darn sure Trudy is going to heaven and he wouldn't want to get left behind — no one else would know all the little stuff he needs. Besides, the night the kamikaze hit his ship in the Pacific, the force that propped him and his mates up in life preservers till rescuers found them had something of the supernatural about it.

A young black man in a jacket with gold lettering waves as he rides a lawnmower across the front lawn.

There was a time when a strong coloured buck like that wouldn't have it so cushy, wouldn't be doing much more than washing dishes.

Larry, he tells himself, *you live in the best country in the world.*

Larry goes exploring. The hobby room is on the third floor. Needlepoint and knitting at one end, workbench with tools at the other. A slender young woman in spike heels comes out of a small office. He would have preferred someone with her neat classic looks for his son instead of the dumpy bo-he-me-an that boy married. The woman says her name is Ann. He tells her his. She is the Activities Coordinator and can teach him to use "the net."

"What do I need a net for?" Larry says. "Ain't goin' fishing."

She waits till he's stopped laughing.

"Most people want to check the obituaries," she says, as if promising a child a treat.

He sits down in the chair beside hers, facing the monitor. He notices her bare ring finger. Up close, her skin is like Trudy's when Trudy was between thirty and forty. This woman should be married. He wishes he had a younger son to whom he could introduce her.

"Your perfume — what's it's name?" He's always had a sensitive nose.

"Celine Dion."

"Frog perfume," he says. "Knew it."

"She's French-Canadian."

"Same difference."

"You want to learn?" she says.

He may as well find some old friends. "Make sure my name isn't listed," he tells Ann. She pecks at the keyboard.

"You can go right by the ones with that Star of David beside them," Larry says. "Don't have any Jew friends."

Larry's own obit will be like his older brother Eddie's, with the Stars and Stripes beside his name. After that he won't have to see the flag burned or trampled by un-American peace "warriors" moaning about unilateralism and flying the UN flag higher than the flag of their own country.

When he leaves, Ann shakes Larry's hand and tells him her last name as if he were deaf, which, despite his other ailments, he is not. "Bernstein."

Jews can be so over-sensitive.

A few days later, the woman across the way in number 102 is talking so loud Larry comes out into the hall in his skivvies. She doesn't want the young administrative assistant sticking up an eight-by-ten photo of young Bush on the wall near her door.

"Put it up with the Halloween decorations," says the woman.

The boy bites the inside of his cheek. Like Eddie when he didn't know what he was supposed to do.

"Let *me* have that," Larry says. "I'll put it up in our living room."

The boy shrugs, hands it over and slouches away.

Larry stands with his belly hanging slightly over the waistband of his shorts, wishing the hall felt warmer. He points to his scar and tells the woman from 102 how he got his Purple Heart from taking a bullet after the kamikaze, during the strafing. He was fighting the Good War, sacrificing time he could have spent drinking beer and kissing Trudy. Eddie was killed in action off the coast of North Africa, he tells her. "We get behind our President in a time of war. The government always knows something we don't."

"You line up right behind Bush along with the other sixty-two percent, sheep all of you," she says. "You approve of him, just like the Germans got behind Hitler. And look what happened to them — they followed that madman right over the edge. I didn't vote for your smiley warmonger, nor did the majority in this country."

"So Al Gore would have done a better job of dealing with terrorists?"

"It's Bush who's the terrorist," she says, and slams the door.

Larry takes the Bush photo in and tells Trudy all about it. He gives it to her, but Trudy doesn't put it up in his living room or outside his door. Not that day, nor the next. And she smiles at the peacenik next time she passes her, smiles with Larry right beside her as he escorts her to the dining room. That smile is good for an hour of bickering like he and Trudy haven't had in years.

Larry thinks "terrorist" again when he visits Dr. Bakhtiar, the raghead at the adjoining medical clinic, who has checked his pacemaker every month since he and Trudy got on the waiting list for their condo. He can't not think "terrorist" — he's been watching enough Fox and CNN to hear it every three minutes. He gives his

Medicare and Medigap cards to the terrorist's secretary, the girl who calls herself a medical assistant.

"Just don't send the bill to me," he says, and laughs.

She doesn't look up.

Nothing's free. Larry would like to tell Dr. Bakhtiar that freedom isn't free, either. It took young men like Eddie — strafed by the Luftwaffe — and him with his Purple Heart to hand it to the likes of the raghead. On a platter.

He takes one of the straight-backed chairs in the waiting room and grabs a *Newsweek*. The cover photo shows a GI standing someplace in Iraq, whining, "What's Plan B?" That man probably can't imagine things Larry can, like being captured by Germans and digging trenches or being tortured in a POW camp in Japan.

Dr. Bakhtiar's pension's going to be bigger than his own, and Larry doesn't like that one little bit. He bets the raghead got a scholarship someone like Ronan could have gotten, if Ronan had ever wanted to go to college. Larry is glad there won't be much left in Social Security for the raghead's retirement — except that means there won't be much left for Ronan either.

Goddamn immigrants nowadays, they have it easy.

Larry's pacemaker kicks in. He's remembering how his grandpa bought a hundred and sixty acres from the land office for ten dollars after he passed through Ellis Island, how he paid two dollars to the land agent, cleared the land, built a home and farmed five years to keep it. Larry still has the land patent that transferred the title for six dollars, signed by Abraham Lincoln.

Doctors didn't send their bills to Medicare in his grandpa's day, either. You got sick and you paid. Often you — or the doctor, if he was a soft touch — went bankrupt. Medicare is progress, even if the pharmacist gets Larry his Coumadin pills from Canada.

Sitting alone in Dr. Bakhtiar's examination room, Larry's

almost bicepless arms dangle from a blue cotton smock tied behind his neck.

Maybe the raghead kills Americans slowly, turning up the heartbeat, turning up the pace, till millions of hearts drop dead from exhaustion.

His son's going to drop dead from exhaustion — moving so fast he doesn't have time to get his computer to remind him to call Trudy.

Dr. Bakhtiar comes in at last.

The raghead doesn't apologize for keeping Larry waiting. Brown hands flip through Larry's chart. Dr. Bakhtiar's black brush moustache bobs as he purses his lips.

Larry has never noticed Dr. Bakhtiar's touch the other times he's been examined, but today the doctor's hands feel as soothing as Trudy's on his chest.

Larry pulls away: *the raghead could be gay.*

Dr. Bakhtiar says the cholesterol that has hardened the walls of Larry's coronary arteries is thickening, "like an octopus squeezing your heart. Be more careful — eat margarine, take walks."

Larry says, "I haven't eaten margarine since the war."

"Which one?" the raghead says.

Larry realizes he's serious.

"World War II. You've heard of it?"

"Ah well, we've had so many since then."

"Skirmishes," says Larry. There's the ship he so often sees in his mind, Eddie at the rail, with that Rhett Butler moustache he was growing back then. Eddie standing on a deck by the lifeboats, waving his cap. That moment before the explosion and the smoke.

Dr. Bakhtiar says nothing.

He has nothing to say.

. . .

A week later, Ronan comes to visit. Twenty years old, in his McDonald's cap, the logo shirt stretched tight across his muscles. The Elvis grin he had at three. He tells Larry his heart is telling him to marry his girlfriend.

Twenty years old and just dying to hand over his freedom to a wife and babies.

"What's her name?" Larry asks, stalling. This is what Ronan, his grandson Ronan, wants to do with his freedom — the freedom that cost him a bullet, cost him a brother who could have shown him how to grow this old?

It gets worse: the girlfriend's name is Maria. "You're going to marry a Mexican?"

"She's Catholic," says Ronan.

"So's the Pope," says Larry, "but we don't have a lot of wops in our family. Older than you, I bet?"

"No, she's eighteen."

"I was eighteen when we got married," says Trudy. Larry yearns for the old closed kitchen. "And you were twenty," she finishes.

The boy isn't asking Larry's permission. He's telling him.

Ronan puts his arms around Larry. "Bye, Granddad."

All the times Ronan put his arms around him before. All the times he carried Ronan when that boy got tired.

When Ronan is gone, Larry goes up to the hobby room.

He has learned to Google. He can't find a law against them getting married.

There has to be one. There ought to be one.

When he returns to the apartment, Trudy says she thinks Ronan and Maria have already been sleeping together.

"That's her problem," says Larry.

"Oh, it'll be his too," Trudy says. "A paternity test is all it takes."

He could swear Trudy is feeling better than he is, but she doesn't feel up to cooking much. She wants to go downstairs to the dining room every time there's music, which is almost every night. But the residents' talk kills his appetite — their organs have lives and histories of their own.

"It costs us six ninety-nine apiece," Larry says. "I can't afford it every night."

"Remember when we'd jitterbug till three in the morning? You held me up on the floor." says Trudy. "It's not like you have to learn tap-dancing. Just live a little."

That's what Eddie used to say. Maybe she's still Eddie's girl.

After lunch the next day, Trudy is taking a nap. Larry cannot stand one more nap. He doesn't want to be babysat by television. He doesn't want to play Bingo in the lounge. He's read *Prevention* and all his *Reader's Digest* magazines. It's raining and he can't go for a walk like the raghead advised.

Back to the hobby room, to the white screen, the little box at its centre. He sits down in the plastic chair in front of it.

Trudy, Eddie. Eddie, Trudy. All Eddie had to do was last a few more hours in the water and rescuers would have picked him up. And he would have come home.

Trudy might have married him, even if he had been wounded. Then she might have lived a little. Jesus.

Larry takes his glasses from his pocket and polishes them against the ribbing of his shirt.

When the kamikaze hit Larry's ship, Eddie kept him going all night, yes he did. Larry was damn well going to tread water in the Pacific longer than Eddie had in the Mediterranean. He wouldn't let his mother get another telegram saying her son was missing in action. And after a whole year, another telegram informing her he was killed in action. He didn't know if Trudy had mourned for Eddie — she was only seventeen, after all — but he swore he wouldn't let her mourn a second time. And he swore he'd propose to her if he ever made it out of the water.

Ten thousand dollars insurance and compensation of five thousand — that's what Eddie was worth to his parents, said the government. But what happened to those lifeboats? How long was he in the water — longer than Larry? Why wasn't he rescued, as Larry was? How come no one ever contacted Larry through the Legion or Navy in almost sixty years to say, Hey buddy, you know that ship, the *Paul Hamilton*. I was on it, and I survived. I remember your brother . . .

Someone must know. Someone must remember Eddie.

Larry types "Edward Reilly" in the little white box. A fine name, but there are Reillys aplenty out of Ireland; he adds the ship's name and hits Google Search.

As he blinks, Eddie's name comes right up in front of him. *Personnel Lost at Sea*.

Larry clicks left, clicks right, hitting anything underlined, ignoring that his pacemaker has kicked in.

Here's something. He leans forward and reads. *April 20, 1944: The SS Paul Hamilton was torpedoed by a Junker JU-88 off the coast of Algiers. It carried high explosives and bombs along with five hundred and four men.*

What stupidity.

No wonder Eddie's body and those of his mates were "nonrecoverable."

Scrolling and clicking further, Larry learns that a British steamship loaded with explosives and cotton bales exploded in Bombay docks, sank eighteen merchant ships and injured over a thousand in April 1944. That a Japanese Navy destroyer was torpedoed by a

US submarine and one hundred and thirty-six died, also in April, 1944. But these do not cause his tears.

Eddie.

He prints what he can, turns off the light and heads back to his apartment. He stops opposite the peacenik's door. In that second, he remembers what he said: "The government always knows something we don't."

A singer, bass player and guitarist play on a stage in the corner of the dining room. Larry watches Trudy's foot beating time to the music. She's one elegant lady in her light pink jacket dress and pearls. And even if she was Eddie's girl once, Larry's the one she married. He's hidden the printouts under his mattress, because he wouldn't know how to comfort her if she cried.

The singer would look better in any colour but black. Most young women would look a lot better in any outfit that isn't black, but they seem to follow some Taliban dress decree.

Some of the residents in wheelchairs can't even clap between songs. On the bulletin board, Larry read the names of those who have "passed on." Two people added to the population of the dead today. Two who won't take up any more food, clothing, shelter, social security or medical care.

Time to take the raghead's advice — he'll take a walk before it gets dark. Leaving the building, Larry stays in its shadow alongside the lawn.

The flag jutting from the side of the building is parallel to the ground.

"Jesus, Mary and Joseph — doesn't that jackass know what that means? It's at half-mast."

Larry is the only man who can set that flag back to its proper forty-five-degree angle.

His building key opens the garage and the maintenance shed. He chooses a stepladder about six feet high. He lugs it back outside, places it beneath the flag and climbs up level with its two-socket bracket on the wall.

The end of the flagpole rests in the lower socket, instead of the upper. Larry grabs, twists, and yanks it out.

Larry is flat on his back on the lawn. How did he get here? The pain in his chest might have something to do with it. The coloured guy is leaning over him. "Hey! Hey! You okay, mister?"

He remembers, and right as the coloured guy is punching cell phone buttons for help, gasps out, "You — the flag . . . it . . . was . . . half-mast."

Dark hands cover Larry with a gasoline-smelling jacket that says "Security" in large gold letters. "The flag?" says the coloured guy. "Yeah — for my brother. He was blown up yesterday."

"Your . . . brother?"

"Yeah, maybe the day before, but I got the call yesterday. Wasn't doing nothing but trying to show him some respect."

A landmine, he tells Larry. Under his brother's Humvee. Blew a hole in its armour, flipped it over into a Baghdad canal. His body will be coming home next week.

Larry wants to tell the security guard about Eddie, but now wheels are rolling beneath him and obits scrolling before his eyes. He wonders if his name is listed there, but all he sees are stars.

Faces collide and combine in his mind. Grandpa cranking up the telephone, Trudy the day Eddie brought her home from the USO. Eddie with his Rhett Butler moustache, waving from the SS *Paul Hamilton*, the moment before the explosion. And there's the guy who called him a mick fifty-seven years ago.

When he opens his eyes again, everyone has gathered around

him. Trudy, the coloured security guard, the kike in number 109, the kraut in number 111, Ann Bernstein, the peacenik from number 102, his son, Ronan and some young Mexican woman who must be Maria. And Larry is, like the flag in the anthem, still there.

As he is wheeled off the ambulance, Dr. Bakhtiar comes forward. Warm brown hands buttress Larry's cold clammy hand. Right this minute, Larry needs this raghead's skills, his experience and all his compassion.

So this time, Larry doesn't pull away.

Nocturne for a Blue Day

Jon's obit mentioned Fay Anne. She hadn't been back in Madison for years. Probably hadn't heard her dad's last composition before, either. When Gino entered from the sunny back garden, stepping through the French window, she was curled up on the couch, reading. "Nocturne for a Blue Day" welled from the Bose speakers — the part where the melody crept like a vine along a wall.

Her book thumped to the carpet, and she started from the couch.

"It's me," said Gino, awkward and guilty as a burglar, though he'd come through that window hundreds of times. "Jon always left this window unlatched for friends."

He switched his tuning case to his left hand, held out his right.

She relaxed and slipped her feet into wedge sandals.

Jon would have called any woman wearing shoes like that a lesbian.

She came up, shook hands. A small hand, unlike Jon's.

"Thought I'd stop in about the piano." Gino gestured at the white shape of the Schimmel concert grand dwarfing the couch. All week since Jon died, he had to keep doing everything he'd always done for Jon, along with anything Jon might have forgotten or that needed to be done. And concert after concert, on tour or at home, Gino's job was to keep each string in Jon's piano vibrating in harmony.

"Gino. Sure, come in." Fay used the remote to turn the volume down, but he didn't need sound to hear the music, its seeming calm, its underside of pain. Maybe it would replace the auditory hallucination induced by the current hit on his car radio, "My Heart Will Go On."

Fay was taking in Gino's silver — okay, grey — hair, the suspenders holding up his black jeans, probably thinking he could have used suspenders for his saggy face.

She had a genuine tan — the only tans in Madison before spring break would be the tanning-bed kind. One shoulder beneath the beige knit turtleneck and cashmere sweater was set higher than the other, one hip beneath her cotton skirt seemed set too low. Rings on every finger, gold watch, tennis bracelet. Gino noticed jewellery, which, according to Camille, most men didn't.

Gino muttered the same bumbling condolences he and Camille had tried at the funeral dinner.

Even her little pot-belly fit poorly with her slender frame. Five babies, she told Camille and Gino during dinner, a boy and four girls, all from her first marriage. None of them musical, and not a one who'd trekked to Wisconsin for their grandpa's funeral.

Gino followed Fay in, picking up the smell of her perfume. And cigarettes. Had to be Fay, Jon gave them up back in the sixties.

At the funeral dinner, she had lit one and tossed the match into the leftovers on her plate. Truth was Gino didn't like to see her smoke because it made her look old. And if Fay was old . . . well, Gino'd be even older. A year up on Jon, so Gino always felt responsible for him and his family.

He put the smoking down to grief and listened for wavering notes, as he did with instruments. Somewhere in this husky-voiced, fiftyish woman was the little girl who used to call him Uncle Gino. A little girl dressed in a wine velvet tunic, frilled white socks and black patent leather shoes who warbled, "Oh Give Thanks to the Lord for He is Good," back when Jon played at weddings and funerals.

By the time coffee and wedges of sweet clay-like cheesecake showed up, Fanny — Fay Anne — had told Gino, Camille and everyone else within earshot she was now called Fay. And that she wasn't sure she'd attend the family gathering to discuss Jon's estate next week, and that she lived in some town in California with only one streetlight, where the streets were all cul-de-sacs.

Why did she have to live in California? Well, they say it's the place to be. She sure didn't like the folks there — called them health nuts.

"People are getting that way here too," said Gino. "More kids jogging by Lake Monona, sailing around Lake Mendota every day."

Fay reached for a pink packet of fake sugar and said she didn't believe the human body was made to be shaken around that way. Gino laughed as if she'd made a joke, but it got him thinking. What the heck was the human body made for, and how did hers stand having five babies and his Camille's not a one? And if guys like Jon, indestructible through endless nights of composition followed by days of practice and travel, were checking out, just how long did he and Camille have to go?

Now setting the tuning case by the piano, Gino asked if Fay was doing okay. She was doing okay. Would she be all right? She would be all right.

"That's good," he said. "Your dad and I were friends so long, I can't get used to him not being here." A friendship closer than brotherhood, Jon called it.

"Yeah, you probably knew him better than I did."

Uh-huh.

He took his tuning fork from the case and approached the Schimmel, rolled back its quilted cotton drill cover, lifted the great white wing and the keyboard lid. He bared the keys under the scarlet felt strip and sat down.

Fay clicked the mute button and "Nocturne" went silent. But it lingered in Gino's inner ear, playing itself out in the background. The piece always spoke directly to him. Heck, to any listener.

It came to Jon at night, of course, in London, after a recital English music critics dubbed "eccentric" in the next day's newspapers. Interviewed after the debut of "Nocturne," Gino said, "After the concert, we went for a walk on Hampstead Heath, and I could feel a part of Jon was absent. It was like watching God at work, patterns forming, flowing and being discarded before his eyes until the whole stood ready and all he had to do was write it down. A few clues would surface as he hummed a phrase or two — that's all."

The reporters lapped it up. And Jon was pleased. Gino didn't mention the months of scrapped notes and preparation preceding the actual creation, or that Jon had stayed awake three days and nights writing the first draft, or that it was another year before the piece was refined and ready for performance.

Gino explained Jon's music in program notes and longer notes for record sleeves, then his CD jacket copy. He gave quotes "from Jon" to magazines. He organized his upgrade from audiotapes to CDs. Even persuaded one of Jon's students to make him one of those new computer billboards where anyone in the world could learn about Jon. A web site, uh-huh. He had done the best he could for Jon; a wife could have done no better.

"Knew Moira too. Kind. Gentle. A good woman."

Fay said, "My mother's motto was peace at any price. I swore I'd never be like her."

Gino placed his tuning wrench on the strings. Every piano has nuances, a few delicate hammers, a few touchy pins or a slightly thinner section in its soundboard. No one knew this Schimmel like Gino, but it could still surprise him.

"Unlike my brother Earl, who trades on my father's name — never could understand that."

Gino reached into the tuning case, grasped a tangle of red and green felt temperament strips, selected a green one, and threaded it through C, isolating the sound of a single string.

"When I was in school, Mom kept track of the finances and my father would go out and buy extravagant presents for her. I used to go with her to Gimbel's, where she'd try returning them without a receipt. Usually she ended up juggling money to pay for them."

Gino smiled.

Peace offerings. That's what we called them.

The richer the offerings, the merrier Jon's memories. And Gino's.

"I forget what you went to school for . . ." he said. He forgets a lot of things these days. And sitting in Jon's seat was bringing back Jon's note-head figure, that large head jutting forward from an erect body. Bringing back how Jon's hands and heart moved and music leapt from the page, from two dimensions to four.

"Earl was studying business, and Dad told me I'd flunk the math if I did the same, so I took theatre. I figured drama comes naturally to our family. When my youngest followed my lead, I told her, you have ten per cent talent and ninety per cent chutzpah, whereas when I went on stage, I had ninety per cent talent and ten per cent chutzpah."

Gino struck his tuning fork and tightened till C rang pure at 523.3 cycles, then began tuning relative to the note. Jon used to say music is created for the human ear, so Gino tossed away Strobotuner and software ads promising pitch-perfect notes for each key. And he didn't tune dead-on like the modern fellas, because the maestro liked all the notes relative. Jon was no synthesizer, reading notation like a fundamentalist reading his Bible — he played to each audience differently.

Was that from talent or chutzpah? Both. Had to be both. If he had to guesstimate, he'd say fifty-fifty.

He plinked on, listening for the telltale wa-wa-wa of quarter-tones. Jon was too sick to play in the last couple of months — the spring weather must have affected the instrument.

"Anyway, I gave up the theatre," said Fay. "Got tired of ketchup sandwiches. I said, I'm outta here."

"When were you last back here?" he asked. A memory of Fay as an adult might help connect his cute little girl image to the woman before him.

"Fifteen years ago, when Mom was in the hospital," she said. "Nineteen eighty-three."

Gino had comforted and stood by Jon when Moira died, but darned if he could remember seeing Fay that year.

"Didn't stay in this house, because Dad was practising for a tour. Stayed with Earl and his wife. You know Catharine? When Mom died, she tried to make me go along with their ideas."

Jon and Earl had wanted Moira buried, and Fay had wanted her cremated.

"Why should I go along? I said. Burial is a stupid tradition. It makes no sense, takes up land. Besides, she was buried her whole life. She was a star pianist at the conservatory when they met, but Dad always treated her as if she didn't know anything about music."

"What did Catharine say?"

"Catharine said I should agree with Earl because he'd been so helpful and loyal to my parents. She meant, whereas I had followed my husband to California. Ha! Well, the Spanish Inquisition thrived in the name of being helpful and loyal, so I said, Tough. Deal with it. My sister-in-law told me it would hurt Earl's manhood and my dad's if Mom were cremated. I said, you can hurt someone's feelings or religious ideas, but *manhood*? No, it would hurt his manhood, she said. So I said Tough. Deal with that too, because, you know, I didn't want peace at any price. See, unlike Earl, I always wanted to think for myself, always said I'd keep my soul my own. But Dad and Earl wouldn't listen and buried Mom anyway. So after her funeral, I was outta here."

Jon and Gino had left Madison too, after Moira died. Jon had been complaining that audiences in the US were pale-faced and greying. Or ruined by rock, pop or whatever simple rhythm stuff it was that Michael Jackson started. He needed extravagantly subsidized concert halls and more patronage than he could beg from the National Endowment for the Arts. That tour, his most successful ever, lasted a whole ten months, and, as Gino told the press, "His grief seemed to pour through the music."

Gino tuned, repaired, packed, wheedled, booked, scheduled, rescheduled and coached, while Jon premiered his seventh symphony. Gino did everything Jon forgot to do, and, oh yes, he even called Fay from West Berlin to wish her happy birthday "from Jon."

Gino reminded her of the phone call.

"I was so angry you remembered to call and Dad didn't. Never figured out why or how my mother stood his ways all those years."

Fay was like Camille, talking non-stop when she figured no one was listening. Maybe nobody had ever listened to her, like he'd never really listened to Camille till recently.

"All my daughters have problems with men," she was saying. "One thinks she's being smothered and can't breathe every time she goes to bed with a guy. My second daughter went to a shrink and then called to tell me she was sexually molested by her stepfather — my second husband. She said to me, Where were you, Mom? And I told her, truly, I didn't know. Tried telling my dad, but he said I was making it up so I could get divorced again."

Gino played a few chords with pedal; the sound swelled to a resonant sostenuto. A new-fangled digital wouldn't have strings that could vibrate in sympathy like Jon's Schimmel.

Fay clasped her elbows and leaned on the far edge of the piano. "Maybe we all say peace at any price in some way. Just not as quietly as my mother."

Discord irritates worse when someone points it out, and dampening checks its vibration only momentarily.

She went silent, moved over to the bookshelves, then into the kitchen. The Schimmel was struggling against Gino's attempts to tune it. At least sixty, it was allotted the same lifespan as Gino — three score and ten.

Fay was back. "Did you ever meet my first husband, Art? Suave and handsome — kinda like my father, I guess, but quite a lot shorter. I knew Art had many women on the side, but he always convinced me that unfaithfulness had nothing to do with our marriage." She gave Gino a warm rueful smile. "I believed him till I went to San Francisco for a convention. I was negotiating teacher contracts, though I never trained as a lawyer — should have. I was thirty-eight and the city was decked out to celebrate the Spirit of '76."

"I went out for a few martinis with a consultant who also was married, and after maybe three or four he asked me up to his room. And what do you know, he had wine and flowers and candy. There it was, laid out for me when I arrived. And all I could think of was how much trouble he'd gone to, just to get me in the sack. We talked, and after a while he said to me, When I talk you listen, but whenever you say anything, it's about your husband or children. So I think we should just say good night."

Pin after pin turned into the maple beneath Gino's tools. Camille was that way too, never saying anything about herself. But she could talk about Gino all day, having listened for years to Gino talk about Gino.

"So nothing happened, but I did go back to my room thinking that unfaithfulness has everything to do with marriage. I should know that from watching Mom with Dad."

"The next night I was still at the hotel, and Mr. Consultant asked me out for a drink again, at the lounge on the top floor, and we both knew it was for the same reason. This time, all it took was a couple of shots and he had to take me down to my room. And he undressed me and put me to bed. When he left, he said, I don't take advantage of helpless women. And I lay there drunk, thinking oh-my-god, there are men in the world who think women are people."

Gino wanted to tell her there are many men in the world who know women are people, but he hadn't been so good at remembering the principle himself. Fay had barely stopped for breath, like if she stopped talking she might drop dead. For Jon's sake, Gino listened. Jon would have walked out by now, but no matter.

"I went back home to Art, and a couple of months later I had a hysterectomy — I'd been bleeding badly every day. Art came to the hospital and told me he was soooo depressed, and did I think it was male menopause? And all I could think was, I'm in the hospital, gushing blood, and the only thing my husband can talk about is his own male menopause. A couple of days later, I got a box of chocolates and a note: If you call me, I'll be there. My consultant friend still thought I was interesting."

The high A twanged like a saloon piano. Could the Schimmel's sound board have warped? A slight arc can put so much tension on the strings that a piano can sound too sharp. Gino gazed at the blankness of the ceiling as he listened to it and Fay at the same time.

"When I left the hospital, the doctor said, You're tight as a virgin again, and I thought, A second chance at virginity isn't a gift for just anyone, especially a jerk like Art. And now there was no fear of getting pregnant, either. So once I'd healed I called my friend from San Francisco and arranged for him to stop by our district office for some consulting. He came, and we had a nice time." She looked away with a coy expression, as if a bout of old-fashioned Midwestern discretion had trumped the uninhibited Californian act. "A *very* nice time."

"And then you got divorced?" Gino's head bowed over the instrument.

"Oh no. First I went to a shrink. I told him my husband brings work home every night and we have a compromise — work after the children are in bed. Which was of course when we might have been talking to each other. The doctor said, If he was a violinist and brought home a violin and played it all night, wouldn't you object? If he was a construction worker and brought home a jack hammer, wouldn't you object? Well, yes, I said, that might be a problem."

"And then you got divorced?"

"Oh no. The next time, I took Art with me. Doc, he said, I need Valium. She gets Valium, why can't I have any? So the doctor gave him a prescription and warned him what would happen if he mixed it with alcohol. And then we sat there for an hour, listening to Art tell us he didn't have any problems. When he left the shrink's office, he went down to the drugstore, then over to his favourite bar and mixed those pills with alcohol anyway, just because the doctor said he shouldn't. Oooh, was I pissed. It was the kind of thing my father used to do."

Gino tuned and tuned as if adjusting some misalignment between earthly music and its cosmic equivalent. Fay going on and on like this made him wonder how many times Camille must have toyed with the idea of leaving him.

Certainly in the days when Jon and he caroused all night, bar-hopping down State Street. She and Moira stuck it out even when Gino and Jon went over the state border to Chicago and didn't come home for days — as if they were radical rock musicians instead of straitlaced symphony hacks.

He was down to the red felt temperament strips, and the Schimmel was as pliable as he could make it. He played arpeggios and a few Hanon runs till Fay brought coffee. Then he put away his gear, brought the wing down, closed the lid, and took the velvet armchair beside the couch.

The coffee pot, cream and sugar stood on a gilded wood tray Gino remembered buying in Florence. A gift "from Jon" for Moira. The coffee itself was nothing schmancy, just the regular-smelling brew, the kind with which he and Jon would try to cure their hangovers.

"Why did you stay with Art?" he asked as she poured and handed him his mug.

"I worried what he'd do to himself if I left him. But eventually we couldn't pay the bills so we paid a smart you-know-what lawyer a thousand bucks to put our papers before a judge. We sat with seven hundred other luckless deadbeats in a lecture hall and got ourselves declared officially bankrupt. Afterwards, Art said, Let's find a bar. So we found one. He had two martinis, maybe three, to decompress, and I had my usual sugarless something — Tab, that's what I had. I didn't think much of it then, but that personal bankruptcy would be a monkey on our backs, stay on our record for years. But that night all I felt was the bankruptcy of my spirit."

A husband should be a good provider, Gino thought, whatever else he is. How did Art feel that night? Art wasn't around to tell his story. "Was that the last straw?"

Fay shook her head.

What is the last straw for women? How much can they take? Gino had dumped a ton of straws on his Camille — disappearing for days, coming home drunk, throwing up, demanding sex, never violent but just never thinking about her in those days. Or never thinking what he was thinking now: maybe Camille didn't leave when most women would have because she wasn't like most women.

"Oh no, Dad kept telling me Art was just young, that we were just immature, that divorce would harm the children, that I'd lose all my friends. So I didn't divorce Art till '84. By then my old friends were born agains, and they were shocked. Shocked! It's amazing how God loves you and will forgive you anything, even murder, before you become a born-again Christian, but he won't forgive a little divorce afterwards. I had to go get me some new friends, I'll tell you."

Gino gave a rinky-tink laugh. "Never was much for religion," he said. "Jon and I figured music was worship enough."

A look of surprise. "He sure played a lot of religious music. In churches and cathedrals," she said.

"You can't take God out of classical music."

"Well, no fear of anyone wanting to do that these days," she said. "Now everyone's born again, not just my old friends. Did you know you can become a born-again Christian anywhere if you just raise your right hand and say, I'm born again? One of my friends would do it every so often — in my car, on the porch, on the back forty, in a bar. Sounds like sex, doesn't it? Only not as much fun. Now even Art's joined those sanctimonious Promise Keepers — they take your membership money no matter how many promises you've already broken. He's become a family man since he lost his kids. He goes out, guys only, to a stadium every Friday and all of Saturday and then quotes Leviticus about homosexuality."

"Some men need to do things a different way."

"Now you sound like my father."

He didn't — couldn't. "No one sounds like your father." Gino took up the tongs, dropped a sugar cube in his mug and stirred. "You know the way every musician in an orchestra depends on the next? Time after time, I saw Jon mold that, saw him smooth the over- and under-confidence of the rank-and-file musicians. In his hands their very dependence became his sound. His sound was the sound of other people's unexpressed feelings, the effect of all their emotions."

"Yeah, yeah, Gino," said Fay. "But I wasn't talking about Dad's music. The sound of other people's unexpressed feelings was deafening in this house. But he sure expressed his own feelings — shouting, hollering. And how he could hurt with his sarcasm. What does it matter what his music sounded like? What's important is what he believed, how he treated Mom. And me. How he never noticed Earl wasn't the only one who had kids — I couldn't get even one of my kids to come with me for his funeral. You make excuses for Dad the way he always made excuses for Earl."

Gino focused on the swirl in his coffee. "Because he was a genius. After performing or conducting all evening, after all the bows and applause, the next day Jon would be sitting right here at that piano. And he'd hear the merest trace of melody in his head and construct another piece. Pure genius."

"Yeah, a musical genius. And I used to get walloped for interrupting him. But it's not that difficult. You just need to hear it in your head and write it down."

Gino laughed, shaking his head. "Fay, if only it were that simple! I might have done it too. But I didn't have Jon's creative energy or his persistence."

"It *is* simple. Used to compose myself, you know." An ashtray scraped the table as she drew it towards her.

"Uh-huh?" Gino tried to keep his tone indulgent. "I didn't know."

"Till I was fifteen or so. He never mentioned it? I performed for him several times. On that piano." She produced a pack of cigarettes and a lighter from a handbag beside the couch. "Oh, he never approved. Once he said he agreed with von Karajan — a woman's place is in the kitchen, not in a symphony orchestra. And that was the end of my composing."

Two equally steep and dimly lit paths seemed to open before Gino. "You know," he said, sidestepping the one that might imply criticism of Jon, "he's left you such a legacy. Whenever we listen to Jon's music or a musician plays what Jon wrote, we'll forget he's gone. And each performance will be a new interpretation. As if we're communicating with the spirit realm."

"Spirit realm." Fay laughed. She lit up and took a long drag, blew a smoke ring. "He sure communicated with the Jack Daniels realm. But you save that line for a concert program, Gino. You know what shocked the hell out of Dad? That I opposed the war in Vietnam. And then that I marched for peace, even after a fertilizer bomb carved a crater into the Army building on campus."

"Well, he was in the service. Both of us were. Anyway, the explosion was such a long time ago — 1970?"

"Right." Fay tapped ash from her cigarette with an admonishing forefinger. "And I shocked him even more with my divorces. After that, when Newt Gingrich and his goons took over Congress, I came in wearing a Civil Liberties pin and he said, Now you've really turned into a goddamn liberal. And when I told him liberals got him a National Endowment for the Arts, a musicians' union, Social Security and Medicare, he just laughed. Maybe he thought conservatives give a shit about art — I told him they just want to be seen attending concerts. A couple of years ago I sent him a book about that mean-spirited radio guy he always listened to" — she went over to the bookshelf and ran a glazed fingernail down a spine: *Rush Limbaugh Is a Big Fat Idiot* — "so I'm proud to say I disappointed him."

"Oh no — never say that. You two just didn't agree on some things."

"That's putting it mildly. I'm glad I told him he was responsible."

Gino frowned. "For what?"

"For Mom being buried long before she was dead."

Gino opened his mouth to say something about Jon to defend him yet console her. Something fatherly and preachy. But he too had laid off the booze and women only when it was too late for Camille.

Did Camille feel like Moira? Buried before she was dead?

"Fanny — I mean Fay — women didn't think of married life as being buried in those days. And they didn't think of complaining. Heck, if you're any indication, women still don't complain."

Fay held up a hand. "Gino, I've been down some very wrong roads, busted my ass for two husbands." The smoke haze grew to a thick screen. "You never know where you'll end up. I mean, you set off on a path that's all laid out for you, soon as you're born, and along comes a day when you veer off, and pretty soon you have no explanation for any of it."

Her heavy-lidded eyes were bright, defiant. "You can only think about where you changed. You could go on regretting all the roads you didn't take and never do yourself a bit of good."

She snuffed out the cigarette and sat back in the sofa. Had anything he said brought her closer to harmony with Jon — or Jon's spirit?

Only a little coffee remained; Gino put his mug back on the tray.

"I don't know if it's in writing," he said, "but we always talked about my being Jon's music executor. He was working on an authoritative edition of his music when . . ."

"And you'll complete it for him, won't you. Be Constanza to his Mozart, Romain Rolland to his Beethoven."

"Of course. It'll take a bit of judgement. Well, guesswork.

Jon tended to play his music slightly differently each time — like Chopin or Liszt, you know."

"It will take imagination. A muscle we could all exercise sometimes."

"Editing, more like."

"And what will you learn from it?"

"Me?"

"Yes. Will it tell you more about my father? Will you gain some new insight?"

"It may help future musicians play his music as Jon intended."

"Oh yes, I can see it now — debates over authenticity. How do you know what anyone intended, Gino? You can't escape our time and return to when he began performing and composing. When was that — the sixties? Will you try and recall what he intended? Even if you were there, Gino, it's impossible."

"Yes, it will be a speculative business, but it's important."

"And you think you'll find some over-arching pattern to help you understand my father?"

"No. I don't think the music is a guide to the man. But the man guided us to hear the music."

"And that was the purpose of his life?"

"Yes."

"What about his other decisions — to marry, to have children, to ignore them and his grandchildren?"

"Incidental," he said, before he could stop himself.

She turned away.

What a cruel SOB I am.

"I mean, the music doesn't reflect his actions or attitudes. Listen."

Gino set his mug on the table and rose. Though he could have done it remotely, he went to the CD player, turned up the volume and pressed repeat. "Nocturne" played again, softly.

He allowed it to course through him for a while, watching Fay, hoping for magic. "It sounds wonderful on CD. Some of Jon's early recordings should be reissued on CD."

"And you'll select which ones? You'll decide which of his works will be rearranged, which can be heard in elevators and airports?"

She crossed one leg over the other, digging her heel into the carpet.

"Well, someone has to make his work accessible. Do you want to do it?"

"You want him back, you do it, Gino. Who else would be interested — a few academics, maybe? I'm sure Earl will give his permission too, though he might strike a hard bargain on royalties."

Gino turned up the volume. "Listen. What do you hear?"

She uncrossed her legs, leaned forward, elbows on her knees, hands clasped beneath her chin, and closed her eyes as if making a superhuman effort.

"Pride . . . violence . . . anger . . . grandiosity . . . arrogance. And you?"

"All that, yes, and intelligence. Wait . . . now here's a suppleness, a breezy elegance." He closed his eyes and let the music take him into the next movement.

After a while he said, "I hear such a sinuous gentleness. Do you?"

"No."

"I wish you could."

"Well, Gino, you tell the world that's what they oughta hear." Crockery clattered into the music as Fay cleared empty mugs, the cream and sugar, the smell of ashes. "Next week, after the gathering of the clan, I'm outta here. Though I doubt anyone in my family wants to see me. I may have to call an escort service — they go anywhere with anyone, don't they? Do they go to family gatherings?"

A huge earthy laugh.

Some little girls get so warped along the way. So broken they can't be expected to sing pure as they once did. Maybe we are all like notes — some louder, some softer. With fleeting links, contrasting, each becoming the cause of another.

"I better be going." Gino took up his tuning case and made for the French window, pushed it open and stood on the stone terrace overlooking Jon's garden.

Those purple petunias — a self-branching variety called Madness — were drooping. And if he hadn't talked to Fay, Gino might have, no, he would have busied himself here with the sprinkler.

But Camille was waiting, as always. Suddenly Gino needed to be with her, hear her voice.

"I'll be back again, I promise." Fay leaned out to the terrace and placed her small hand in Gino's.

But will I be here next time you sweep in?

"And I'll make Earl send you all Dad's music — every scrap we find."

A latch clicked; the French window had locked behind him.

The Distance Between Us

Fourth of July weekend e-mail: two rejections from academic journals, requests for revisions from another, four student assignments, seven Viagra solicitations, three days' worth of newsfeeds from the *New York Times*, the *Los Angeles Times*, the CBC.

A translation of Windows commands into Punjabi. Minni and Gagan will laugh when they read that. They're asleep right now. Karan forwards it — Santa Barbara to New Delhi in seconds.

Google Alerts on the Guantánamo Bay prisoners. Sikh Coalition Bulletin: another Sikh man beaten up in New Jersey. Weekly digest from *The Onion*. And — a message from someone with an all-too-familiar last name. It's highlighted in Karan's inbox. His cursor floats over it.

Click.

Campus sounds outside his office blend into background. He rubs the back of his hand across his throat; it comes away damp.

This one didn't take seconds — it's been years in coming. Like the plate shift that sent a sixty-foot tsunami racing outwards from Indonesia to swallow a hundred and fifty thousand people. Now of all times, when suspicious looks at his turban and bearded brown face are becoming less frequent.

He pulls a deep breath into his lungs, slowly releases.

He should move the message to trash. He can't send it to trash. Two teams tug a rope that passes through his chest.

He shouldn't even think of replying. Could be entrapment: remember "special registration" that turned out to be a roundup? Twenty-four hundred men were deported. And remember the OSHA industrial safety meeting that turned out to be a Homeland Security roundup of illegal Latinos?

Sticky air hangs over his shoulders. He flicks on the table fan.

He expands the message to full screen and scrolls with tingling fingertips. He sends it to print. When it materializes, he carries it to the window. Reads it again.

> *Hi. Are you the Karanbir Singh who married Rita Ginther on Jan 7, 1980? I'm her daughter. And yours. I'm 23. Born in August 1982 after you guys split. Mom kept tabs on you from Madison to Montreal, Amsterdam, St. Louis and now Santa Barbara. All I know is that you teach economics at the university and come from India. Mom said I should look you up if anything ever happened to her. In case you care, she died three months ago. Kidney failure. Am leaving tomorrow for Los Angeles. So I googled you. Found a Wiki entry about you too. Will be spending the July Fourth weekend with my friend Ashley. Plan to visit till Friday. I could come see you the weekend after that.*

Some mistake here. He doesn't have a daughter. That marriage — a transaction, for god's sake. Just a transaction. Rita was the capitalist selling Resident Alienhood, and he was buying because he panicked — well, he *was* paying almost double as an international student, was ineligible for student loans and still had a thesis to complete and defend. All she had to do was make it last two years till his INS interview. She had loans to pay, needed the money. And it was cheaper to live together.

Consenting adults.

Oh, what had he consented to? Making love with Rita was like sinking into heavy cream — but hadn't he told her: no complications? She had assured him — the Pill, the foolproof Pill.

There was no daughter. No child, full stop.

Then how does this girl — woman — whoever she is — know his anniversary date? How come she's born in August, eight months after Rita moved out?

He twirls the shade-pull, dims the room. The screen glows. The cursor blinks. The table fan spins like karma on steroids.

It's signed Uma Ginther. Indian and German. Uma. Rita wouldn't pick Uma to complement his ancestry. Named after Uma Thurman? No. The actress would have been about nine in '82. If she is Rita's, the Hindu goddess's name reflects Rita's New Agey side. Ginther — old German name obscuring the Greeks populating Rita's mother's family.

Two years older than him — Rita'd be only forty-eight now. Who must she be now? Serve her right if she were reborn black and poor in sub-Saharan Africa — might learn a thing or two about economics. But kidney failure. She didn't deserve that.

Moments, images reappear: two hundred and forty pounds encased in acres of luminescent pale skin. Pink doughy face with owlish glasses. Rita lifting rosettes from hot oil in the narrow kitchen at the International Students' Center. His brown hand lightly touching hers as he helped her dust sugar over butterfly, pinwheel and star shapes. He remembers himself talking about crisp orange jalebis in India that would put those Norwegian rosettes to shame, telling her the name Rita is Indian — Sanskrit for cosmic order. Reciting a recipe for butter chicken he'd read in Madhur Jaffrey's cookbook. The first unrelated woman whose hand he'd ever held.

What an idiot he was, mistaking culinary for cultural curiosity! Rita could have asked how he tied his turban, maybe sent him a card on a Gurpurb or Baisakhi day, or been a little curious about his relatives. Not Rita, before the wedding or after. She couldn't picture him anywhere but here, adult and a-historical.

Her laugh — oh yes. A tremor passing across her Buddha-belly. Filled with indulgence at the beginning. "Oh, Karan-be-er!" she'd say — mispronouncing his name. And later, with exasperation, "Kar-an!" — the name that now represents him in America.

Karan returns to his desk, crosses his ankles, leans forward, lets the gel in his wrist rest cool his pulse.

Don't reply, implore his mother's eyes from her frame on his desk.

His fingers are poised between thought and word.

"Dear Ms. Ginther: I'm sorry but you must have found the wrong person. Like Ginther, Singh is a common name . . ."

No.

Tension sharpens to a knot in his back.

"Dear Uma Ginther, I'm afraid you are quite mistaken. Rita and I met at UW-Madison. We were married in 1980, divorced in 1982. She moved to Detroit. Never once did she mention a child."

But then Rita wouldn't, would she? Said she never wanted a husband for life. Even one who didn't mind a Rubenesque woman and was as irresistible as Karan used to be. He'd believed her motives were pure — pure economics. But every woman must have a baby, na? Probably stopped taking her pills.

But fathers have duties! Most women drag men into court, sue for child support, garnish wages. Not Rita. She must have done okay. First in her family to move off the farm, a degree in industrial engineering, why wouldn't she?

Don't fathers have rights too? But Rita wouldn't want to share her child; after two years of living with her, he wasn't fooled by her softness. It surrounded a hard little heart.

What he could say: "Dear Ms. Uma Ginther, I'm afraid you are quite mistaken. Rita and I had what in the old days would be termed a marriage of convenience. We divorced after the required two years. I paid her in full. She moved back to Detroit. Never once did she mention a child. There must have been another man after me."

He draws away. Such a reply cannot be written. Homeland Security or the FBI or the CIA could still be monitoring his e-mail. They'd be only too happy to deport him. And campuswatch.org denounces more than professors of Middle Eastern Studies. He should know that, even if Homeland Security hadn't "interviewed" him. And just a few weeks ago, lusting for tenure and spurred by the interview, he'd paid an attorney to apply for his change of status from resident alien to citizen. He mustn't jeopardize that application.

A brown scent insinuates itself under his door. Scorched popcorn. He closes out of his e-mail program and heads to the faculty lounge down the hall.

It's Thayne Grey, UCSB's star history prof, almost setting off the fire alarm again. An otherwise intelligent man. Never learns.

A cup of orange pekoe fortifies Karan. He returns reluctantly to the e-mail.

Why isn't he more surprised by this contact? More certain that this girl, woman, female, whoever she is, is not his offspring? But the blood spinning his heart chakra says she is, the quickening in his breathing says yes, she is.

Think of it! A daughter. Someone of his blood on this continent, a member of his family who isn't in the next country or hemisphere. Is she fat like Rita? Thin like him? Is she a natural blond, or dark-haired like him? Eyes? Dark — brown genes trump blue. She could have attached a photo. If she is his daughter, how might he explain her existence to his sisters? Gagan will look down her jewelled nose, then probe gently but relentlessly in her professional way. Minni will be voluble about the double standards he applies to his wrongdoings in contrast to hers.

He stops, rereads the e-mail.

"In case you care . . ." An implicit accusation. Indignation raises its head, offers a mute bark. Minni, Gagan, his mother — when she was alive. Always accusing him of not caring, forgetting how much he remitted each year. And this from a woman who might not even be his daughter, who doesn't even know him.

So maybe he had hurt Rita, but Rita could survive. If nothing else, he'd given her reason to tell her anti-male jokes for a few more years. And now this child born of Rita's maternal longing, like Ganesh to Parvati.

At some point, he must have stepped over the threshold that permitted him to be guilt-free about that marriage, so American is he. It made him a legal resident. Which is more than many in California can say.

American enough to go on TV and tell all about it? American enough to meet his long-lost daughter on Oprah? Not *that* American. Contrary to textbook economic models, all transactions are not equal. Suppose it were drugs — Rita would be forgiven for buying, but a brown man would never be forgiven for selling. And similarly, she'd be forgiven for selling herself in marriage, but a brown man would never be forgiven for buying himself a green card.

What to do? His brain clicks into high gear, throbs against his skull. At least the girl has given him a few days notice. Hai Rabba! — what if she'd just waltzed in, asking anyone to direct her to his office?

They say when a tsunami hits, you either disappear, survive or die. Can he disappear? As of last December, one can't even apply for asylum in Canada anymore.

What is he thinking! Walking out of his well-built life because a girl of twenty-three wants to visit?

It's taken twenty-five years of withstanding ignorance and prejudice, starting from long before it was cool to be Indian in Silicon Valley, to gain this office in North Hall with this window, this computer, these shelves groaning with books, this inbox full of scholarly papers and assignments. He isn't the next Amartya Sen, but it is possible he's changed some perspectives in the US-centric West by working within the English-speaking educational establishment.

And he has commitments here, assumed like an elephant takes on lading. Classes, committees, upcoming conferences, research papers, a new home. A mortgage. And he is beholden to money-lenders, just as he could be in India. And at the same interest rate, twenty-seven percent, from charging two weddings and associated dowries on credit cards. Expensive Delhi weddings, first for Gagan, then for Minni. Almost paid down after fifteen years, but still — commitments.

A wife might demand and deserve explanations, but uncles, aunts and cousins in Delhi gave up introducing Karan to eligible "girls" on his annual trips once his mother passed away, the tacit assumption that he would now dedicate his life to supporting them. Gagan said apologetically once that his divorce had lowered his value on the marriage market, and couldn't he have just kept quiet about it? Might be different now. Many school friends in Delhi have divorced and some have remarried.

But something in him turned away after the two-year marriage, became irretrievable. An empty space that scarcely bothers him, except when his mind collides with it and retreats. Other men may be curious about interior unknowns, but one person is too small a sample size. Ergo, he does not use himself as fodder for analysis.

In lieu of a wife, Karan has Adela, his bi-weekly housekeeper. And he has had women friends over the years, the kind who cannot resist cooking and caring for a single man and expect a professor to be absent-minded. He's slept with a few — maybe twenty-two — but he's not counting. Sex is much like healthy exercise in California. His only rule: no students. No career complications.

Outside his window lies an emerald lawn, an unwrinkled sky, students rollerblading down palm-shaded walks, each carrying a backpack. Summer flowers, leaves turning mirror faces to the sun. And out of sight, though resident in consciousness, the graceful curve of Goleta Beach, the silver glint of the infinite Pacific.

Santa Barbara, his American Riviera city.

The publication of his first un-co-authored textbook earned him the offer of a three-year contract here, and he leapt at it like a migrant farm worker at the gates of a corporate plantation. Each year he must write and publish articles with titles like "Non-Parametric Efficiency Analysis under Uncertainty" and fill them with windy prose and formulas to justify his existence to the dean.

Dean Bradnock. Seated behind a very wide desk, light flashing off reading glasses. Bradnock, who counselled Karan to call in and register with Homeland Security, "since *you're* not an illegal." Bradnock saying, "You don't have anything to worry about — right?"

Nothing to worry about but scandal. What a Victorian word.

If Bradnock senses the smallest shadow of illegality, he will "err on the side of safety" again. He'll "suggest" a leave of absence. And there'll be no guarantee he'll renew Karan's contract — or health insurance.

Perhaps this Uma girl doesn't know there was a green card deal.

She must know. Rita never let Karan forget it for a single day of that marriage.

The real question: is Uma a benign or retributive being? And if she is some vengeful churail, can she be propitiated? At what price?

Karan worries all of Tuesday, even as he draws demand and supply curves showing summer students that billion-dollar-a-day farm subsidies in developed countries enforce the poverty of millions elsewhere, even while watching Dr. Sanjay Gupta reporting on CNN, even while listening to an hour-long public radio program about successful Indo-Americans.

On Wednesday, Karan hears himself explaining to students that, by "invisible hand," Adam Smith meant to describe the outcome of buyer and seller relationships. The term, he tells them, wasn't a coded reference to some god-like hand meddling in human affairs. But he's not convincing them — or himself, really.

Worry expands in all directions till evening, when Karan loses his weekly squash game with Nadir.

On Thursday, Karan wanders into the faculty lounge where the foul smell of popcorn lingers. And there is Thayne with Dean Bradnock, paging through a pocket brag-book of photos. He waves Karan over to see: here he is marching down State Street in the Fourth of July parade last weekend, carrying the black POW-MIA flag before the Vietnam Veterans banner.

And here's a photo of Thayne's long-unknown half-Vietnamese son, now thirty-five years old. Karan gazes at the photo, taken in Ho Chi Minh City last year — the young man poses astride a scooter. The woman in long white opera gloves riding pillion is the prof's daughter-in-law. Thayne found out he has two grandchildren — see, here are their photos.

Dean Bradnock is admiring.

"If we never met," says Thayne, "I'd still be wondering what he's like, you know?"

Karan returns to his desk. What is this Uma like? Who is she like? He fires up his e-mail and hits Reply. He replies contrary to all his drafts. A reply that introduces himself and becomes an invitation.

On the climb between the university and his home, Karan's white Toyota groans beneath the weight of its rust. He'll buy a Jeep Cherokee when he's more settled. Solidly American, somewhat reminiscent of a Mahindra Jeep in Punjab, and it won't outshine the dean's Volvo.

Alongside the road, the ocean extends and recoils along the shore. Per MapQuest, the ocean is south, even though he feels as if it should be west. Or something like that — directions are not his strong suit, and he hasn't lived in this neighbourhood long enough to auto-pilot home.

Joggers. A cyclist. Each with the sun-drenched insouciance of the native Californian; they seem to know exactly where they are going.

Friday evening, now. The girl is arriving tomorrow. He turns on the radio, finds KCLU. Lakshmi Singh reports, "Bombs exploded yesterday in three subway stations and on a bus in London." Casualties . . . the death toll so far stands at thirty-four. Suicide bombers are suspected. Terrible. "Barbaric," says a politician. "The civilized world will not stand for this," says another.

Thank you Bush-Cheney-Rumsfeld, Bible-waving evangelists waiting for the Rapture, and car-makers whose SUVs guzzle Middle Eastern oil. And, it must be admitted, even people like himself — anyone who drives at all. Will Prime Minister Blair bomb some other country or treat it as a crime? The British have a few centuries of experience in putting down dissent — Indian freedom fighters, the IRA. They'll deal with it more sensibly than Bush dealt with 9/11.

Karan turns the radio off.

Receipts, Twix wrappers, unpaid parking tickets. Punjabi, Hindi and Urdu audiocassettes, napkins, travel mugs without lids — he really should clean up his car and pay his tickets before the girl — Uma — arrives. If she does. He'd bought her Amtrak ticket online rather than send her money. He couldn't bring himself to ask for a photo, either. She'd seen his picture posted on the university web site — hard to miss. Only faculty member with turban and beard.

The house isn't new, but it's freshly painted, tangible evidence of the advance for *Economics: Basic Relationships in the Twenty-First Century,* by Karanbir Singh. Better than his old studio apartment. And, thanks to Vaheguruji, a good word from the dean, and a preferential mortgage rate for faculty, the monthly auto-deduction from his account is only sixty cents more than his former rent check.

Can't do much about the mailbox — some prankster cracked its supporting post last week. Probably the sandy-haired freckled kid next door or someone in his gang. The kid looks fifteen or so. Just a few years younger than Karan's students. Has nothing better to do till September but slouch around smoking weed with his pimply friends and make a nuisance of himself.

But the car . . .

He won't clean up. Let the girl see him as he is. Decide if she wants any more to do with him. She's probably like his first-year students — bored, sullen and given to quoting themselves with a prefatory "I'm like."

But it is a good thing he had the windshield replaced. Someone — probably the kid, but he can't accuse anyone — hit a baseball that splintered it the day he moved in. He waited two days for a parent to come over, apologize, insist on paying for replacement, but no one showed up. Even after the insurance, it was still $218 out of his pocket.

He slides a tape in. The car fills with Rabbi Shergill's voice: ". . . Bulla ki jana mein kaun?"

Who knows who I am?

Twenty-three and she hasn't been to college. His daughter — if she is his daughter — isn't a college grad. For this Uma can thank her mother. If Rita had called Karan once, wouldn't he have found a way for Uma to go to college? One of his cousin-nieces in Amritsar is writing a PhD on racism in Joseph Conrad's novels at his expense. He's helped pay for another in Ludhiana to study chemical engineering and encouraged at least three in Delhi who are now working in multinationals. Two generations ago . . . well, everyone in the family was village-schooled and muddy from the fields back then.

Karan parks, enters his home, opens one of the moving boxes and takes out a backpack. Returning to the car, he begins filling it with junk from the back seat. When he's finished, he opens the hatch, leans into the boot, pushes the black bag all the way in so there will be space for the girl's luggage.

No question of a hotel, Uma must stay with him. Maybe she'll want to study here in Santa Barbara — it's a beautiful city.

The Santa Barbara Train Station has, Karan is proud to note, been remodelled lately. On this Saturday it's full of people who will never make it to Karan's classes without Pell grants. Flyers hanging over the red, white and blue bunting warn of a Yellow Alert. He takes a seat and waits for the train from LA, hands clasped around a rolled up page from a legal pad on which he's written her name.

Smell of onions. A tanned tattooed arm appears beside Karan's. Impression of leather and polished rivets. The hair at the base of his turban is rising. The man leans closer, digs his elbow into Karan's side.

"Go home, Bin Laden!" Karan turns. Two inches away, a single-browed glare radiates from a stubbled face.

Karan's skin tightens. Fear hits in a galvanic rush, then anger. *Ignorance — just ignorance! Don't allow yourself to react to Philistines.*

He swallows. One, two, three, four, five.

A flush is rising beneath his beard. "I am home, mister." His voice is as even as if he is lecturing in class.

And he smiles.

Then hates himself for smiling.

He gets up, moves to another seat a few feet away. Sits down. Presses his palm on his knee to steady its tremor.

This idiot couldn't pass his SAT even if there were a GI Bill for bikers. But surely a basic education should have taught him something. In the absence of better schooling, one of Karan's much-rejected papers argued, the US will need more immigrants.

The man hauls himself off the bench, slings his backpack over his shoulder and swaggers off to catch his train; Karan pretends he doesn't notice.

A mute television above his head repeats the clip of bodies being carried out of the subway. The death toll is now fifty-two, maybe more. Sad! And now mug shots of suspected Muslim men.

A few minutes later, the same images again.

In 2001, one of his colleagues said the scene of the planes and the twin towers was replayed so often that her five-year-old thought all the planes were falling from the skies and crashing into buildings.

At least this time it isn't New York or Washington.

Now a close up of Osama Bin Laden. Karan is much better looking — plenty of women would agree.

Eleven o'clock. The train has arrived. He stands up, unfurls his paper.

Uma will never be able to read it from a distance.

He sits down again, takes out his pen. Darkens his handwriting.

The passengers have alighted. One girl — woman — remains. She walks toward him immediately. He crumples the paper — he always forgets how much his turban stands out in a crowd.

Not obese like Rita. Not thin, either. Proportionate. Tall, well-endowed as any Punjabi girl. Shoulder-length dark hair — did he expect she'd have hip-length hair like his own? Caramel colouring. A pink camisole baring an expanse of skin that makes Karan wince. White Capri pants. Sunflower sandals — retro fashion from the seventies.

Oh, she is his all right. No paternity test required. Those are his mother's dreamy eyes, the set of his father's chin. The slightly pouted lips — those are Rita's. And between her lower lip and chin is a round stud of polished steel.

Not a nose ring — a stud.

He approaches her, extends his hand. Suddenly wishes he had thought of bringing flowers. "Uma? Karanbir Singh." It comes out as if he's at a wine and cheese gathering.

Dark eyes spark. A quick tug at his hand. Hers is cooler.

"Hi. Uh, hi."

He reaches for embrace. She doesn't, so he stops. His voice wobbles forward again, stalls, balks.

She gives a faint smile; that's something.

Her tapestry bag has wheels but he carries it out of the station.

Welcome to Santa Barbara. How was the train ride? Good. Had a good time in LA? Sure. Did you go to Disneyland? Oh, yeah. And the beach? No, didn't have time. Well, then, we must visit a beach in Santa Barbara. Can't go back to Detroit without experiencing the ocean!

Thank god for ritual small talk.

In the car, Uma puts on a pair of boxy sunglasses and flicks a lighter without asking permission, takes a deep drag on a cigarette.

Karan debates reproving her, but it's minutes since he met her, and she is — no question — his daughter. His only daughter. Maybe she doesn't care that smoking is against his religion. No, she just doesn't know anything about Sikhism. And she's from Detroit, where they don't frown on smoking as much as Californians.

Karan starts the car. A cell phone appears; Uma calls someone.

"You okay?"

Someone she cares about, she doesn't say who.

At least she can care — many of his students don't seem to care about anyone but themselves.

State Street. Left or right? Karan's interior compass oscillates. As usual, the earth's magnetic field refuses to attract his directional core.

Vaheguruji!

He turns right.

"Later!" she says, and hangs up.

Despite invoking the Name, Karan finds what must be the longest route home. Along the way, he points out the towering Santa Ynez mountains, the impressive Spanish-era courthouse and its clock tower, the Santa Barbara Mission. He drives her past the golf club on Las Positas because it's beautiful, not because he plays. He shows her the red tile roofs, the arched facades, the wrought-iron gates of houses. He's comparing Santa Barbara's cleanliness and spacious boulevards to Delhi, of course. He compares everything to Delhi. Is she comparing Santa Barbara to Detroit or LA or Madison or — where? He can't stop his tour patter long enough to ask.

On Cliff Road, he grips the steering wheel tight. The car could veer off, take both of them over and down. Is she enjoying the ride? She nods, but the sunglasses guard her expression.

She's over twenty-one; he is not responsible for her. His sperm was merely a catalyst between Rita and her child. Maybe Uma thinks he's rich. How much will she ask for silence?

Behind her sunglasses, Uma wishes she hadn't come. After she calls Ashley to check on her, she rolls down her window so the smoke has someplace to go. She takes a last drag and flicks the butt out.

In Ma's stories, her pa — Karan — looked like an actor called Omar Sharif, so she married him. "So I could have you, baby," she'd say. "Only an immigrant woulda married a woman the size of your ma." And she'd laugh and laugh as if that was funny.

Karan isn't as tall as Uma expected. The turban, the moustache. Jeez, a Toyota. Pretty uncool. Were all Indian men so dark? She hadn't met any Indians up close in Detroit. Only seen bright fluttery figures entering a Hindu temple. When she was little, she never told Ma how she punched the kid who asked, "What's a Hindu?" and the one who answered, "Lays eggs." She figured her dad was Hindu — which was why she'd tried to read that Bhagavad-Gita thing — but last year Ma told her he was a Sikh. So Uma found reams of stuff about Sikhism on the web and printed out pages and pages. From what she read, it wasn't anything like being Hindu. But Ma got worse right after, and what with work and hospitals and the funeral, pretty soon nothing Uma read seemed to stick in her head.

Karan is going on and on about the scenery. Lecturing like she had to taste it, eat it. Hasn't mentioned Ma once. Ma, who can't see this, can't hear, taste, touch or smell anymore. Who does he think was with Ma till the end? Who drove Ma to dialysis appointments three times a week, kept her pill schedule, cooked her special food? Uma rolls her left shoulder, then her right — taut muscles from lifting Ma.

Shouldn't have come. Seemed like a good idea a couple of weeks ago when Ashley invited her to cheer up and visit Disneyland and sent her a frequent flyer ticket. Uma was functioning semi-okay after the week-long rummage sale of Ma's belongings. She still had two kidneys. Goddamn genes from the guy at the wheel here had made hers useless — "incompatible" they said — for a transplant.

But . . . think about Disneyland.

The day at Disneyland was the only one that seemed real all week. On Saturday morning when she arrived on the red-eye, Ashley met her at the baggage claim at LAX and said she was scheduled for a "birth prevention" on Tuesday morning after the long weekend. "Two months. Didn't want to tell you on the phone — you wouldn't have come. Can't be pregnant right now — my agent says I've got a chance for this great part in a Spielberg blockbuster. You're the only one who can help me through it."

And Uma did — sucker! What else was she to do? Tell a friend she'd been with from kindergarten through high school that she wouldn't drive her to the doctor, wouldn't wait for her, drive her home, clean up, cook lunch and watch her in case she began hemorrhaging?

No, that wouldn't be her. Even though she'd decide differently than Ashley in the same circumstances. And even though it meant she never got to see Universal Studios. But the Ashley thing made her almost forget she'd written to Karan on Friday night before leaving Detroit. She hadn't expected a reply to her Shock and Awe bombshell — Hey, Pa! Here I come, fully grown, and you didn't even know. Or the invitation to stay at his home. He probably guessed there was no way she could afford a Santa Barbara hotel — that was kinda nice of him, yeah.

But she could have said forget it after the week with Ashley and headed home — now why didn't she? Freakin' geography and curiosity, that's why. Kill two birds . . . oh, that's real funny. Especially when you're driving along a cliff and you're a turn of the steering wheel from one helluva drop to the ocean below.

Ma is dead. Dead. Dead. And Uma's going to carry that loss forever. But she did her best. No guilt. Because Ma said, "You blame yourself when I'm gone and I'm sure as hell gonna come back to haunt you."

Look, Ma, I'm blaming myself — just come haunt me. Show up already!

Karan yields his right-of-way to let a car pull into his lane. The other driver doesn't signal thanks.

A few minutes later, an SUV cuts in front. Passenger yells, "Fuckin' Ay-rab!" and gives Karan the finger. Fucking idiot — her dad is *not* an Ay-rab.

Karan didn't react; it's just road rage. Californians!

It's fine. Everything will be fine.

Ma always said, Expect nothing and you won't be disappointed. No use. Uma can't stop expecting. Not from Karan, but from herself. Where is the warmth? She should feel it rise spontaneously for the father who went missing, the dad she always wanted. But this guy. He doesn't look like her — or rather, she doesn't look like him.

Ma, couldn't you have shown me pictures of him — something?

Karan swings into a neighbourhood of neat houses. Homes — each is different. Definite curb appeal. People who don't mow their own lawns live here. No apartment buildings in sight. Up a gravel driveway to a tiny red-roofed house set against a backdrop of trees. The car rocks Uma to a halt before a garage door freshly painted rust red. Sprawling letters of underlying graffiti. Readable if she narrows her eyes: "How to stop wars — kill the ragheads."

"Oh, that. A gang of kids, about three weeks ago," he says. "Needs another coat of paint." And he gets out of the car.

"Awful mean," she says.

If this white-turbaned guy carrying her bag across the lawn and into his home is her closest relative, Uma better get to know him and his life this weekend. She won't make enough money bartending to get out here again any time soon.

Look, Ma, your baby made it all the way to California. And I can't even send you a wish-you-were-here postcard cause you went and left me, didn't ya?

Okay, be honest now, Ma, listen up. Is this visit gonna heal me or kill me?

It takes Karan only a few minutes to show Uma around. Cardboard boxes stacked in each room. Accumulation of his years in four different countries, different cities. He still isn't sure what should be tossed out, what he needs to keep. Now that he's no longer renting, he tells her, he might decorate typically American, say, Posturepedics instead of the old futons in the two bedrooms. And a curio cabinet to display the trophies from his field hockey days. He'll add Indian touches, of course — mirrorwork cushions, some big brass planters, wool durries — and maybe, someday, Kashmiri carpets.

He pours Uma a glass of orange juice while she freshens up, then leads her into the green glow of the one room he's carved off for living, the screened veranda. She calls it a patio, as Rita would have. No boxes here. Just bookcases across two walls, his reading chair and footstool, two wicker chairs angled on the tile floor to face a small TV, and a collapsible coffee table of painted wood. He watches approvingly as Uma examines the books spread face down on his two-drawer steel file cabinet in the corner — books are his true community, beyond religion or time.

Karan sweeps file folders off a chair and into the cabinet.

"My taxes." He laughs ruefully. He used to have his taxes completed by January, when paying them was a privilege, the price he paid for smooth roads, clean water, future Social Security. But he's been procrastinating since he began paying for two wars, torture and detention. Still, he pays. Because he's one of the good kind, the hard-working white collar immigrant — so he told his interviewers.

The veranda, surrounded by lush foliage, is dark and cool, but from this angle, the rest of the house looks half-built or half-ruined.

"Had a break-in a few days ago," he tells Uma. "Kids, I'm sure . . . can't prove that, unfortunately. Took a couple of boxes. They didn't need the stuff — tossed it down the hillside."

He doesn't believe himself. It had to be Homeland Security. Those chaps don't need warrants now and don't have to know or tell you what they are searching for. He inserts a CD — Vikram Seth's selection for *An Equal Music*. A violin launches into Bach's Partita in E major.

Uma takes a sip of orange juice and makes a face. "Got a beer?"

"Kingfisher — an Indian beer. Want to try it?"

She looks dubious.

"Or a very elegant fumé blanc."

"I get sleepy from wine."

Tipsy, is what he would have said. A word that no longer belongs anywhere.

"You don't have much of an accent," she says, obviously intending a compliment.

"Everyone has an accent of some kind." He smiles. He is always conscious of lilting phonemes long excised, accents on the wrong syllable.

"Got any pictures? Of Ma and you, I mean."

He nods, having anticipated this one. "A few."

"Videos?"

"Only a couple of Betas."

"What's Beta?"

"A video format — it's not around any more." He brings a shoebox of photos, places it before him on the coffee table and sits down. He rifles through them and hands her one.

"Rita and I. At school."

She sinks to the floor beside the table, legs folded beneath her, and supports her head on her hand as she looks at it closely.

Without the photographs, he might persuade himself that Rita never existed as his wife, that she was just a one-time helpful friend with whom he'd lost touch.

Uma looks up, holds his gaze.

"How much did you pay her?"

He can all but taste the anger in her words. Silence is his best defence.

"I heard twenty-five hundred."

He nods. Decides repentance would be dishonest. "You'd pay a personal matchmaker about the same."

"Yeah, but this was *citizenship*."

"A resident alien card," he corrects her. "After two years, if you can prove you're still married. And the *possibility* of citizenship, if you apply, after another five. In fact, I've only recently applied. And I'm sure Rita had her reasons." Feelings are layered, inaccessible. He wants to be precise, bring them into words for her. "We were friends. At least, at the beginning . . . I thought of it like an arranged marriage."

A hooting laugh. "Bet you Ma didn't." She takes a cigarette from her pocket and lights up.

"Nor did her mother," says Karan. "She didn't want us to stay married after the two years unless I cut my hair and no longer tied a turban."

"Makes sense. Grandma's practical."

"No, it doesn't make sense. No one should ask that."

Uma taps her cigarette on the edge of the table; ash falls on tile. "Yeah, I guess. I don't know her very well — she got remarried and moved to Chicago after Grandpa died. Ma said Grandma had to be someone's wife or she didn't believe she was alive. She'd call Grandma every Sunday morning and hand me the phone, and Grandma would tell me how I should try giving Ma cod liver oil pills or green tea. But she never showed up to see us for more than a day."

She blows a smoke ring. "What about your ma? How did she take it?"

"Not well. Only son marrying a gora woman — I mean someone non-Indian. It was uncommon in the early eighties. But she put a good face on it, sent jewellery for the wedding."

"Wow. So who got the jewellery, you or Ma?"

"Rita."

"Hmmm. She must have sold it when we were having budget troubles." Uma leans forward. "So you both stuck it out two years. Was it worth it, you think?"

Karan strokes his moustache. The answer Uma expects plays through his mind like the drone of a repetitive raag. He should be so grateful to live in the land of the free and the home of the brave. But there were bad times, better times, okay times, good times. Any immigrant would say that.

Some very bad times after 9/11.

"Dr Singh, tell us: why did you travel to Pakistan in 1997?"

"A bus service had opened up between India and Pakistan. My mother was dying and I knew she wanted a picture of the house in Multan where she was born."

"You want us to believe you went to Pakistan to take a photo? Which other cities did you visit? Who did you meet? Were you ever in Afghanistan?"

His alien registration card said he was a permanent resident on Day One. But they took till Day Five of harassment and solitary to let him go.

No apology.

This happened in God Blessed America. It happened to him.

And for the five days and nights he sat alone in a cell in Sacramento, no one asked where Dr. Karanbir Singh was. Adela is illegal — she wasn't going to call anyone, even if she had known whom to call. Nadir thought he'd forgotten their squash game — in his experience, "interviews" only happened to Muslims. His students waited ten minutes and left. Bradnock said later he thought Karan was sick. Karan didn't believe him.

The dean, a supposedly well-educated man, seemed to believe that the constitution was suspended and would be for the foreseeable future. He didn't think it could protect foreign-born people or non-citizens in a time of war. National origin, he said, that was the key.

What if they'd kept Karan longer? Who would have called an attorney, organized protests or demanded his rights? It was the only time he'd wished Rita was there. Or any wife. Or a single relative living in the USA. He has called civil rights attorneys since his release, but they're swamped with Guantánamo cases or simply unwilling to take his.

So what should he answer? Was the marriage worth it? Is it worth it now that fear has replaced love?

"It was worth it in the beginning," he says. A fluted space

appears between him and Uma, magnifying each word, his meaning. She regards him solemnly.

"Got an ashtray?"

"No," he says. "Smoking is against my religion."

"Against — no kidding!"

She rises. Goes to the veranda door, steps out, grinds the cigarette beneath her toe on the tiled stair and skips the stub into a flowerbed.

"You're real religious?" she says, returning.

"Not very. My sisters say I'm a Sikh out of habit. Habits from the seventies. They tease me, say I'm more observant than many Sikhs in Delhi."

"Delhi. In India, right?" She takes the chair beside him. "So, do I got relatives there?"

He restrains himself from correcting her English.

"Oh yes," he says. "You have aunts, cousins."

"Grandparents?"

He places a black and white photo before her. "First of all, here's my grandfather. My father's father, Dadaji — he's ninety years old." The photo is circa 1943, before he was jailed by the British, and Dadaji is wearing a plumed turban and kurta salwar. Karan tells Uma how Dadaji fled Pakistan in 1947, taking the last train from Gurdaspur to Delhi before the British-decreed borderline between India and Pakistan came down. How he found out a few months later that Gurdaspur ended up in India after all. But Dadaji couldn't go back there after what he'd seen.

The patriarch's birthday, he tells Uma, brings Karan and his cousins back to Delhi every year. He does not mention his memories — the petulant roar of the aged tiger demanding love as his due, the tribute to be paid for the treasure each of them hosts in blood and bone: his hardy seed, his memories in their genes. If she ever meets him, let her make up her own mind about him.

Uma has what he came to America for. Economic freedom,

intellectual freedom. She can be anything, do everything he once wanted to do, more than can be accomplished in one lifetime. *You are born here,* he wants to tell her. *You cannot be deported. You have light skin; you will never understand.*

"And what," he asks, changing the subject, "do you do?" and nearly adds, with your freedom?

She works at a bar near an auto plant. The customers are mostly auto workers. Good people, she says. All just trying to get by. She makes good tips. Flexible hours, so she could care for Rita. She still lives in Rita's apartment — in Indian Village, by the way — "not your kind of Indian, ha ha." She works out with weights, has good friends from school — Ashley, for instance.

"Do you have a boyfriend?"

She hesitates, seems to weigh her answer. "Not right now."

"Pretty girl like you?" A clumsy attempt to tease.

She looks away. Picks something off the coffee table. "What're these?"

"Gandhi slippers." Minni sent them last year, courtesy of some Indian traveller.

"They look like real silver."

"They are silver."

"Wow. What are they for?"

"For? Nothing. Just beautiful," he says. And his reminder of one man's ability to bring about change in a whole economy, one man's struggle against colonialism in every soul-diminishing form.

Uma puts the slippers down.

"Ma loved the movie. I liked Ben Kingsley better in *House of Sand and Fog.*"

Karan is unwilling to reduce Mahatma Gandhi to the film version, though he'll admit that harnessing religion in the cause of independence was an act of cruelty against a newborn country.

He moves the slippers to the lower level of the coffee table.

Another picture. "My mother. A widow. But she managed to raise three of us. Me, my two sisters."

It's safe to say his mother would have loved to meet Uma, since it's an untestable hypothesis, so he does. Uma glows at this comment; his breath catches in surprise.

"In fact, I'm sure they'd all like to meet you, get to know you. Here —"

Wedding pictures of Gagan, then Minni. His princesses in their flame-red lehngas, festooned with gold hand ornaments, hair ornaments, necklaces, bangles and nose rings. Henna curlicued all over their hands, kajal ringing their large black eyes.

"How come they aren't wearing turbans?"

"Only Sikh men wear turbans."

"Yeah?"

"A few Sikh women in North America wear them, but I've never seen a Sikh woman wearing one in India."

"Doesn't seem fair."

"To the women, you mean?" Protest poises on the tip of his tongue — the only religion in which women and men are equal, etcetera etcetera —

"To the men," says Uma, turning the page. She sighs and exclaims over more wedding pictures. "Bet you miss India."

"Sometimes."

"But you love it, right? Then why didn't you go back?"

"Wasn't much to go back for." Karan had escaped it all once the Emergency was lifted. Escaped two thousand rupees per annum with scooter allowance, dearness allowance and government housing in seven-storey tenements, escaped the years necessary between application and receipt of a telephone, escaped the corruption, the pidgining of English as it mixed with Hindi, replaced them all with different cares. But . . . "You have to leave to learn how much you love people. I missed my mother, and I do miss my sisters."

He tells her about his cousins, aunts and uncles all over the world. "We're a globalized family," he says and laughs.

She laughs, a little uncertainly.

"Where's your pa?"

He shows her a picture. "My father — your grandfather — died when I was seventeen." He doesn't add that he was seventeen when Prime Minister Indira Gandhi's thugs dropped off his father's blood-spattered, turbanless body. Seventeen when he lit his father's funeral pyre, travelled to Hardwar by train with his father's ashes resting on his knees. Someone said his father had written articles critical of Mrs. Gandhi's sterilization programs. In later years he had studied the correlation between WHO's population targets and the PM's quotas, but that data was no comfort. Oh, the slow torment of learning to live without Papa, the need to invent a gilded version with wings. Even with loving uncles who had pooled their resources to send him to school in the US.

"Speaking of fathers, what did Rita say about me?"

Uma rises, moves to the screen wall, and looks into the foliage. She turns back to him after a moment.

"Ma said you were smart, tall, thin — she wanted me to be thin." Palms on hips, Uma rolls her eyes. "Never showed me a single picture, hated cameras. Any time I got bad grades in school it was your fault. When I was real small, I used to ask if we could go live with you, but she said she didn't want a husband, just me."

"Yes, Rita was like that only."

"Always thought she was joking around about that — but now I think maybe she did mean it and I just didn't want to believe her. Said you had moved back to India when I was a few years old and she didn't know where. I used to bring it up every once in a while but never heard any different till last year."

Rita! A sardonic laugh escapes him. "Moved back to India. Either Rita didn't know me very well or she didn't want you to try to find me."

Even now, when he goes back, more than twenty years fall away on landing, as if the North American continent hid itself in a pre-Columbus fog, as if five thousand years of touching the feet of elders suddenly evaporated his years of cultivating a firm European handshake. Even his American accent melts in Delhi, replaced by the silent head-wobble yes, and the Arey-yar! Rushdie-style speech rhythm of the Delhi University lad he once was. But live there again?

Maybe he no longer knows how.

"Or she didn't understand the news from India in the eighties."

Since 1984, when politicians gave tacit permission for riots and thousands of Sikhs were killed in Delhi, he can't imagine living in India. After the riots Karan turned into one of those swaggering Non-Resident Indians, an ugly NRI, making every member of his family aware of the favour he bestowed by his presence each year in a country he now abhorred. Oye! Such a bastard he was then!

Then came Montreal. He actually felt safer wearing his turban in Montreal than in India. It calmed him down. Allowed him to explore the economic rationale underlying the pogroms.

He can't describe these things. Context, nuances, qualifications, time frames. He has one weekend. One weekend in which to counter all that Rita must have filled Uma's mind with in twenty-three years. Or one weekend in which to fill in a whole lot of blanks.

"So what happened last year to make Rita break her silence?"

"We were watching TV," says Uma. "May or June? The news came on after *Cheers!* and Ma saw this skinny old guy and she sat up in bed. That's a Sikh, she said. And I'm like, What is? He is! she says. See his turban? Like your pa, she says. First time I ever heard you wore a turban. See his beard? That's like your pa. So we kept watching as this guy was getting sworn in as Prime Minister of India."

"Manmohan Singh."

"Yeah, I guess so. Any relation?"

"No, all Sikhs are Singhs."

"Oh. Anyway, after that she convinced herself I needed to look you up. But not till she was gone. She'd decided she was going, and when. Couldn't get her off of it, so I promised."

"Well," Karan says with a smile, "I'm glad you keep your promises."

Uma thinks a Leinenkugel would taste much better than the orange juice right about now. But her dad is saying the only beer he has is Kingfisher. She's not in the mood to try it.

So many books in one room, and it's not even a library. Ma kept five or six for show in the living room. Karan's are spread face down all over. One is marked up, highlighted, indexed and footnoted in tiny precise writing: *The Trial.* Tom Cruise could play the guy on the back cover, Joseph K. Maybe Sean Penn — no, he's too old.

It's going to be fine. Uma can just flow into Karan's life. She'll start from babyhood. Tell him how she won a swimming trophy at twelve, was captain of the Lush League softball team last year, and how she's been to Windsor, Canada, and seen their cute coloured money. He'll place his hand on her shoulder. She'll tell him how she hoped he'd walk in one day and rescue Ma and her, and Ma would get better and all of them would live . . . oh, sure.

Right now if she were dreaming there would be a dad who'd say what Ma did: Kid, you done good. You couldn't have done more than you did. Can't he say that just once?

But she doesn't know this guy. No clue where he's coming from.

So what? He's still her dad. She has a dad.

Part of her is trying very hard not to get mad. Why did he not know? Wasn't there some kind of father's intuition? How come he didn't figure out Ma was pregnant? Why didn't he call Rita at least once if he was still in the States or Canada? Ashley's parents are divorced but her pa calls her ma sometimes. And he *always* calls Ashley for her birthday.

That's because he knows when Ashley was born — he was there when Ashley was born.

Pretty mean of Ma, telling her Karan had gone back to India and she didn't know where he was. One time, when Uma asked too many questions, Ma hinted she didn't contact Karan when she found out she was pregnant because she thought he might kidnap Uma and take her back to India with him. And that night Ma rented the movie *Not Without My Daughter.* Uma got the message.

Karan has pulled out photos. In colour. How come she'd expected them to be black and white, or even sepia? Maybe cause the eighties are in the last century. All of Ma in colour, taking up most of the shot. Karan smiling over her shoulder, like he's hiding behind her. They don't look like enemies. But they don't look in love, either. He put in his two years and then split. Kinda like going in the army. Well, Ma was great most of the time, but often so pig-headed German that you had to find a lot of love to put up with her the rest of the time.

Maybe Ma put in her two years and was ready to split too?

Was it worth it? She really needs to know.

Karan hesitates a long time before answering, "In the beginning."

He could mean it was worth it only while he and Ma were married, or that he thought it was worth it for a few years and now he's not sure. She tries to read his face.

It's harder to read a brown face. Especially one you don't know.

It was worth it while he and Ma were married. She's sure of it.

She needs another smoke, but he says it's against his religion. That's gotta be bullshit — she's never heard of a religion that forbids smoking. But then he's born into a religion that says no cutting your hair. Even women? What do Sikh women do about underarm hair? Do they shave their legs? Can't ask a guy something like that. It'll be on the net somewhere. But even if your religion does forbid smoking, can't you have an ashtray for guests? Can't you just do it anyway — like Catholic girls do the Pill?

He's off lecturing again, telling her his ancestors — and hers — once lived together in a haveli, a mansion with suites of rooms that opened onto verandas and courtyards. Generations rubbing up against one another, the young educating the old, the old receiving respect and ruling with iron authority over the young. And then.

He pauses dramatically.

And then came Partition.

"It was a vortex of violence. Every man became aware of himself as animal, every breath became a gift of Ram, Allah or Vaheguru. Some escaped on trains to places where they had family ties, marriages made as alliances were now called to account. The old haveli fell to the battering ram of Islam, and its occupants took every possible transport and fled from blood and slaughter as far and wide as they could."

Now her relatives wander in London and Winnipeg, in Fiji and Hong Kong, in Sydney and Singapore. And some remain in India. Karan shows her wedding pictures of two "aunties" in Delhi — Aunty Gagan and Aunty Minni. Much younger than Karan. Only a few years older than her. They don't wear turbans. Uma does look a bit like them. And she doesn't — they're beautiful.

"We're a globalized family," he says and laughs.

Uma isn't sure what the joke is, but laughs because he does — like she does with customers sometimes.

"Do you have a boyfriend?"

Does she? There was no parting screaming match last year. No tears. Will came in one evening when she was bartending and made a long loud speech about Indians draining away a call centre job that should have been his. And an immigrant who took the other one he'd applied for. Said he was ready to join the Minutemen and police the border. Uma told herself he was just tired of troubleshooting for folks who didn't know enough to reboot their PCs.

"Not right now," she says to Karan. Because after Will's tirade she no longer felt anything pour in and overflow inside when he kissed her. And every time she went out with him she wondered how she'd ever loved a guy who could hate so many people, how she could have missed the clues, and if there had been any clues.

"My father is from India," she told him the last night they were together. "That makes me an immigrant's daughter. And if you're not Native American, you're descended from immigrants too." Will never apologized.

Karan asks — *finally*! — about Ma. First he wants to know what Rita told Uma about him. Then what happened last year to make Rita break her long silence. So she tells how Rita made her promise to look him up. He says he's glad she keeps her promises.

An hour later, he asks how Ma died and was she buried or cremated. And Uma is trying to explain, describe, tell him how it was. How Rita just decided one day — no more dialysis. And how Uma had to let go, give Rita permission to die. She's ordered the headstone for Ma's grave. It'll be ready when she gets back.

She's describing a woman performing Uma's life. Someone without her light-headed sense of unreality, without her anger at unfinished conversations. Someone without the ripples of panic that flow through Uma at the thought of moving on without Ma.

"I am so sorry you had to experience that," he says.

He's not real interested in Ma or her final days.

But when he asks, "What are your plans now?" he leans forward, giving her answer his utmost attention.

"Back to bartending next Tuesday."

Suddenly that didn't sound like fun. Especially without Ma to come home to.

"Have you ever thought of doing something else?"

"I could maybe get a job at the auto plant. Keep bartending on the side."

That didn't sound like much fun either. It sounded as if she was heading for the Bermuda Triangle.

"You could — no, never mind," he says.

"Did you ever think of doing something else?"

"Oh, yes. After my PhD I tried to join the army."

"The army? Why would they need economists?"

He laughed. "Oh, it wasn't that they need economists, but the army is, well, sort of a traditional occupation for Sikhs."

"No kidding? I'm trying to picture my aunts in camouflage helmets."

"No, no, just traditional for Sikh *men*. Though there are women in the Indian Armed Forces . . . Anyway, my uncles kept saying I should join."

"You mean the army in India?"

"No, the US Army — it would have been a way to get my citizenship."

"Jeez, you'd be in Iraq right now."

"True, except that the US services didn't allow turbans. Not allowed today either."

"Why not?"

He shrugs. "Ignorance."

"And you wouldn't wear a hat? Oh, I get it, it's like when Grandma wanted you to take it off."

He gives her a nod and a wry smile. "Their loss, really. Sikhs are either the bravest or the foolhardiest chaps, depending on one's point of view. "

Chaps, meaning guys.

Could be he doesn't notice how people talk in America. Or he hangs on to old words the way Ma used to hoard clothes that didn't fit anymore.

The photos in the box dwindle. Karan turns on a lamp.

He putzes in the kitchen and brings two mugs. "Orange pekoe tea" he says, as if it's special. And some cookies he calls rusks.

Uma watches TV as she sips and nibbles. He seems so pleased that she likes his tea.

What's a father supposed to be, anyway? Teacher, coach, older brother, friend and boyfriend all at once? And if she wasn't the kind of daughter he wanted, then . . . ?

She's still hungry. But for details, or food, or for something else this guy can give her?

Karan can't find the right pots and pans; he says he has to take Uma out to dinner.

"Suits me," says Uma.

She'd have chosen any place where they serve chips with salsa or where you can get Singapore noodles, but he's paying so he gets to choose. She doesn't know restaurants and their prices in this city anyway.

A few miles out of town she follows him into Bistro Balti, a restaurant that could be a transplant from Detroit — it's just like the one Ma sometimes called for delivery. Takeout menus on a sign behind a counter, only two other couples occupying diner-style tables and booths. Incongruously, each table has a white tablecloth.

Karan asks for the owner and he comes over, a slight, dark man with a moustache but no turban, dressed in a tuxedo with a purple cummerbund, like he's just come from a wedding.

"Sat Sri Akal, Doctor-sahib!"

"Salam Aleikum, Nadir!" Karan rises for a half hug and shakes hands.

"Nadirji is from Karachi," Karan says. "Excellent squash player. Has to play very hard to work off his wonderful meals."

Karachi — where has she heard of Karachi?

Nadirji laughs and pokes Karan in the stomach. "I say, eat much and you'll keep playing as well as you do!"

Karan is smiling and talking in Indian. Obviously explaining who she is. Nadirji's eyebrows jerk up and down and he glances at her uncertainly a few times.

Daniel Pearl, the journalist, was beheaded in Karachi. Karachi is in Pakistan, not India. And there's going to be a movie about it.

And what does any of that have to do with this man? Nothing. Absolutely nothing.

Nadirji says, "Dr. Karanbir has told you how we met? At the courthouse — we were being fingerprinted together. All day we sat there waiting, waiting. So we started talking. Do you know, we found out both our grandfathers are from Gurdaspur. Only mine fled to Karachi, his to Delhi. At least they chose the capital cities of the time."

He laughs and slaps Karan on the back. "Dr. Karanbir said Partition was all because of economics. I said, Rubbish! All because of religion. So we started arguing and arguing. So then this Homeland Security guy, he comes up, says, Hey, are you fighting? So Dr. Karanbir says, No, no, sir! This is my friend."

Nadirji beams.

Karan asks about Nadirji's younger brother — is he back in Karachi?

"Oh no," says Nadirji. "Still he's sitting in the Detention Center in New Jersey. But they're saying they will send him back to Karachi any day."

"And his wife?"

"She's here only, in San Diego. Still calling me every day — do something, call his lawyer. Call Homeland Security. Don't we know anyone with a relative working there? Talk to them in English. I tell her I *have* called, but they don't even take messages on their voice mail. So every week I'm sending the lawyer more money — what I can. And every week I'm giving her advice how to run my brother's appliance shop. But I too have a family."

Jeez! Does he ever, and Karan's like a doctor, asking about the health of each one. Didn't he say he met Nadirji for squash last week? Brothers, parents, uncles — it's a friggin' assembly line.

". . . and your cousin-brother? The one with the PhD in architecture?"

"Subhanallah! He found a job. Temporary, and he's only drafting, not designing, but it's a job." For Uma's benefit, Nadir explains. "He was laid off after 9/11 — his boss told him he was scaring the clients. But he's tip-top in drawing with the computer. He has a wife and child to feed. So. Very difficult."

Everyone has it difficult.

"My Ma did CAD," says Uma. "She worked from home, designing car parts on her computer."

"Your mother?" says Nadirji. He glances at Karan for confirmation. Karan is studying the menu.

"Yeah, my mother was an engineer."

"Vah! A woooman engineer," says Nadirji. Like it's a strange species of baboon. "But this is good, good. Working at home. She must be a good woman."

"She was." Uma's eyes are filling; she tries to bring the menu into focus.

Now Nadirji is all business, bringing water, recommending the raan of lamb, the turkey keema in case she doesn't eat beef, the cucumber yogurt in case the spices are too hot for her palate.

Uma orders a combination platter — butter chicken, daal makhni and naan. Karan orders the same but points to a different bread. Nadir writes it all down, tears off the bottom and gives Karan a number. He hands the order to another black-moustached man behind the counter.

Karan launches into an explanation of how butter chicken is made. Uma holds up her hand.

"Butter chicken was Ma's specialty. She learned to make it in Madison."

Look, Ma — I brag about you all the time.

But hey, who taught you to make butter chicken?

Karan goes to the counter when their ticket number is called.

Turmeric and ginger aromas rise from the compartmented Styrofoam before Uma.

Lentils scald her tongue. She takes a gulp of water and bites into the thick naan. Everything she has to tell Karan, show him, is stored up someplace.

Karan unfolds a soft thin bread on his plate. "Listen, Uma. There's no need to tell anyone about this green-card marriage thing. It was a long time ago. I don't want any trouble. They deport people for less, you know. India's not a bad place to be deported to nowadays, but a year or two in a Detention Center is worse. And the legal expense. Not to mention the indignity."

The chicken glows red on its bed of saffron-flecked rice. Uma takes a sip of water.

Karan, her dad Karan, only invited her to visit so he could keep her quiet. She should get up and walk out right now. Except that she doesn't have enough money for a fucking hotel.

How can he think she's going to tell anyone that her ma took money for a green card and sex?

Don't worry, Ma.

She gets that Karan is afraid of her. He totally should be. One word from her . . .

Maybe you took the money from him because you needed it. Maybe you didn't want him to feel he had to stay with you. How come you didn't tell me more of your reasons, Ma? All our years together?

Like it or not, she's related to Karan. By blood and secrets.

She gestures at the salt cellar, he passes it across the table. "Who's gonna ask me?" she says, shaking a fine mist across her food.

Back home, around midnight, conversation fizzles. Karan opens the futon in the spare bedroom, fetches clean sheets, helps Uma make her bed.

Later, when he goes to check on her, she is in pyjamas, with headphones over her ears. She puts her CD player next to her pillow and waves goodnight.

He reads a bit of Galbraith's *Getting and Spending*. Then he returns to her room, turns off the bedside light, turns off her CD player to save the batteries. Her face, nude of expression as she sleeps, carries little imprint of time. What did she look like at five, ten, fourteen?

His fears of entrapment, of Homeland Security, of extortion all disgrace him now. She's right — who is ever going to ask her?

People in novels have reams of thoughts; why is his mind blank? If only he had something other than economics, some profound life lesson to share with Uma. But at this moment anything he's ever learned eludes him. Like an echo, she reminds him of the courage he once had, the optimism that drove him to candlelight studying, the desperation that made him look around in the late seventies and cry, "Not this!"

Her shoulder feels warm beneath his palm. How did a chance and loveless combination like his with Rita have produced such a beautiful being? Think of it! Rita raising this child all by herself. No — not so. Thank every babysitter, teacher and friend who also raised his daughter for him.

He tiptoes out. In his room, he switches off the bedside lamp, closes his eyes.

The men. In suits, with look-alike FBI masks, pale as though bred in Washington — worse than the clones in *Matrix*. One looks like Prince Harry, complete with swastika armband.

A blade, sharp and cold against his jugular.

Questions prickle under his skin — he's being asked to explain the twenty-five hundred dollars. Uma appears. They ask her.

Then they cut up his alien registration card.

Rita, grown huge, stands in a corner of the room. A sea-green silk sari swirls around her. She seems to be wearing a spiky crown. She raises her right hand high above his head — she is holding a massive cone with a flaming diya at the top. The flame flickers and sputters as the men feed it the shreds of his card.

Rita begins to weep, and Karan is surprised by an urge to console her, but he cannot move.

And then he is flying without a plane, without a net, without a swing to grab overhead. Over the bomb-ravaged mountains of Afghanistan. A Stinger missile rises toward him.

Impact!

It has shot right through him without a sound.

He is falling, falling.

Then suddenly he is being torn limb from limb at the centre of a huge riot. Desperate, angry men. All dressed like Dadaji.

Chanting, *"Amrika murdabad."*

America, may you die.

An electric rush of fear. Uma — his little Uma — she's a born American. She's in danger.

His eyes spring open.

The word "father" has taken root somewhere at the base of his spine.

On a normal Sunday morning Karan would be at the gurdwara in Ventura. After listening to shabads and prayers till noon, he'd sit cross-legged on the floor with everyone else and be served langar: rice, lentils, gobi allu. Maybe even super-sweet kheer.

But he can't take Uma there. She might light a cigarette. She may not want to remove her shoes. She may balk at wearing a chunni or even a scarf to cover her head, or refuse to bow her head to the ground before the Guru Granth Sahib. She might laugh. Some might think she's his girlfriend. Next time he'll be able to prepare people in the community. *If* she visits again.

If this were any other Sunday, Karan would drive back to North Hall after langar and let himself into his office like a yogi or a monk performing his rituals — Sundays, not being a Guru-prescribed Sabbath, do not feel very different from weekdays. Self-imprisoned in his book-lined cubbyhole, he'd be scrolling web sites for statistics, typing, thinking.

Instead, Karan's just-washed hair lies like a limb upon his spine, dampening and cooling his back through his T-shirt. He has found and unpacked a frying pan. Bacon sizzles in its fat. He adds a jalapeño to egg bhurji while Uma showers.

He has never thought about eggs. Or chromosomes. Or genes. All he knows is every human being has anywhere from forty to sixty thousand and more are derived from the woman. And as for sperm, his sperm — he has given no thought to the whereabouts of his sperm. He's probably thought more deeply about the ratio of US Foreign Aid to its Gross Domestic Product.

Water rolls and chugs in the kettle. He pours it over an orange pekoe teabag for himself, Folgers instant for Uma. It's ready just as she appears.

She's wearing a bathing suit, shorts and the sunflower sandals; he is grateful he didn't plan on going to the gurdwara today. He puts the bacon and eggs before her and serves himself.

Uma toys with the bacon and looks confused. "I thought — Ma said she couldn't remember whether . . ."

"Whether I eat pork? Of course. It's Muslims who don't."

"Oh. I didn't know."

"Well, how could you? I eat beef too. Of course, we have our share of vegetarians, but I'm quite omnivorous. And you?"

"I'm allergic to eggs."

"Oh, dear — I didn't know."

Her expression, as he removes her plate, says there's a lot he doesn't know that a father should. There's no autobiography he can read to bring himself up to date.

Let the egg bhurji twirl down the vortex of the garbage disposal or keep it? Spices preserve; he shoves it in the fridge.

Achcha! He pulls out a box of raisin bran for her. Is proud of himself for having fresh milk.

Today, he shouts from the bathroom, as he ties a fresh white turban over his topknot and underturban, they'll cycle to the beach. He'll ride his old bike, she can use his new one.

"And afterwards, we can come back here, change and drive to the Faculty Club for lunch. If we run into the dean, I'll introduce you. It will be a treat to see Bradnock inspecting us to see if we look alike!"

He laughs and Uma joins him.

Yes, he will say, Dean Bradnock, this is my daughter. Like Thayne Grey showing those photos.

Then to Stearns Wharf to see the sailboats, do some shopping. He'll find out what she likes, buy her whatever she likes.

Dinner someplace.

"You decide," he says, showing her a visitor guide.

In the garage, Karan hands Uma a bicycle helmet left by the former owner.

"Don't you wear one?" she snaps the clip beneath her chin.

"My turban is protection enough."

Tires sing on asphalt. Karan floats down lanes of carob and palm trees. He breathes in the scent of grass and sea mist. His bicycle bell pings, pure as the end note on a jal tarang. He looks back. Uma waves.

Gold light. Time slows.

Sunwarmth glides over Uma's shoulders, back and legs. Sweat trickles between her breasts. A few feet away, Karan's white turban lies beside him on a beach towel. He rests his bearded chin on his forearms. A dull silver bangle shines on one of them. His hair is swept up into a knot and covered with a black kerchief. She's never seen anything like it.

He's real brown-faced, but his back and stomach are lighter.

Seagulls squawk their conversations. Seahorse waves stumble and leap over black rocks. A motorboat zips the seam between water and sky. Sail triangles lean into the wind.

Right about now Uma's got good attitude. This minute she could die with no regrets, just like Ma. The hospice, obits, funeral and farewells, the details of closing down a life are behind her.

Ashley is left behind in LA. Strange — she can't remember the last time she didn't have someone, anyone, to worry about.

She called Ashley last night. Told her Karan was a bit old-fashioned.

Ashley said, "You were going to take a picture with your cell and send it, remember? I want to see if you look like him." Uma was going to but she hasn't. She's not ashamed or anything, just not used to him.

"He's different. But nothin' special," she told Ashley.

Whenever Uma thought she was nothing special or if some wise-ass told her so, Ma would say, "You're special to me."

Karan, her father. Strange foreign guy, but he doesn't seem like a terrorist. A two-inch dagger hangs from a chain around his neck — a kirpan, that's what he called it. Said the charm is religious, to remind him of his duty to defend the weak. Boy, all that education and he's superstitious as a Lions fan.

And he really believes in God. Uma usually flies under God's radar, but she could easily believe in God on a day like this. God's a typical guy, Ma used to say. Gets all the credit, never the blame, never apologizes.

She hears the distant howl of sirens. Fire trucks, ambulances.

Can't stop bad things from coming at the people you worry about. Madmen fly planes into buildings, kidneys fail, pregnancies happen when you don't have your own act together.

She rolls over. Warm sand shifts beneath her spine, grits into the midriff of her tankini and fills her navel. Maybe she'll plug her navel with a stud when she goes home. Every woman her age on this beach has either a stud or a navel ring. Each seems so sure of herself.

Coming to Santa Barbara, she expected to arrive magically at a station and see a sign that said Answers.

Blue above her. So much blue.

The earth's coordinates lie within her.

Karan leads the way home. Warm and cool bands of wind alternate on his cheeks. He's pedalling under a canopy of trees. He'll have tortilla soup and the chili-marinated ahi at the Faculty Club. Maybe Uma would like to try their soba noodle salad — that is, if it isn't made with eggs.

A sickening odour of burning.

He sails around the corner.

Five red trucks. Big ones.

He squeezes his brakes. Uma comes to a stop beside him.

From the Storke Road and UCSB stations. Firemen, hoses. A small crowd keeping a safe distance.

A black-orange nebula billows and floats over a lawn.

Hai Rabba! That's *his* lawn.

A ragged blot spreads across the sky. A whoosh like ghee igniting over a body. A crack like a skull bursting from heat. The pungence of ash and uncertainty.

His home! His new home!

Karan scrambles from his bike and runs as he's never run before.

Smoke-steam. Hot, hot, hot, like the open throat of a dragon. Padded arms come at him from all directions, snagging him like branches. Hands claw at his back. He feints, evades, elbows them away, runs toward his goal.

"My books — all my books!"

Shouting. "Easy! Easy now!"

Uma is screaming, "No, don't! Don't!"

A blow takes the air from his lungs; someone's arms have him around his stomach, and another grasps him across his chest. Karan goes down hard on his hip. His turban tumbles from his head, falls, unravels. Hot grass grinds against his cheekbone, slicks into his beard.

Gasping, choking, shrugging them off, he struggles to his feet.

Arcs of water, clouds of steam.

He gulps searing breaths, shakes men off him. Stands, absorbing each lick of flame in his gut. Boundaries of skin and time fall to thin lines. His eyes burn and tear. He is on fire as his home burns.

A man is running, dragging a spurting garden hose across the street to help. Uma is coming toward him.

The kid. Sandy hair, pale freckled face. By the mailbox, with three or four look-alikes standing right behind him. Watching the firemen. The kid turns.

A smirk passes across that face. Then quickly affixed innocence.

Blood gusts in. Karan's heart pounds against the barricade of his ribs. Events align themselves in orbit around him. A broken windshield, the mailbox, kill the ragheads, the break-in, this fire. Events past and present, people, things, moments. Each hyperlinks, connects like a giant nerve system.

The kid backs away one step, then another, and he's running. The other kids scatter. Karan lunges a fraction of a second later, and he's off, sprinting after the kid through intervening trees, picture-perfect lawns.

He's caught the kid. He's rolling in mud and wet grass and smearing mud into the smirk and all over the face and hair of the little bag of stupid stupid malicious ignorance till it yells, coughs, spits, begs and weeps. Whistles, strong hands grasp at his shoulders, pulling, pulling him back.

"Maniac! Criminal assault!" cries a man. The kid's father?

A great weight rests on Karan's chest, pinning him to the grass. Air, he needs air!

Paramedics are helping the kid up, wiping his face. The kid is wailing, shocked — never expected Karan to fight back, did he? Somewhere above, Uma is crying, pleading with someone to let Karan up.

The weight lifts. Air rushes in. He lies there till he contains himself again.

Yes. He, Karan, was going to keep on beating the shit out of that kid.

Lawn chair behind him; Karan staggers to it, sits down. Fire truck beside him. Uma comes up, hands him his besmirched white turban. What is she thinking, feeling? That he's a violent awful chap to go after a kid, a fifteen-year-old kid. But did she see that smirk?

It's over. She'll never want to be with Karan again. She'll tell them what she knows.

He smoothes his hair up into his topknot. Re-ties his turban slowly.

Hands shaking.

A black policeman holding a scarf over his nose and mouth with one hand approaches Karan. Asks the questions he should ask. Takes Karan's alien registration card and reads its number over his radio. Snaps his PDA shut and gives Karan a long hard look.

"This here could be careless smoking, overheated stove, faulty wiring," says the cop.

"I don't smoke."

"Yeah, well, someone else might have lit up? Like your little white girlfriend, maybe?"

"That's my daughter."

"Uh-huh. You lucky you and your, uh, daughter weren't inside. And how come you're sure it's arson and it's him? You gone and had the trial all by y'self, made up the sentence y'self. And what if some other guy did it?"

Karan's gaze travels over the policeman's face, then back to his eyes.

"I know, I know. You think it's racism. You don't know jack shit about racism. Us Black Muslims could tell you a thing or two about racism, going back to Elijah Mohammed and Malcolm X. But you — d'you understand anything? You assault somebody, people gonna think all Muslims are —"

"I'm not Muslim."

"You ain't gotta lie to *me*, brother."

"I'm not lying."

"Okay, okay. We're going to question the young gentleman, seein' as you accuse him. All I'm saying is you could be mistaken."

Sensations cascade over Karan so fast he cannot name them. The flames are subsiding now, rustling, creaking, hissing less and less. The walls, the floor of his home are caving in. The air stings his eyes. Sweat trickles down the back of his legs. A membrane rises between him and the policeman.

"I am *not* mistaken," he says. Words taste acrid in his mouth, go up with the smoke.

A crackle sounds at waist level. The cop takes the radio off his belt and listens. "Your resident alien card checks out. No prior record of violence — that's good, man. Checks out that you're a prof at UCSB too. But we're gonna talk to you some more. I'm going to have you report to Goleta Station, with your green card and passport."

My passport. It was in the house.

These things happen. You call the Indian Embassy, you apply for a replacement. You have your green card, your driver's licence and credit cards. That's all this chap wants.

"Monday morning, ten o'clock. Got that?"

The kid, his blackened hair and face perched on the white pole of his neck, gives Karan the finger from the paramedic van.

Karan goes over to Uma. "I was angry. Couldn't stop myself. I'm sorry —"

"Don't you know a cop might have cracked your head? Could have killed you!" Her face is contorted with what seems like anger. She looks away. "It would be too much — both of you."

A Red Cross woman interrupts to offer Karan a hotel voucher.

The guy who ran across with the garden hose waves her away. "You come stay with us tonight," he says.

Karan begins to say, "Thank you, sir, that's very kind." But his mouth feels sealed; no sound comes.

If Uma could click Undo she would return to the bright shining morning at the beach and forget the lick and snap of flames, the taste of burning wood.

Ma, you were right. Life is just one goddamn thing after another.

Like Uma didn't have enough problems. Like she really needed this. She's always the one that gets stuck looking after someone.

But what's she supposed to do? Leave her dad and just walk away?

Karan's eyes were like red blisters on his face.

Concentrate on small details. Hold it together. Accentuate the positive, as Ma used to say. Here goes: Karan's neighbour, Chris, turned out to be an okay guy. His girlfriend, Jena — he calls her his partner — is about the same size as Uma, hence the Diesel jeans Uma is wearing, along with a T-shirt from Belize.

The living room where she's sitting is scattered with do-dads from all over the world — Chris and Jena joined the Peace Corps in the seventies. Karan is sleeping in the bedroom that belonged to their son. The son is now almost thirty and, Jena says, is cool with the idea that his parents have never married. But then, he's Californian.

Oh, and Uma's figured out how to wash and fold a turban so Karan can put it on when he wakes up. He's exhausted and in shock but so freaking worried about having new underwear for tomorrow that he gave her his credit card to go buy some right away — his "kachcha," he calls it. Rhymes with gotcha. That's in his religion too. First she's heard of a religion that says you gotta wear clean underwear every day.

What needs to be done now?

She calls Ashley, changes her return from LA — luckily, there is a frequent flyer seat on Wednesday. She calls a friend to cover her shift, then calls her manager at work. She gets on Jena's PC and uses Karan's credit card to order some new clothes for him, for her. And a suitcase for each of them. Details jump and swarm through her mind, each begets another.

She calls information, gets hold of Karan's dean. "I'm Dr. Karanbir Singh's daughter," she tells Bradnock. "Visiting from Detroit."

Did she really say "daughter?"

This morning at the Goleta police station, a stiff-backed Karan swore it was another racist attack. A hate crime, he called it. The cops didn't believe him. Particularly the black guy, the cop who was at the fire — and you'd think *he'd* get it.

"You smoke, don't you?" he'd said to Uma. Like it might be her fault.

Uma told the cop she saw a creepy smile flick across that kid's face right when she first saw him. If homes were built closer here, like some in Detroit, the kid could have burned down a whole block.

And the father — he's going to press charges for criminal assault. Rita would have had Uma doing a year's community service if Uma had given anyone a look of such hatred as his little turd son had.

The black cop warned Karan he could end up with a police record. Assault is criminal, he said. They could start deportation proceedings for that alone. There might be mitigating circumstances, like if the fire inspector finds arson and it can be traced back to the kid — but that's up to a judge.

"Right this minute, you don't have no country," he said to Karan as they left the station. "If I was you, I'd get my Indian passport reissued pretty damn quick. And I'd call my immigration attorney and have him check the status of my application for citizenship."

Uma thinks of Will, of telling him she's an Indian immigrant's daughter. Words that meant little then. And now? She's just met her dad and now he can be sent away to prison — who knows where, or for how long?

She leans back on the couch and closes her eyes. In a second, she is back in that bright spot of shock when she first saw the fire.

Her psyche has been reformatted; she could just scream.

The next day Karan's footsteps squelch on marshy ground. Heat lingers over the stinking mess that covers his lawn like an oil spill. Smog hovers over the wreckage, as if a piece of LA sky were snipped and pasted above Santa Barbara's. The skeletal remains of the house will be cordoned off with yellow tape until the fire inspector's job is done, but Karan can grope through a mess of salvage splayed beneath the tattered trees.

A flutter of black ash. A beam shifts and thuds in the debris.

What's left of Karan's belongings lies bare, cardboard boxes in each room having capitulated to flame and smoke. The Gandhi slippers are a smudge soldered to the remains of the coffee table. Moldy smell of wet charred books. Impotence rebukes him, leaves the odour of humiliation. He replays the moment when the kid smirked and everything clicked into place.

He flexes his hands. Detained or not, he will add the fire to the other incidents logged in the Sikh Coalition database. He'll donate more to the American Civil Liberties Union. Some of this failure is his — he should have been more cordial. Should have introduced himself to the family next door, to all the neighbours. He could have held a housewarming party. Explained, wooed, befriended, charmed the kid and his friends.

He can't imagine doing any of that — he's always lived separate in every city, except when he lived in Madison with Rita.

And would it have made a difference?

Thanks to the quick response of the firemen, the Toyota is damp and soot-speckled but miraculously intact in the garage. A wash and day with the doors open to the sun — that's all it needs. The other salvageable item is the steel file cabinet containing the folders for his taxes.

Uma tosses the remains of her tapestry bag back on the rubbish heap. She's been sifting ash, searching for the shoebox of photos and her CD player, but she hasn't found them.

Karan cannot believe he is still here. Each limb feels thick and leaden, and he hasn't found his passport.

Maybe Uma didn't report what she knows to the police because they didn't ask her. She never said she wouldn't. If she lets it slip, even inadvertently . . . he cannot think of that now.

"What will you do?" says Uma. "I mean, if the judge lets you off."

Karan sinks to a squat, picks up a stick and jabs at the debris. His blackened frying pan shakes loose.

"I've lost relatives and friends before now. These are only

things. This is nothing! Nothing! My grandfather — your great-grandfather — survived Partition. And this is not as bad as the Delhi riots in 1984 — fires everywhere, then. Three thousand Sikhs slaughtered."

"What's any of that got to do with this? You need to leave this area. You can't wait till it gets as bad as — whatever. Or until thousands of people are killed. Thousands!" She stamps her foot. A cloud of ash rises, starts her coughing. "Jeez, if it happens to one person, it's too much!"

If the judge issues a deportation order, the insurance company will low-ball and stall, knowing Karan won't be around to sue. And Karan won't have much time to sell the plot before he's sent away somewhere. But if the judge believes Karan or the fire inspector's report points to the kid, Karan can press his claim. Then the insurance will pay and Karan will replace this home.

He won't buy or build right here, but close by. Nothing and no one will decree his self-elimination.

Uma is stomping and shouting. "Shit, you should go teach in some other university. You could move to Detroit."

The books. Some irreplaceable. His marginalia — gone. These ashes will someday mingle with the Pacific.

Karan rises to his feet. "I am where I am supposed to be," he says. "Why should I walk away from what I've built because of one halfwit American? Why should *I* be the one to leave? How many places can I leave?"

"You can leave this one, anyway. Oh, you're as pig-headed as Ma!"

He looks at her, wounded. "No, I'm not. Unlike Rita, I continue learning. That's what being a Sikh means."

"Learning what?" says Uma, obviously exasperated.

At this moment, speaking feels like trying to paint darkness.

"I've been focusing on aggregate data; I've never truly understood till now how a man feels when his slum home is bulldozed.

How a villager feels when they build a new dam and flood his home. And tsunami survivors — how must they feel?"

Uma runs a hand through her hair.

"You're pretty crazy, aren't you? How about taking that turban off, or at least wearing a cap?" She sounds scared. Even worried. Didn't she say, It would be too much — both of you? And just now, didn't he hear, You could move to Detroit?

She's thinking about her own welfare, isn't she? Self-interest — the American creed.

"No," he says. "If not my turban, people like that kid will find other things to hate or envy. This is about economics and power. The rest — just cover."

"So how will you fight it?"

He sighs, "One person at a time, Uma, one person at a time."

Two days later, Karan drops Uma at the main entrance of the train station, then goes to park. Walks into the station, glances around, consults the schedule. Uma's is the last train of the day.

There she is, sunflower sandals crossed one over the other. Beside her, the new bag he bought her.

"Want coffee?" He strives for nonchalance.

"Sure. I'll get it."

His hand extends a five dollar bill, like a ticket-spitter.

She returns from the coffee kiosk carrying a cardboard tray. Two cups.

"Orange pekoe," she says.

Uma thought of him. Beyond emergency assistance, voluntarily. Optimism shakes loose, like snow-melt from a mountain, pours into Karan's empty space.

He cannot demand love, anyone's love. Like oil, it's in limited supply. But there's always hope for equilibrium.

Is it better for Uma to be with him or on her own? The answer to that question will drive her.

He slips his kara from his wrist and holds it out.

"A little gift," he says. "It's the steel bangle Sikhs wear to remind us of birth, death and rebirth. And karmic justice. You should have one."

She slips it onto her hand, twirls it on her wrist, then slides it up her forearm.

"Rebirth?

"Rebirth? Cool," she says. "And that's what you believe will happen? Like, to Ma?"

"I'm sure of it," he says. "She's probably a baby yelling her lungs out at this very moment, driving her new mom and dad insane."

That's uproarious. He's laughing. And Uma is laughing. Now he's doubled over, laughing. Can't stop. He trades a glance with Uma and she starts up again. Her laughter circles and sidles around him, twining itself about his thrumming heart.

People are staring — let them. He is accustomed to being their education, and if Uma plans to see him again, claims him after this weekend, she will need to become inured to stares.

The train to LA is announced.

"Hey," she says, boxing his arm lightly. "Just so you know — I wouldn't say nothing to a goddamn soul about your green-card wedding. That would be like saying Ma was a prostitute."

"No, no. Don't put it that way," he says, with a twinge of hurt for Rita but relief, all the same, for himself.

On impulse, he holds out his arms. She comes into them. Her scent — so different from his own. Then the solidness of her arms closing around his waist.

"Call me when you get to Detroit," he says. "Then the distance between us won't seem so much."

She nods. "You be careful, will ya? Let me know what the judge says. Don't you get sent off someplace without me knowing."

He takes a place in line with her, hands her bag up once she's climbed the steel steps. He watches till she's seated inside. The train begins to move.

Is that her bare arm waving? He can't be sure.

But her hug still tingles through him.

Outside the station, the sheen of a rain-scaled night. Smudged silhouettes dart to and fro at the fringes of the street.

The spot where his Toyota should be is empty. Could he have forgotten where he parked? He walks up and down the aisles, retraces his steps.

Not a familiar tail light in sight.

It's gone. Stolen. His rusty old Toyota. Goddamn bastards, whoever they are this time.

Let them have it.

Karan is not going to report it. The police didn't believe him after the fire. He'll be like the Pakistani chap Nadir told him about. The one who was attacked, robbed and stabbed three times, but when the police came, he told them he had stabbed himself. That's it, Karan robbed himself!

Half an hour later, a security guard volunteers a simpler explanation: the Toyota was towed. Hauled away. "Either you didn't make your car payments or you didn't pay your parkin' tickets."

Parking tickets.

Meteors rush past in dyads — the receding tail lights of cars heading toward the mountains.

Car-free, Karan follows on foot in what he hopes is the right direction.

Acknowledgments

These stories began in the creative spaces provided by the Banff Centre for the Arts, the Ragdale Foundation, and Redbird Studios. For their time, attention, and comments as they matured I thank Edna Alford, David Baldwin, Elaine Bergstrom, Brian Brett, Judy Bridges, Annie Chase, Stefan Honisch, Olena Jennings, Bisakha Sen, Ena M. Singh, Gurdip Singh, Alexander Yaroshevich, and Theresa Yaroshevich.

"Naina" received a prize in *Prairie Fire*'s prose competition when it was published in 2000. It was translated for the *Belles Étrangères* anthology (Philippe Picquier, 2002) and anthologized in *The Harper Collins Book of New Indian Fiction*, edited by Khushwant Singh (Harper Collins India, 2004). "The View from the Mountain" was published in *The Capilano Review* (spring 2006) and reprinted in *Asia Literary Review* (fall 2006).

Among many sources, I acknowledge and recommend *Ablaze,* by Piers Paul Reid; *Chernobyl: The Forbidden Truth,* by Alla Yaroshinskaya; Discovery Channel's *The Battle of Chernobyl*; *Soviet Women: Walking the Tightrope,* by Francine Du Plessix Gray; *Tangled Routes: Women, Work and Globalization on the Tomato Trail*, by Deborah Barndt; and *The Subcontinental*, 1:3. Taras Schevchenko's poems are quoted from translations by John Weir and Vera Rich.

For expert advice, research assistance, and background interviews,

I am grateful to Dino Aguilera, Ilena Burshteyn, Dr. Kimberley Chawla, the late attorney Earl Hagen, Mavis Hubbard, Indira and Jit Pasrich, the staff of Froedert Hospital in Milwaukee, and the many dedicated librarians of the Milwaukee Public Library.

My editor Laurel Boone shared my vision for this book, and I thank her. Many thanks also to my agents: Bruce Westwood, Natasha Daneman, and Carolyn Forde.